Curse of the Fairfield Witch

A T. J. Jackson Mystery

By

Paul Ferrante

F & I
by Melange Books

Published by
Fire and Ice
A Young Adult Imprint of Melange Books, LLC
White Bear Lake, MN 55110
www.fireandiceya.com

Cover Art by Stephanie Flint

To the thousands of teachers and students I've known:
There's a little bit of a lot of you in these stories!

Acknowledgements

There were many people responsible for the completion of this book. Special thanks to Elizabeth Rose and Walter Matis at the Fairfield Museum and History Center for their assistance in my research of 1600s Fairfield, Rev. David Spollett of First Church Congregational in Fairfield for sharing his knowledge of the church's history and giving me access, Jill Campoli for her insights into the Paranormal and Wicca, Lieut. John Cronin of the Fairfield Fire Department for educating me on Confined Space Entry, my neighbors at Vista Royale in Vero Beach for all the great material, Caroline Ferrante for giving me the plot idea, Sarah Martin for her sharp eye, Deb Perry for her help with all things T.J., and my editor, Denise Meinstad, for her continued patience and guidance.

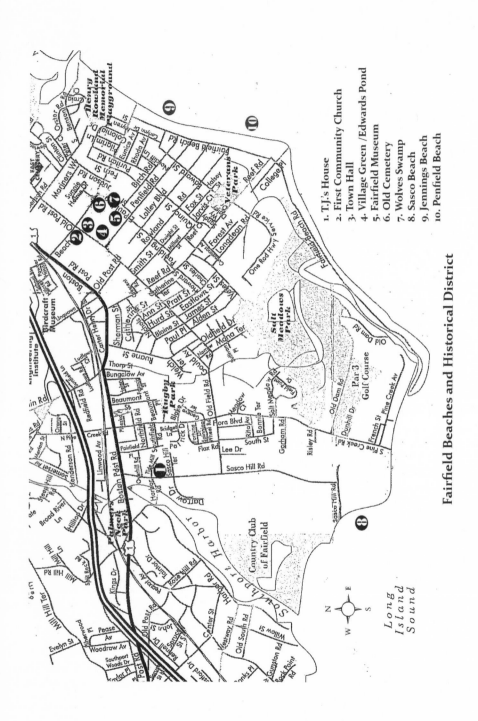

Fairfield Beaches and Historical District

1. T.J.'s House
2. First Community Church
3. Town Hall
4. Village Green / Edwards Pond
5. Fairfield Museum
6. Old Cemetery
7. Wolves Swamp
8. Sasco Beach
9. Jennings Beach
10. Penfield Beach

Prologue

July, 1662

"I tell you, it is the mark of the devil!" declared the shrieking woman, strings of iron-gray hair protruding from her close-fitting white linen cap. "Goody Nichols and I have seen it for ourselves!"

The somber group of men gathered in the first room of Reverend Jonathan Melrose's residence either nodded slowly or looked away in embarrassment. The physical description of any woman's privates was cause enough for discomfort, especially in the presence of a man of God. Melrose, a tall, gaunt figure with a shock of gray hair tied back, wiped a bead of perspiration from his brow, his black waistcoat heavy with sweat and high clerical collar chafing his skin in the summer humidity. "If you would be so kind, Mrs. Ogden," he said steadily, "please describe it as best you can—"

"It is red!" blurted Harriet Nichols, a stout woman with a florid face. "Just below the hip on her left side. Larger than a seagull's egg and heart shaped. This is not natural! Even a blind man can understand she is the daughter of Satan. You can see it in her eyes!" From the corner of the room could be heard the pathetic sobbing of the accused's mother.

"And you are sure this mark is not natural?" asked Melrose, glaring toward the distraught woman in the corner.

"As sure as I stand here before you and God," declared Goody Ogden.

Melrose breathed deeply and shut his eyes for a few seconds. When he opened them again they were sad and tired. "Very well, then. I thank you fine ladies for carrying out this most distasteful task." The women gathered their ankle-length brown skirts and bustled out, no doubt in

1

breathless anticipation of announcing their findings to the kind townsfolk of Fairfield, Connecticut. After the crying woman excused herself to the other room in which the accused girl lay, Melrose sighed and faced the men. "As the Town Council of Fairfield, you are aware that we are authorized to begin an investigation of satanic possession, if any, if the grounds for such are evident. We have, to begin, 'notorious defamation by the common report of one or more persons'. Is this so?"

The men nodded as one.

"Has the accused 'quarreled or threatened mischief to other parties'?"

"She has," said a tall man with a hard face dark and cracked from years of toiling in the sun, "on numerous occasions."

"And, as we learn today, the mark of Satan is evident upon her. We have no choice, then, but to proceed with further measures which may lead to a hearing for the purpose of determining whether she is a witch among us."

"And God help us all," wheezed an elderly man with a black eye patch.

"I will let you know where and how we will proceed," said Melrose in the stifling room. The lowing of nearby cattle could be heard through the rough-hewn walls of the wooden four-room house. "I ask you in the meantime not to speak of this to anyone outside of the Council. No need to create hysteria amongst the congregation. You are all good men and I trust your better judgment. Go with God."

The handful of town elders filed out and Melrose sat down heavily in a crude wooden chair with a leather seat back and bottom at his oaken dinner table. Wearily, he regarded his surroundings. As the pastor of the First Community Church, he possessed a few amenities that others did not, among them a cupboard brought over from England, the country of his birth, and pewter utensils and plates. But the advantages of his station in the community were at the moment far outweighed by the responsibility that rested squarely on his angular shoulders. He stared into the blackness of the walk-in fireplace where cookware suspended from swing-out cranes awaited the commencement of the preparation of the evening meal. The fire, which was never allowed to go out, even in summer, had been reduced to a pile of glowing embers due to the length of the meeting.

Finally, the woman emerged from the other room, her eyes rimmed with red. She had been pretty once, with blonde hair and pale blue eyes. But life in the Connecticut colony had been hard on her, and she was worn out far beyond her years. After tending the fire, she lit the solitary candle that sat atop the table, brushing her hand across his shoulder in a moment of tenderness before seating herself across from him. The candle's guttering flame sent pulsing shadows across their faces. "So there will be a trial," she whispered resignedly.

"If there has to be," was his curt response.

"But Jonathan, she is your daughter," the woman quietly pleaded.

"No, she is *your* daughter, a child begotten of the union of yourself and that infernal ruffian of a husband who drowned himself in drink. Dear God, Mother, whatever possessed you—"

"That is of no matter, Jonathan," she said softly. "I cannot change the past. What is important is that you and I found each other. And has it not been good?"

"Aye," he said, "there's no quarrel with that. But *she* is another matter. From the moment the two of you came under my roof that girl has done nothing but defy me, the spiritual leader of the entire town of Fairfield!" He struggled to keep his anger under control, but his voice was starting to rise as it did during Sunday sermons when his fervent invocations literally shook the rafters of First Community Church.

At that moment, the heavy door to the other room swung open and the girl stood defiantly in its frame, backlit from the orange sunset streaming through a window. Her feet were planted shoulder width apart with her arms crossed over her bodice, which was still in a state of disarray. Her dark red hair, having come undone during the struggle to examine her, fell in cascades to her shoulders. She fixed her catlike green eyes upon the minister and sneered, "So beating and starving me is not enough, I gather. You'll not be satisfied 'till I dance at the end of a damned rope."

"Hush!" cried her mother. "Do not blaspheme, child!"

"You've brought this on yourself," snapped the minister, returning her glare. "Ultimately, it will be up to a court of your peers to determine your innocence or guilt."

She laughed sardonically. "My *peers*, indeed. Those forthright souls who have been conspiring to do me in for as long as I can remember. Well, we'll have our trial, then, but remember this, *Father*—if I am condemned to the fires of hell, I'll make sure to save a place for *you*."

Chapter One

During late August 2011, the natural disaster that would come to be known as Hurricane Irene originated from an Atlantic tropical wave that began to gather strength east of the Lesser Antilles. It achieved tropical storm status on August 20 when it made landfall in St. Croix. The next day it slammed into Puerto Rico, paralleled offshore of Hispaniola, then surged through the Bahamas, packing winds of 120 MPH as a Category 3 hurricane. By the time Irene made its first landfall in the United States, on the Outer Banks of North Carolina on August 27, it had "weakened" to a tropical storm; then it churned up the East Coast from southeastern Virginia, blasting the tri-state region of New York, New Jersey, and Connecticut on August 28 and 29.

Irene cut a swath of death and destruction as it tore through New England, inflicting $15.6 billion in losses for those US states affected.

In the coastal town of Fairfield, Connecticut, residents were urged to activate their emergency plans, stock up on food and supplies, and secure their homes, vehicles and boats. A state of emergency was declared, and many residents along the shoreline, whose houses of precarious stability faced Long Island Sound, evacuated inland or to higher ground and hoped for the best.

The residents of Tide Mill Terrace, a half-mile from the public beach of Sasco Park, feverishly prepared for the worst. Although they lived near the crest of Sasco Hill, far above the beach, the only thing between them and the oncoming destructive winds of the storm would be the palatial beachfront estates that had been constructed in the late 1800s by the wealthy as summer vacation residences. Those who lived in the Historical District, which stretched for a couple miles behind Jennings and Penfield Beaches, however, were vulnerable not only to wind damage but the projected storm surge of the waters of Long Island Sound.

At 65 Tide Mill Terrace, widower Thomas Jackson, Sr. and his teenaged son, T.J., fitted plywood inserts into their east facing windows and moved any outside furniture, as well as their barbecue grill, to the basement. The cars, including Tom's beloved Jaguar XJS coupe, were somewhat secure in their garage, but nearby older trees, which Tom had judiciously pruned, still posed a threat. Their house, a large updated Colonial, had been fortified by the senior Jackson—a respected architect—but there were no guarantees when dealing with what promised to be a storm of major proportions.

The Jacksons also invited their neighbors from across the street, Pippa Bortnicker and her son, a close friend of T.J.'s, to join them so they could ride out the storm together. The Bortnicker residence, though attractive in its own right, was simply not as formidable structurally; ancient oak trees, which loomed over its roof, heightened the threat to its integrity in a windstorm. The Jacksons' huge GENERAC generator would also provide power for both families in case of a major outage.

Pippa was more than grateful for Tom Jackson's invitation. As a single parent, whose husband had walked out on her and her young son years ago, she was unnerved by the dire forecasts of the storm, which she'd been tracking via the Weather Channel for the past week as it roared through the Caribbean. Besides, her son and T.J. had an unbreakable bond formed in early childhood and strengthened during their exploits as fledgling ghost hunters; the most recent adventure happened a couple months earlier, when the boys, aided by T.J.'s adopted cousin LouAnne, had solved the mystery of a Bermudian pirate captain who was terrorizing visitors to his plantation estate on that tropical island. The teens' experience had been chronicled in a reality TV special produced by The Adventure Channel entitled *Junior Gonzo Ghost Chasers: The Bermuda Case* that was due to be aired in the fall. Pippa, who made a decent living as a Feng Shui consultant to the wealthy of Connecticut's "Gold Coast," was thankful for friends like Tom Jackson and his son, especially because her boy, who could generously be called "eccentric," was somewhat of a social outcast and considered T.J. a brother.

As they stowed the last of the lawn furniture, Tom turned an eye to the darkening sky. "It won't be long now," he said resignedly. "Let's go inside and take stock of our emergency provisions."

The Jackson kitchen had been turned into a command post. Cases of bottled water had been stacked neatly against one wall; bins of cereal and tinned meats were arranged on the center island. Flashlights with new batteries and candles were lined up on the kitchen counter next to cell phones hooked up to chargers. Surveying the tableau, Tom ran a hand through his stylishly cut salt-and-pepper hair. "Have we missed anything, Son?" he asked.

"I don't think so," replied the boy. "I mean, don't you think the generator will get us through?"

"I'm hoping it will. If we can keep the fridge going, cool the house, and stop the basement sump pump from conking out, we'll be okay. I think now would be a good time to take a shower. I'll use the upstairs bathroom and you use the one down here. Then, rinse the tub before you fill it with water."

"Got it. Hey, Dad, you scared?"

His father smiled tightly. "Of course I am. Listen, no matter how much you prepare for something like this, Mother Nature has a way of throwing you a curveball. I'm concerned most about wind damage, to tell the truth. Tree branches and other flying stuff that hasn't been tied down. It's the people down the hill at sea level that are going to get the brunt of this. A lot of the houses on the beach aren't stilted high enough for my taste. If we get anything near the storm surge that's been predicted it could be catastrophic for them. So go get your shower. I'll call Pippa and tell them to come over in a half hour or so. We'll cook up some food, hunker down in the basement rec room and ride this out together."

T.J. gave his father an awkward hug. "We'll come through this okay, Dad," he said. "We've been through worse." He was referring to the untimely death of his mother from ovarian cancer when he was only five, an event that still prompted bouts of melancholy in both the Jackson men.

"She's watching over us," Tom replied. "Let's get moving."

Bortnicker, his wild mop of curls nearly obscuring omnipresent Coke bottle glasses, arrived with his mother that evening. Pippa, who had a bit of the 60s counterculture in her appearance and personality, was urging her flighty son to think pacifying thoughts, but he was having none of it. "They've got fire trucks crawling through the streets down near the beach, urging people to evacuate," he reported. "Lots of people from the low-lying areas are headed inland. They're setting up a shelter in the gym at the high school."

"Wonderful," said T.J., brushing aside his Beatle cut that made him resemble a young Paul McCartney.

"Could I interest you in a glass of wine, Pippa?" offered Tom. "Might as well make the most of it."

"That would be nice." She sighed. "I hope we're not imposing—"

"Nonsense. You can have the guest bedroom and the boys can share T.J.'s. That is, unless, the wind gets really bad. In that case, I have air mattresses and sleeping bags ready to go in the rec room downstairs."

The foursome made the best of it that night, talking and playing Monopoly to the tune of the Jacksons' rock 'n roll CDs, most notably the Beatles and Bortnicker's former favorite, Steely Dan. But despite the fact they were fairly secure below ground level, they could sense the wind ramping up outside until it began to howl. A decision was reached to sleep where they were, and they arranged the already inflated mattresses to afford maximum space for each person. Bortnicker was a prodigious snorer, but that couldn't be avoided.

By the early morning hours winds in excess of 70 mph were blowing in off the Sound, bringing with them torrential rain that lashed the house above and rattled the windows, despite the plywood. Every once in a while they could hear the cracking off of a large tree branch followed by the explosion as it crashed upon someone's roof, deck or garage. Wails from police or fire department sirens wove in and out of the stormy darkness.

T.J. finally fell asleep in the wee hours of the morning, but was tormented by strange dreams of being submerged in swampy water, then clawing his way out of quicksand-like mud. A woman's laugh, piercingly mocking, made him snap awake in a cold sweat. As he took his bearings in the dark rec room, his buddy's snoring was somehow reassuring. Grabbing a flashlight, he quietly padded upstairs to the ground floor and peeked outside through a small window that was plastered with wet leaves. Branches were everywhere, and the trees were swaying precariously around the house. It was at that moment he understood the total blackness in the surrounding area—the power had gone out. But his dad, always thinking ahead, had invested in the generator, and it was probably humming away outside. "This is gonna be bad," T.J. whispered to himself, and crept back downstairs, where he crawled into his sleeping bag and zipped it closed around him.

Chapter Two

By the evening of August 28, Hurricane Irene had moved northward and out of Fairfield County, leaving destruction and misery in her wake. Rivers had overflowed, and trees had been uprooted, taking down power lines that led to widespread blackouts, some of which would not be restored for days. The beginning of the school year was delayed in many districts. The governor declared a state of emergency after surveying the devastation from 1,000 feet up in a Black Hawk helicopter. It would not be possible to put an estimate on the monetary worth of the devastation for weeks.

The town of Fairfield had taken a direct hit. Along parts of Beach Road, it was hard to distinguish where the beach ended and the road itself began. For many blocks inland, the seawater was at least ankle-deep; basements were either soggy or completely flooded. Downed trees and branches blocked roads and prevented rescue vehicles from gaining access. Some residents had taken to paddling about their neighborhoods in kayaks or canoes. In places where the water was receding, piles of sand, seaweed and garbage remained. The town's beaches, most notably Jennings, Penfield and Sasco, were littered with the remnants of docks, buildings and boats that had washed ashore in the storm surge. Some of the beach houses that Tom Jackson had worried about had been knocked into the water or had their view of Long Island Sound expanded thanks to the shearing off of their facing wall. Decks and small garages collapsed, and downed power lines hissed menacingly. Lines at supermarkets and gas stations were long as residents tried to restock perished food, ice for coolers, and gasoline for small generators. The late summer heat only added to the misery, and tempers were short. The

Bortnickers' overnight stay at the Jackson residence would stretch well into the week. The days were filled with cleaning up around their houses (the Bortnickers were lucky to have only a few small puddles in their basement, while the Jacksons' sump pump, kept going by the generator, didn't allow a drop of moisture) and those of their neighbors. Everyone pitched in to clear branches that blocked utility company vehicles from entering side streets. Those who owned chainsaws added to the continuous buzzing of the overworked Town of Fairfield and Connecticut Light and Power crews. The fire department and police were run ragged.

* * * *

As the night of August 29 descended upon Fairfield, the pastor of the First Community Church, Reverend Daniel Melrose, distributed the last parcel of donated food to a family whose house on South Pine Creek Road was inundated with seawater. The surge had petered out halfway to his church located at the corner of Old Post Road and Beach, where it had existed since the mid-1600s.

Melrose, a middle-aged man who looked much older due to an ongoing weight problem and receding hairline, stepped outside the main entrance of the church and surveyed the nearly empty Old Post Road and Colonial-styled Town Hall, a series of connected white clapboard buildings with ornate cupolas, green doors and window accents. It sat on the Village Green adjacent to verdant park space that featured a pond, some restored structures from the 1700s and 1800s, and behind them, the Fairfield Museum and History Center, a modern structure that had been opened only a few years before after being housed in an outdated facility next to his church.

Some low-lying areas of the park were pooled with rainwater, but they were of little concern to Melrose, who had been pastor of First Community since 1985, assuming the leadership of this prestigious congregation that was created under the stewardship of his ancestor, the Reverend Jonathan Melrose, in the 1600s. Daniel Melrose was proud to take on the responsibility of continuing the family name in Fairfield, and as such, he was filled with worry on this night. His church had been spared, thank God, but there were two other locations that might be in jeopardy. First was the Old Cemetery, which was situated on a rise not far from the Museum, bordered by a low New England-style stone wall. Jonathan Melrose's marble slab, with an impressive headstone dedicated by the church only a few years before, commanded the highest point in the cemetery, and the current pastor hoped it had escaped ruin. However, there was another place removed from the view of current day Fairfield residents for which he feared the worst. That was the secret tunnel, which ran from his church underneath Old Post Road and Town Hall to the burial ground. Although it was never used—only a select few even knew of its existence—it did have to be inspected periodically for cave-ins caused by the freezing and thawing of the ground during the harsh New England winters. But Melrose could afford to wait a bit before sending a DPW crew down there. Despite its ceiling being reinforced with wooden timbers, the passage was precarious at best. As for the good reverend, he absolutely refused to enter it. For one thing, he was claustrophobic. And on top of that, the very idea of its existence gave him the willies.

* * * *

It was not until October that the tunnel was deemed safe enough for inspection. Reverend Melrose contacted the director of the Department of Public Works, Jim Welsch, over at Town Hall and asked if he could spare a man or two for the task. Welsch, whose department had been working overtime since the hurricane, was finally restoring some semblance of normalcy to the beach section of town, including the Historical District, but his men were frazzled. It was because of the potential danger of this particular task—as well as its secrecy—that he tapped two of his most capable workers, Paul Jarboe and Ken Trishitta, to explore the tunnel. Both were strong, able men in their mid-30s who could be trusted not to blab about the tunnel's existence, which could lead to trespassers who considered themselves "urban explorers".

Paul and Ken met Melrose in the church sanctuary on an overcast afternoon for their instructions.

"Thank you for coming, gentlemen," said the somewhat anxious clergyman. "Have a seat in this pew so I can fill you in."

The men positioned themselves on the cushioned bench of the first row, and Melrose sat facing them at the foot of the altar. "To begin," he said, "this is a very old structure. A church has sat on this site since the 1650s, though the present building has only been here since the late 1800s.

"The first structure, all wood, was burned to the ground by the British when they invaded Connecticut in 1779 during the Revolutionary War. Since the church served the town as a seat of government and meeting hall as well as a place of worship, its destruction effectively knocked out the nerve center of the town of Fairfield. What the British didn't know, however, was that a tunnel linking the cemetery over a quarter-mile away to the church had been dug."

"Wait a minute," said Jarboe. "Are you saying this tunnel runs under Old Post Road *and* Town Hall?"

"Indeed it does," said Melrose. "This was quite an undertaking at the time, though of course no paved road or town hall existed. As for its *original* purpose, that remains a mystery."

"And the British never discovered it?" asked Trishitta.

"No, thankfully. The Town Council had known in advance of the British invasion at Compo Beach in Westport some 15 miles away and had time to move the church's valuables, as well as village records and such, to vaults burrowed into the sides of the tunnel."

"Wow," said Jarboe. "And you're afraid the tunnel's integrity has been compromised by the hurricane?"

"Perhaps. That and the heaving of the ground caused by the changing of the seasons, year after year."

"What's the clearance, height wise?" asked Trishitta, who stood six feet tall.

"It will be a tight fit for you boys," replied Melrose coolly. "The height is maybe five and a half feet, with a width close to four. I hope you're not claustrophobic, as I am."

"Not really, Reverend," said Jarboe, "but I'm not totally thrilled about the thought of a cave-in, either. That's why we brought a set of walkie-talkies. We want to be in touch with you the whole time, just in case."

"I understand completely. Well, shall we proceed?"

"We're as ready as we'll ever be," said Trishitta.

At that, the workers donned hardhats and Melrose led them downstairs towards the boiler room. As they passed through the basement, which was now used mostly for storage, Melrose pointed out the charred ceiling timbers from the Revolutionary War burning. "They rebuilt, of course," he said with a sigh, "but the structure which replaced the original, though far more formidable and ornate, was also fashioned from wood. It caught fire in 1880 and burned to the ground. A wealthy family in the congregation stepped forward and volunteered to finance its restoration, but only under the condition that it be constructed totally of stone. Which is why our church has its fortress-like appearance. However, this unfinished basement is original to the site." With the assistance of Paul and Ken, Melrose moved aside some metal shelves to reveal a waist high wooden portal about three feet square. "Once you climb through you'll be able to stand, stooped over, but watch your head. There are no lights, so I hope you brought flashlights."

They tested the walkie-talkies to make sure they were operational, and Melrose pried open the wooden hatch with a crowbar. Dank, musty air hit the DPW workers immediately and they regarded each other dubiously.

"You can still back out if this bothers you, gentlemen," said Melrose.

"Nah, that's okay, Reverend," said Jarboe with a stiff upper lip. "Give me some light, Kenny. I'll go through first, but I'll need a little boost up."

In a flash Paul, the shorter of the two, was wriggling through the hole and dropping down on the other side. After another minute Trishitta was inside as well, the two workers dusting themselves off and flicking on their flashlights, which were only adequate for a few feet. They checked out the walkie-talkies with Melrose, who gave them a thumbs-up from the basement.

"Okay, then," said Jarboe. "Let's do this."

The pair started inching ahead, the taller Ken shining his flashlight over Paul's shoulder. After about 50 yards their hunched over posture was starting to wear on them.

"We must be under Old Post Road," said Jarboe. "I think I can feel the vibration of cars on top."

Now they were encountering some shallow puddles here and there. Jarboe wondered aloud just how flooded the tunnel had become during the hurricane. Had the light been better, the men might have been able to discern a water line on its earthen walls. They crept onward. Then Paul heard Kenny say, "Is it getting colder down here?"

Jarboe stopped. It *was* a little chilly, now that he thought about it. "Hey, man," said Trishitta, "I can see my breath. Shouldn't the temperature down here be kinda constant?"

"You want to turn back?" asked Jarboe over his shoulder.

"Not if you don't. Where do you figure we are now?"

"Under Town Hall. Which means the cemetery is just—"

That's when both their flashlights winked out, as did their walkie-talkie with a loud *pop,* instantaneously followed by a wailing, rippling scream that sounded like all the pain and suffering in the world. The men, suddenly disoriented, almost collapsed in fright. Then Jarboe, the quicker and smaller of the two, effected an about-face and attempted to run right over his buddy in an effort to get out fast. Unfortunately, the result was that both went down in a heap, the wind knocked from Trishitta. After some flopping around on the muddy floor the workers scrabbled to their feet, practically crawling on all fours back the way they had come, as a cackling laugh reverberated through the tunnel.

"Hurry, it's right behind us!" cried Jarboe. But any attempt to get upright was met with a whack to the helmet, which caused dirt to fall from the ceiling, giving the impression of an impending cave-in, thus intensifying their desperation and panic.

Finally, Kenny, who was now the lead, could make out the outline of the entry hole in the distance, and the silhouette of the clergyman's head—he hoped—within its frame. "Out of the way!" he screamed, power diving up and through the hole before landing hard on his shoulder on the other side. Seconds later Jarboe was on top of him, panting and sweating profusely.

Melrose, aghast at the sight of the muddy, thoroughly terrified men lying before him, could barely croak out a shaking, "What in God's name happened in there?"

"I don't know," said Jarboe, the first to catch his breath, "and I don't want to."

"But I'll tell you what," added Ken between whooping breaths, "you've got yourself a *problem.*"

* * * *

After the debacle in the tunnel, Melrose again boarded up the hole and covered it with the shelves. As a personal favor to him, Jim Welsch—who was astounded to hear of his men's harrowing escape— swore the workers to secrecy with the understanding that loose lips would lose jobs.

Indian summer gave way to the brilliant hues of autumn in New England. The town of Fairfield tried to put Hurricane Irene in their rearview mirror and look ahead to Thanksgiving and the holidays. As this was always the busy season at First Community Church, Reverend Melrose was able to divert his attention from the sinister implications of what had happened in the tunnel and throw himself into his work.

But then, on a raw, windy night in early December, it all came apart.

Melrose, who had not been sleeping well of late, attributing his condition to acid reflux, awoke with a start just after midnight. The full moon poured through his rectory window, while the branch of a nearby willow raked the glass. The clergyman tried to roll over and get back to sleep, but it was no use. For some unfathomable reason, he dressed in his clerical attire, threw on his black overcoat, and ventured outside. Before he knew it, his feet were crossing Old Post Road towards Town Hall, as if pulled by some magnetic force. He skirted the stately building, now bluish in the moonlight, and found himself at the front of the Old Cemetery, whose cut stone entrance pillars framed a heavy black wrought iron gate that was never locked. Melrose pushed open one of the swinging doors and stepped inside.

The first significant snowfall of the year had yet to occur, but the ground was hard and the patchy grass crunched beneath the rubber soles of his black clerical shoes. Hands in his pockets against the cold, he made his way up the small hummock in the center rear of the graveyard where his ancestor's crypt lay. In the moonlight, after wiping away some dead leaves, he was able to read aloud the inscription in the marble slab:

The Reverend Jonathan Melrose

16

Born in Southampton England in 1595
and was a graduate of
Queen's College in Cambridge.
A puritan divine of the Church of England,
he was the first pastor of the
First Community Church of Fairfield
which he faithfully served
from 1645 until his death in 1664.
A valiant leader of Christ's Soldiers
Holy Man of God

"Ah, such touching prose for a great man," called a bitterly sarcastic voice from beyond the crypt.

Melrose straightened with some difficulty. "Who's there?" he croaked. The moon, which had slipped behind a cloud, revealed the silhouette of a woman atop the wall some 30 feet away. When the cloud parted, however, Melrose was astonished to see that the female, who appeared to be in her late teens and dressed in 1600s garb, was not actually standing on the wall but hovering inches *above* it. Her long, wild reddish hair blew in the wind, and her green eyes were riveted to his. Recognition flooded over the cleric, who fought to retain his composure as he said, "You."

"Indeed it is, *Your Holiness*," she mocked, cocking her head. "Are you not surprised to see me? Or have you simply been marking time until this inevitable moment?"

"Wh-why now?" he managed, his heart hammering.

"Why? Because I was waiting for *you*, Daniel." She pointed an accusing finger. "Because I want *you* to feel the weight of this community as I did many years ago. Because there is a score to settle, and I'll not give you—or this community—a moment's peace until it is!" By now, her voice had risen to a shriek.

Melrose, trembling with fear, suddenly felt like he'd been hit in the breastbone with a sledgehammer. He toppled forward onto the marble slab of his namesake where he was discovered, barely alive, the next morning by two youngsters playing hide and seek among the monuments.

17

Chapter Three

T.J. had been in some strange situations his life—especially the past couple years—but he'd never felt more mentally uncomfortable. That being said, he had no one to blame but himself this time, though he also felt justified.

The Cooperstown investigation had left the boy shaken, especially Roberto Clemente's final words to him regarding his mother watching over him. And Mike Weinstein's remark that he might be "sensitive" to the spirit world was both intriguing and frightening. T.J. had also caught Bortnicker and his cousin exchanging glances in Cooperstown as he described "feelings" he was having. So, upon his return, he'd summoned up his courage and called Mike in L.A., where they were editing the Cooperstown Special.

The host of the wildly successful *Gonzo Ghost Chasers* was at the very least unusual, but he did have his serious moments. After raving about the rough cut of the show, he'd proudly told his protégé that The Adventure Channel was going to air the program opposite the Major League All-Star Game, and that they would have their ears open for any future investigation ideas that either Mike or the kids themselves could think up.

Although T.J. was proud of what the three of them had accomplished, he wanted nothing more than to return to Bridgefield High and quietly finish out his sophomore year. Grade wise, he was about normal, in the A-/B+ range, so that wasn't an issue. And as for athletics, his baseball fortunes were on the upswing after his impromptu midnight fielding lesson with Clemente's ghost at Doubleday Field, which seemed to give him a much-needed confidence boost. He had also reached a deeper understanding with his coach, Mr. Pisseri, who had accompanied the teens to Cooperstown as a chaperone and gotten more out of the trip than he'd bargained for. Coach P. didn't talk to T.J. or Bortnicker much about it, but their shared experience of interacting with the Hall of Famer's ghost had forged a special bond among them that went further than the normal teacher/student relationship. And there was a rumor floating around school that the varsity baseball coach, who had been there for over twenty years and was enduring the latest in a series of mediocre campaigns, was thinking about hanging up his whistle at season's end, thus paving the way for both Pisseri and T.J. to move up to the varsity together next year.

Of course, T.J. still enjoyed running cross-country, and had no plans to give it up next fall. The sport, which offered him an opportunity for self-challenge and contemplation, was also a bridge between him and LouAnne, who was trying to salvage her junior year of spring track down in Gettysburg after a near disastrous personal setback during the winter. With the support and love of her cousin, she'd managed to pull out of her funk, but the last time T.J. had spoken to her she was still playing catch-up in a sport she'd dominated until now. Nevertheless, with her internal tribulations behind her, LouAnne was also looking forward to a smooth end to the year and her summer job as a Civil War reenactor in Gettysburg, where they were already gearing up for the 150th anniversary of the battle in July of 2013. Of course, it had been the annual commemoration of the event in 2010 that had spawned the creation of the *Junior Gonzo Ghost Chasers*, as well as the tricky romantic relationship of the cousins by adoption. LouAnne had promised to visit T.J. and Bortnicker this coming summer after Reenactment Week, and he was determined to hold her to that. With each investigation, their romance—if one could call it that—had deepened. T.J. wanted nothing more than a pleasant week with no ghosts or drama, just himself, LouAnne—and Bortnicker, of course—chilling out and enjoying summer in lower New England.

Which was why he'd contacted Mike to inquire whether his ghost hunting mentor had anyone he could recommend that he'd met throughout his travels who could talk to T.J. and help him sort out his feelings and experiences of the past two years. As it happened, Mike had made the acquaintance of a woman while on a case in Vermont—something about a farmhouse built on a Revolutionary War battle site—and gave T.J. her contact information.

When T.J. had called Jill Rogere, she was at first a bit wary, but when he mentioned Mike's referral, the ice was broken. Although he was a bit over the top, women found Weinstein utterly charming, and passionate about his role as a ghost hunter. And though she had not seen the Bermuda Special as of yet, Jill had sensed the sincerity in T.J.'s voice and agreed to meet at her converted farmhouse home in Wethersfield. T.J. had not informed Bortnicker or LouAnne as to this visit—he could always fill them in later—but he needed to tell his father, who was his only means of transportation to this small upstate town an hour away. Tom had taken the Jag, dropped his son off at the renovated farmhouse where Jill lived alone, and had gone sightseeing. "If it's important to you to talk to someone, Son," he'd said, "then I'm all for it, because I just can't help you with this sort of thing, and I see it's troubling you." Thus, here he sat, facing the woman whom he hoped had some answers for him.

On the surface, Jill seemed totally normal. She was around 40 and lithe of stature, her brown hair pulled back in a bun; granny glasses completed the bookish appearance. Her home's decor was a collection of simple country antiques and modest furniture. Thankfully, there were no incense-scented candles or occult objects around. It was homey and comfortable.

"You're sure I can't get you a cup of green tea or something?" she asked, observing the boy's anxiety.

"No, that's okay, ma'am—"

"Call me Jill."

"Okay, Jill. I really don't need anything, but thanks."

"And your dad is fine with us talking."

"Oh, yeah. He's out driving around in his sports car, taking in the sights."

"Well," she said, "then he's come to the right place. We have some scenic waterfront vistas and an outstanding historic district, dating all the way back to the 1700s. Of course, the town goes back even farther than that, to the 1600s, when we had our witchcraft trials—"

"I thought that happened up in Salem, in Massachusetts," cut in T.J.

"Let's say the more publicized ones did, T.J.," she said primly. "But Connecticut's problems with witchcraft predate Salem's by decades. Anyway, we're not here to discuss all that; we're here about you. Now, why don't we begin with you telling me all about your experiences so far."

"Well," he began uncertainly, "it all started a couple summers ago when I went to visit my Uncle Mike's family in Gettysburg..." Without getting too wordy or dramatic, T.J. took Jill through all three of their investigations to date. He was relieved when she didn't either comment critically or shout something like "Omigod!" every five minutes. By the time he ended with Roberto Clemente walking into and underneath Lake Otsego in Cooperstown, the most he detected was Rogere's eyes widening a bit at times; whether it was from disbelief or mild alarm was hard for the exhausted boy to determine.

"Interesting," was her enigmatic response at last. "So, what can I do to help you, T.J.?" she asked, placing a comforting hand atop his.

"Could you answer some questions for me, Jill?"

"If I know the answers, sure," she replied and smiled.

Reassured, he returned her smile. "Okay, here goes. First question: Mike Weinstein told me he thought I might be 'sensitive'. What does that mean, exactly?"

"That's easy. It relates to how you feel when a spirit is trying to initiate communication with you. Being sensitive is different from any other form of communication with a spirit. Being a 'sensitive' means that you are the threshold. They can feel you, and know that you might be able to hear them or see them. And if you *are* a sensitive, there will be no doubt, especially if you know this person is dead. It's easier for a young person, especially when a family member is the one supposedly speaking to them, because an older person might misconstrue spiritual communication as the longing for that person. Sometimes it will take a major, life-changing experience, like the one you had in Gettysburg, to give you the confidence to let your thoughts go and be open to communication from the other side. You went down there depressed and alone. But to have that first experience be so clear, that's definitely an indication of your ability."

"So, what's the difference between a 'sensitive' and a 'medium'?"

"A sensitive doesn't really know when it's coming. A medium has to open themselves up before they go into a situation like doing a reading. They can turn it on and off, but constantly welcome it. A sensitive can go on to being a medium…it depends on how far they want to go. But fear of the power can stop them from taking it to the next level, and that fear is well-founded, because you don't want that level if you won't be able to handle it. Personally, I'm happy to leave my ability at this level."

"But when did you first think that you were 'sensitive'?"

"Before I even knew what it was, or that there was a word for it. I was probably six years old when my great-grandmother passed away. It was my first experience with death, but I wasn't afraid. I went to the wake, saw her casket, everything. But I was okay with it, I guess. A six-year-old doesn't even know what grief is. At the time, we were living with my grandparents, because my dad was building what would be our new house. So, my grandparents gave me Great-Grandma's old room. There was this rocking chair in the corner that she liked to sit in. The first night that I slept in my new room, there's Great-Grandma, rocking away.

"The next day at breakfast, everyone was so sad over her death, but I said, 'Why are you sad? Great-Grandma's not gone. She was in my room last night.'

"'What are you talking about?' asked my mom.

"'Yeah,' I said. 'She was in my room, and she talked to me and tucked me in.' Well, my parents were shocked, of course, but I didn't mind. And my great-grandma visited me and tucked me in every single night until we left. I mean, I could *physically feel her* tucking me in. I could feel her as a solid, which doesn't always happen. But, didn't you say that Confederate soldier's ghost touched you in Gettysburg?"

"Yes," T.J. whispered.

"Well, there you go. Anyway, not all my deceased family members have communicated with me, if that's what you're wondering. Some might not have the ability to, and others simply might not want to."

"Did your parents ever come to believe you?"

"Not on that one. They were convinced I was just dreaming. But then something happened that kind of turned the tide. The Indian—Native American—story. Here's what happened. My parents ended up getting a divorce. My dad moved down south, and my mom eventually remarried and they bought a house in a new development in Westport, Connecticut. Well, I was to find out later that the area was at one time home to a North American tribe. But anyway, I was around 14 by this time, and I shared a room with my sister, who's a couple years younger than me. Almost immediately, I began sensing something—in my room, in other parts of the house, and in the yard. I would feel I was being watched, and I would smell pipe smoke. I couldn't see this person but I could feel his touch—this big hand that would stop me, usually when I was about to do something dangerous or go somewhere that I might injure myself.

"Let me give you an example. One night I was sleepwalking, apparently, and I made my way to the top of our staircase, which was pretty steep. My mom heard the creaking of the hardwood floor and left her room. She saw me standing with my back to the stairs, my eyes half open, and I started tipping back until I was almost horizontal. Mom didn't know what to do—reach out for me and risk me falling, or let whatever force was holding me up to do its thing. She elected to let what I firmly believe was the Indian save me. And he did.

"I guess he was confused, too. What did he know about white people, or houses? This was *his* land. Funny thing, he never bothered my sister, but he was always moving my stuff around, turning my radio on and off, that kind of thing. He pulled a rolling chair out from underneath my best friend one day when she was visiting.

"But then he crossed the line. My stepfather and I didn't get along too well, and the Indian did not like it when my stepfather reprimanded me. So he took it out on my parents. My mom's makeup would go missing and then turn up in the attic. Pots and pans would end up in the basement. The refrigerator would be unplugged. Then one day, when my parents were sitting at the dining room table having an argument, he turned the chandelier over the table completely upside down. I was in the TV room, and I could feel his anger at my parents. I said 'Stop!' and when he saw he was upsetting me he righted the chandelier, brushed right by me, and went back upstairs to my room.

23

"Finally, it was my mom who confronted the Indian. She was alone one night in the house, in her bedroom with the door closed, and she felt him, and sensed he was up to no good. By this time, she was losing sleep due to the stress. So, she sat up in bed and told him, firmly, that I was *her* child and that he could not interfere with me, or her parenting, any longer. Then, she dared him to show himself to her, kind of boxing him into a corner.

"Next thing you know, a green light started coming under the door; and then the door opened, and there he was, an Indian chief in full garb, with his arms crossed, staring at her. Mom was scared to death, but she thanked him for showing himself and told him to more or less leave us alone.

"Well, this didn't work too well. Remember, he was a chief—someone used to being in control. And here was this *woman* on *his* land, telling him what to do. That wasn't going to fly; it's somewhat like the spirits you encountered in Gettysburg and Bermuda. One was a cavalry officer, and one was a pirate captain. These guys were used to giving orders. And who's to say that chief even understood English, or her meaning?"

"So what happened?"

"Well, now my mom was totally convinced. She contacted this famous ghost hunting couple who came to the house and did a cleansing. But it only worked for a while. He came back, eventually, but things were toned down. And though I've lived on my own for a while now, when I go to visit I feel him; and although I'm much older, he still regards me as that child he needs to protect. Now, you may be wondering how my mom, or your friends for that matter, are able to see the things that you do. It's because you have enabled them, T.J. It's your sensitivity that acts as a catalyst. You see, my mom and I don't talk much about this stuff. But she did tell me what happened that night in her room, and that was the inspiration for me to start learning all I could about spirits and the paranormal. And the more I learned, the more I understood that I'm *not* strange or crazy. This is who I am, and I'm okay with it."

"But why *me*? What's the attraction for these spirits?"

"Like I said," she repeated, "this is something you had in you the whole time. People who are sensitive usually have a strong will. You're a good kid, at an age where you haven't done things yet to hurt people. Maybe from an understanding you came to—whether you remember being told or not—that ghosts aren't just figments of your imagination, or that they should be feared, you've never closed yourself off to it, even after that first experience in Gettysburg."

T.J. took a deep breath and blew out his cheeks.

"You want to stop, buddy?" Jill asked concernedly.

"Not just yet." He shut his eyes for a moment and gathered himself for the inevitable question. "So, you believe that there is an afterlife?"

"Oh, yes. If you don't have this basic belief, none of the other stuff happens. This isn't to say that I know what it's like—I don't. And, even if one encounters spirits, they won't tell you what it's like. Am I correct?"

T.J. thought hard. "Come to think of it, not one of the ghosts I've met ever mentioned it," he said.

"And they won't, so don't ask, unless you're looking for a disconnect. That's one line you can't cross. The living will only be allowed to know so much. And the reason they won't tell you, either about the afterlife or bad things that might be on your horizon, is that they don't want you to try to change your fate. Some things just can't be interfered with. That's also why, no matter how knowledgeable a sensitive or medium is, they should shy away from ever telling a regular person what the future holds for them.

"Now, some spirits are perfectly happy where they are—there's no 'unfinished business' for them here—which is why, if I heard you right, Roberto Clemente's ghost told you that your mom was watching over you. Whether you ever hear from her directly, who can say? If she does, it might be in a dream, you know. When you're asleep, your third eye, so to speak, is always open. But other ghosts can deliver messages. Looks like you got one up in Cooperstown, and for that you should be happy."

"So, dying doesn't frighten you?"

"What would happen afterward doesn't, but *how* it's going to happen, well, that's always a concern."

"Speaking of concern, I'm wondering if there's any danger in all this for me?"

25

Jill Rogere furrowed her brow. T.J. sensed she was trying to find the right words. Then she asked, "T.J., do you believe in God?"

The boy was taken back. T.J.'s parents had never drilled religion into him; his father was a member of First Community Church on Old Post Road simply because he liked the atmosphere of community and inclusion that it promoted. But he was far from being characterized as a Bible-quoting zealot. Nevertheless, the boy responded, "If you're asking if I believe in a higher power, something that controls our destiny, then I guess the answer is yes."

"Good," she said, "because a person in your situation needs a strong faith, especially one who might be called upon to force out a ghost, as you apparently have been in the past. You can't go into these situations halfhearted. And this goes for clergy, too. It's one thing to go through theology studies and seminary training or whatever, but if that person doesn't truly believe, if there is any hesitation in combating evil, then the cleric has no chance. You can wear the garb, conduct services, the whole package, but you have to believe totally to be able to help others.

"So, to finally answer your question, T.J., yes, there is danger in what you do. Spirits can fool you. And it's not just spirits. I truly believe there are entities created by Satan that have been let loose on the world to wreak havoc and mess with people. God has his angels, Satan has his bad guys. Therefore, if you sense a spirit is trying to get you to allow it to gain more power, *stop*.

"Keep in mind I'm not talking here about my great-grandmother tucking me in. I'm talking about entities that can drive you crazy, even physically attack you. You've heard about people being scratched or pushed by spirits? That really happens, T.J. Of course, in the good old days, if you were set upon like this and tried to tell someone, you'd be ridiculed or shipped off to an insane asylum. Even today, people shy away from revealing these kinds of incidents. The ones—those that are legitimate—that you see on TV are the tiny minority.

"A person like you, who naturally wants to help people, has to make sure you are never so desperate—either in aiding someone or gaining knowledge for your own problems—that you become reckless with your ability. At the end of the day, I'm telling you that from where I sit you're maxed out on what you can do, and should be satisfied with that. Don't push it."

"Understood. Well, Jill, I—"

"There's one question you didn't ask, though," she cut in. "You never wanted to know what I thought of your television exploits."

T.J. felt himself flush with embarrassment. From the serious look on her face, he feared he was about to get lectured or criticized. Thankfully, she only sighed and shook her head, much like a parent might who'd come upon her toddler making a mess in the house.

"Most of the paranormal shows on TV are hysterical. They have to present those cases a certain way or it won't capture an audience. Some, however, do touch upon some true facts or situations. And they do catch sounds or images on their devices at times. So that much I'll give them. But other hosts have no clue what they're doing. What I'd like to see from these people is what they're like when the film shoot is over and they have to go home to their 'normal' life, when they're not the TV celebrity. Do they still have their skill, or interest, when they're not on camera? And if they are sensitive, does it carry over into their home life?

"The good thing is that these shows do open people to at least thinking about this stuff and the possibilities that the paranormal is real. Even our friend Mike walks a fine line at times. On the one hand, he's way overly dramatic on *Gonzo Ghost Chasers*. I've told him this to his face. He just shrugs his shoulders and explains honestly that it's the 'drama' that's kept his show on the air for five years and gets the ratings. Now, I don't know how well you *really* know Mike, but apparently, he had some strange experiences as a young child and is honestly still trying to figure it all out. Fine, I get that. But the confrontational approach he takes at times with spirits is disconcerting to me, and I've told him so. He's a friend, and I'm concerned for him.

"On the other hand, I did finally watch the DVD of your Bermuda show after you contacted me and, based on what you've told me about that investigation, your team—and especially you, as the de facto leader—conducted yourselves in a thoughtful, mature manner. But I fear for you as well, T.J. You're still pretty new at this, though I must say that your experiences these past two years are nothing short of extraordinary. I'm glad you had the good sense to make sure that what made it to the screen reflected the responsibility you feel as someone in your position. I hope that will continue and that you won't 'go Hollywood' so to speak."

"Don't worry, Jill, that won't happen," he said reassuringly. "To tell the truth, the TV fame and fortune stuff isn't all that important to me. But, is it all right in the future that I can still call you with a question or for advice? You've really helped me out here."

"Of course you can," she said with a grin. "You're a good kid, and I see great things for you in the future—generally speaking, of course!" she quipped.

* * * *

T.J. emerged from Jill Rogere's house, relieved and enlightened, to find his father at the curb, the Jag's engine idling. He climbed in and buckled up.

"So, Son," said Tom, easing out into traffic, "was your meeting what you hoped it would be?"

"Totally," the boy replied. "But, you know what, Dad? I get the feeling the two of us will be speaking again."

Chapter Four

Detective Susan Morosko took a swig of foul tasting squad room coffee from a Styrofoam cup and eased back in her rolling office chair. Across from her tiny cluttered office desk on the first floor of the Fairfield Police Department on Reef Road sat one Gertie Bartholomew, the town's designated wacko. No one really knew how old Gertie was, or what she actually did to be able to afford the cost of living in a bungalow off Penfield Road down by the beach. Susan guessed she was around 80 in age, but it was hard to tell. Gertie favored sack-like dresses picked up for pennies at the local Goodwill, clumpy work boots, and an army surplus field jacket. This curious ensemble was always topped off with her signature wide-brimmed straw hat adorned with a huge plastic sunflower.

"You gonna eat the rest of that powdered doughnut, hon?" she inquired of the detective with anxious eyes. "Sure wouldn't want it to go to waste."

"Be my guest," said Morosko, sliding the half-eaten pastry across her blotter, where the old crone merrily attacked it.

Susan shook her head. It was tough being the low man, so to speak, on the totem pole at FPD, at least as far as the dozen detectives on the force. Now in her mid-30s, stocky and compact from lifting weights and bicycling competitively, Susan had started off as a lowly officer and worked her way up to detective, the only female to hold such a title, and one of the comparatively few women on the 110 person force. But her sense of pride and accomplishment was tempered by the reality that she was given a lot of the mundane jobs nobody else wanted. Which was why she was here on a sunny Tuesday morning taking a statement from

29

the citizen best known for pushing a shopping cart around the downtown area and rooting through the dumpsters behind its numerous eateries. Nothing Gertie did was against the law, exactly; but it was a bit awkward and unseemly to have a bag lady—who was by no means destitute—prowling the streets where she blithely interacted with women wearing Versace and men driving Mercedes convertibles.

"Okay, Mrs. Bartholomew—"

"It's *Ms.*," she sharply corrected, shooting a small piece of doughnut from the gap in her front teeth.

"My mistake. Ms. Bartholomew—"

"Just call me Gertie, sweetie."

"Okay, Gertie. If you could just tell me what you saw?"

"Why sure, Detective Morosko, and if I might say, you look quite official in that uniform. What kinda sidearm you packin', darlin'?"

"It's called a Glock," she replied patiently.

"Ever had cause to use it?"

I'm thinking about it now. "Let's stick to why you're here, M-Gertie. Please describe your experience the other night."

"Sure thing." Gertie wiped the white powder from her lips with the back of her hand and sucked her teeth—what was left of them—for a few agonizing seconds as Morosko clicked her ballpoint pen. Finally, she was ready. "It's like this, Detective. As you might know, Wednesday is pickup day downtown—you know, garbage day—so sometimes I go for a dumpster dive on Tuesday evenings, look for some choice leftovers, comprendo?"

"Yes," answered Susan, involuntarily wrinkling her nose.

"Well, I did real good that night. Centro's was having a lobster special—"

"Could you just stick to the relevant information, Gertie?" asked Morosko, drumming her pen on the notepad.

"I was just gettin' to it. So it was round about midnight, and I'm on my way home, pushing my cart down Beach Road, when I saw her."

"Saw who?" Morosko leaned forward. "Please give me every detail, Gertie."

"Hmmm, let me see," said the woman, relishing her window of importance. "Well, I was rolling past the graveyard entrance, and something caught my eye—can you believe at my age I'm still 20/20?—and I pushed open the iron gates to go inside and take a look. I got about halfway into the graveyard, and I could see a woman standing in a small clearing amongst the marsh reeds in Wolves Swamp beyond the back wall, all by herself, lookin' at the moon."

"Could you describe her?" asked Morosko, scribbling notes.

"Not too great—I mean, the moon was up, but there were clouds, and it was past midnight after all, but it looked like she had on some old-timey kinda dress, like 1700s or maybe even earlier, and she wore some sorta cloak or shawl too, fastened at the neck. Maybe twenty years old, give or take. Her hair was long, and kinda wild. Couldn't tell the color—maybe brown or somethin' close. And she was standin' stock still.

"I'll tell ya, I was too shocked to even speak, so I figured I'd just back outta there, quiet like, but then I musta made a noise because she turned her head and, oh boy—you got any more donuts, hon?"

Masking her exasperation, Detective Morosko said, "After we're done I'll run you over to Starbucks, Gertie, and you can get whatever you want—"

"I prefer Dunkin' Donuts. Starbucks coffee gives me gas."

"Okay then, Dunkin'. Now finish the story."

"So, like I said, she turned toward me, and she had these glittering green eyes, felt like she was burning a hole in my chest."

"She say anything?"

"She didn't have to," said Gertie, suddenly quite serious. "That girl just fixed me in her deadlights and gave me this creepy smile... well sir, I grabbed my cart and zoomed outta there, like a contestant on *Supermarket Sweep*. My heart didn't stop pounding till I was back in my house with the door bolted."

"One last question, Gertie," said Morosko, "and you've been a big help, believe me, but let me ask you something. There's no chance you were, ah—"

"Drinking? Is that what you're trying to say?"

"Well, yes. You weren't impaired in any way, were you?"

"Nah, not a chance, dearie. Never touch the stuff. What I saw was what I saw, natural as day. 'Cept, of course, the fact that her feet weren't touching the ground."

* * * *

After arranging for a patrolman to drop Gertie off at the nearest Dunkin' Donuts with a $10 gift card, Detective Morosko returned to her desk and opened the manila folder that would now include Gertie Bartholomew's testimony. She moved it to one side and leafed through the other two reports from the same file that she had personally compiled.

The first involved a night custodian at the Fairfield Museum, Elias Zurita, who was emptying the second floor waste bins when he happened to glimpse something across the parking lot that lay between the Museum and the Old Cemetery. Zurita swore that he saw a young woman gliding—not walking—among the cattails near the cemetery's outer wall. He wasn't sure if she was a runaway or in trouble, so he'd phoned police headquarters, who had dispatched a cruiser immediately. While one of the officers questioned Zurita, his partner searched the marsh as best he could, slogging around in muck that at times threatened to pull off his shoes. But there were no footprints anywhere, or any indication that someone had passed through the dense high reeds of Wolves Swamp.

Then there was the local Boy Scout troop that had camped out on the Village Green adjacent to the Fairfield Museum's restoration buildings. Two of the scouts—who were by all accounts totally credible—had awakened in the dead of night to use a municipal Porta Potty and had spied a young woman, whom they described as wearing "some sort of flowing dress," walking along the edge of Edwards Pond. The scouts had actually called out to her, being far more adventurous than Gertie, but the woman had merely frozen them with a glare before evaporating. The boys had waited until the next morning to tell their scoutmaster, who'd been fast asleep the whole time, of their encounter; he had subsequently mentioned it to his golfing buddy, who just happened to be Susan's division commander, and that's how the Boy Scout sighting had ended up in the file.

And so, although this whole deal was the last "investigation" anyone on the force wanted to be in on, Morosko was more than just a little intrigued. Her nose for acquiring information and her analytical skills were what had gotten her this far, and this morning's interview with crazy Gertie pushed the situation—in her eyes, anyway—past the realm of coincidence. The question was, would anybody above her buy into the possibility of a phantom haunting the area?

Chapter Five

"I really appreciate this, Big Mon," said Bortnicker as they handed the limo driver their bags in T.J.'s driveway. "My mom has a consultation with a big account this evening, but really, I think the whole Boca thing stresses her out. My grandparents can be kinda crazy, and that doesn't exactly fit the Feng Shui profile."

"Still," said T.J., "I feel kind of guilty getting a free weekend down in Florida—"

"Hey, it's paid for," said Bortnicker as the limo pulled out of the driveway. "The tickets had to be used—they got them on some kind of exclusive AARP discount deal where you can't cancel out—so don't sweat it. Besides, they've always wanted to meet you, and after seeing the Bermuda Special on TV, you're like family, in a strange kind of way. And you're sure your dad doesn't mind?"

"Nah," said T.J. while viewing the foliage flying by on the scenic Merritt Parkway as they made their way to Westchester Airport in the town of Harrison, New York. "In fact, once this trip was a definite 'go', Dad called that Lindsay Cosgrove he met in Bermuda and got a flight out this morning. I don't think he's gonna mind three days of golf and sun in Bermuda."

"So they've kept up their relationship, huh?" asked Bortnicker, referring to the friendship Tom and the attractive Ms. Cosgrove had begun when he'd accompanied the kids on their ghost hunting expedition to the island the previous summer. Tom was designing a makeover for a prestigious golf resort's clubhouse on Bermuda's East End when he met Lindsay, who was a member of the resort's board of directors—and unattached. They had hit it off immediately, and had already coordinated two quick visits during the ensuing year. There was even talk of Ms. Cosgrove making the trip to the States in the near future. This all pleased T.J. tremendously. Tom Jackson was one of the most eligible bachelors in Fairfield—a variety of women were calling him on a regular basis—but he'd maintained a sense of caution since the tragic death of T.J.'s mom, Cheryl, some years before. His son felt Tom needed to get out more socially, so he was all for his father jetting off to Bermuda for the Memorial Day weekend. Besides, all father and son would've done was maybe a little fishing and some barbecuing—accompanied by Bortnicker, of course. It was still too cold for swimming in Long Island Sound. However, there would be no such problems in either of the Jackson men's destinations.

They arrived at precisely 4:00 PM for their 6:10 PM flight to West Palm Beach. After checking in and going through security, the boys settled into seats in the waiting area, which was rapidly filling. T.J. read a book, despite having just spent an entire day at school, while Bortnicker fiddled with his iPhone. Among other people, he texted LouAnne down in Gettysburg, who thought it was a hoot that her buddies would be spending the holiday weekend in a retirement community. Luckily, their flight wasn't delayed (Morty and Doris Barrett, Bortnicker's grandparents, would be picking them up at the West Palm Beach airport, and they wouldn't be arriving until 8:45 PM or so), and Bortnicker figured with deplaning and the 35 minute ride to Boca Raton, they wouldn't be in their guest room at Boca Vista Royale until around 10 PM.

Once they were in the air for a while, Bortnicker took off his headset and tapped T.J., who had been watching a baseball game, on the shoulder. "Talk to you a minute?"

"Sure thing," he replied. "What's up?"

"I think I'd better fill you in on the deal with my grandparents."

"Which is what?"

"Well, sometimes they're kinda… out there."

T.J. removed his headset and sighed. "So tell me about it."

"For starters, they're always bickering. They love each other and all… I mean, jeez, they've been married for like a hundred years, but my grandma's always nagging him about silly stuff. Most of the time he just

35

ignores her, but sometimes she pushes him over the edge. Grandma leaves me alone for the most part, but at times, she kinda hovers. She'll probably be after you, too, but in a good way—asking you about your love life and such."

"Great. Just what I need."

Bortnicker pressed on. "Now, my grandpa, he's *really* a trip. See, he used to own this big resort in the Pocono Mountains in Pennsylvania—the Pocono Hideaway, they called it. He ran it with my grandma for years, and it was quite an operation. Anyway, besides just being in charge, he was like the MC at the resort's nightclub. And from what he says, he used to knock 'em dead every night, telling jokes between acts and whatnot. In that region, I guess, he was a minor celebrity, and I don't think he's ever gotten the showbiz bug out of his system. I mean, way back then he even changed his name from Bortnicker to Barrett 'cause he thought it sounded more show-bizzy. The place where they live now, where we're going, Boca Vista Royale, has its own ballroom, and for years he did the same kind of MC stuff at all their functions, but he claims they're cutting him back because of his age. I think he's down to calling out the numbers at bingo night right now."

"Uh-huh." T.J. put the headphones around his neck. "What's this Boca Vista place like, anyway?"

Bortnicker winced. "It's kind of a senior citizens community. Only people over fifty-five can buy a place there. There's all these condos built around a golf course, and it's really pretty. Palm trees everywhere, and ponds and small lakes—I think they even have a couple gators hanging around. And there are four or five clubhouses with pools, tennis courts, shuffleboard, the whole deal."

"Sounds cool. Like a resort."

Bortnicker shifted uneasily in his seat. "Yeah, I guess you could say that. But it's not gonna be like in Bermuda, where we could do anything we wanted. I just want to warn you, this place has *a lot* of rules, and a lot of people there are set in their ways. So, unless there are teenagers like us visiting their grandparents, don't expect to run into anyone under the age of, like, seventy."

T.J. chuckled. "Well, I did tell you that I was up for a quiet weekend."

Bortnicker flashed his trademark crooked smile. "Big Mon, that much I can assure you. It will probably be the most uneventful weekend in your *life*."

"Good. Can I go back to the baseball game now?"

"In a second. There's something else."

"Like what?"

"Like the TV thing."

"What?"

"Well, I told you my grandparents loved the Bermuda Special—"

"Yeah, so?"

"Well, after it was on they were just so proud of me—us—and all…"

This was sounding ominous. "Bortnicker, what did they do?"

His friend grimaced in embarrassment. "What would you say if I told you there was a *Junior Gonzo Ghost Chasers* Night at Boca Vista Royale?"

"Get out. You're making this up."

"No joke, Big Mon. When The Adventure Channel came out with the DVD, my grandparents bought one and had a viewing in the ballroom for all their cronies. There was popcorn and drinks and everything. They didn't charge admission, though. I think that's against the law."

T.J. laughed out loud, causing some passengers in nearby seats to turn around admonishingly. He mouthed "sorry" and then whispered to Bortnicker, "How many people showed up, like ten?"

"Try a hundred," replied Bortnicker. "Or so that's what my grandfather said."

"Amazing. They must be *really* bored."

"Maybe. I guess it's like, if my grandpa can't be a star anymore, he can kinda be popular through me."

T.J. frowned. "Listen, man, one thing I don't want to do down there is call attention to ourselves. I just want a quiet, low-key couple of days."

"I get it, Big Mon. But we have somewhat of a dilemma."

"You mean there's *more*?"

"Yeah, kinda. Now, you know I told my grandpa that I gave the Clemente glove back."

37

"Uh-huh."

"But I never told him I gave it *to* Clemente's ghost. In fact, he doesn't know about what happened up in Cooperstown at all, except that we were up there for some ghost hunting and that the special's gonna be on TV in July."

"So you're not going to fill him in?"

"I don't think so. I mean, from the preview scenes The Adventure Channel sent us, it seems Mike Weinstein did a good job having them edit out the Clemente stuff. See, if I start telling my grandparents about ghosts interacting with us plain as day, well, it might get them thinking about things—"

"Like dying?"

"Yeah, and what comes after. Why fill their heads with all that info? What purpose would it serve?"

T.J. thought a few seconds, then nodded. "I think you're doing the right thing," he said. "Let's try to downplay the TV thing and any ghost talk as much as possible. I just want to go down there and be anonymous—"

"Are you T.J. Jackson?"

The boys turned to find a curly-haired young girl standing in the aisle with a pen and notepad, her eyes wide in anticipation.

"Uh, well, yeah," said T.J. with a wary grin.

"Then, can I have your autograph?" she said eagerly, thrusting the pen and paper at him.

"Sure," he answered, "but... how do you know who I am?"

"Are you kidding?" she replied. "You're on TV right now, on Channel 35!"

Bortnicker quickly punched up the channel on his armrest dial. Sure enough, the Bermuda Special was being shown on the plane. It was up to the part when the boys had just discovered the bell to a sunken pirate ship. "I guess they'll be playing it on TV here and there leading up to the Cooperstown Special," he said, shaking his head.

"Hey, you're Bortnicker!" the girl piped, causing the people nearby to again look at the boys.

Bortnicker offered a sheepish smile. "That I am," he said gallantly.

"Okay, then can you sign my book, too?"

"I'd be happy to, my dear."

She handed the book to T.J. as the suddenly curious passengers looked on. "Who should I sign this to?" he asked disarmingly.

"Natasha," she replied with a smile adorned by a mouthful of braces. "I can't wait till your next show," she said as he wrote. "They're playing the commercial all the time on The Adventure Channel. Looks scary."

T.J. finished signing *To Natasha, thanks for watching JGGC. Stay sweet, T.J. Jackson* and handed the book to his friend, who scribbled *Me, too! Love, Bortnicker*.

"Thanks, guys!" beamed Natasha, snatching back the book and scampering up the aisle.

"And now, back to our game," sighed T.J., clamping on his headphones again.

* * * *

The rest of the flight was uneventful, but any hopes the boys may have had about keeping their TV exploits on the down-low were dashed when they spied Morty and Doris Barrett, waving madly in the front of the waiting area, decked out in matching *Gonzo Ghost Chasers* black T-shirts, which clashed markedly with the tropical wear of others their age. "Jeez Louise," was all T.J. could muster.

Morty stood around six foot, slightly stooped, with longish silver hair swept back on the sides of his head to form a modified ducktail—which wouldn't have looked so weird had he not been totally bald on top. But Doris had him beat, her hair pouffed like cotton candy in a shade that T.J. surmised was platinum. Even so, her hair color paled in comparison to the plethora of gold baubles that hung from her earlobes, neck, wrists and fingers. The slightest movement set off a tinkling somewhat comparable to that of metal wind chimes.

"Sam-ela!" boomed Morty, engulfing his grandson in a bear hug, which T.J. found hilarious, especially because *no one* called Bortnicker by his given name. The only time he remembered using it himself was on the battlefield at Gettysburg when he thought his friend was dead. Morty finished up the hug with a wet kiss on Bortnicker's forehead that skewed his glasses, then held him at arm's length. "What, the big TV star can't afford a haircut? Look at that mop! Don't worry, though, there's a guy in

Boca I go to who does mine for eight dollars. I might be able to get you in this weekend." He released the grateful boy and shook hands vigorously with T.J. "And this is the guy I've heard so much about. I'm Morty Barrett. Welcome to Florida!"

"Pleased to meet you, Mr. Barrett, Mrs. Barrett," T.J. said, flashing his winning smile. "Thanks a lot for inviting me."

"It's no problem, darling," sang Doris, whose skin, like her husband's, was kind of a mahogany shade. "Wait till the ladies get a look at you, you handsome devil. They'll all be on their cell phones to their granddaughters!"

"Uh, I think he's kind of spoken for, Grammie," said Bortnicker, who had taken note of T.J.'s blush of embarrassment.

"Well, don't think I don't have ideas for you as well," she said with a wink.

"We should get our bags," suggested T.J. "I'll bet they're on the carousel by now."

"A capital idea!" said Bortnicker in his oft-used Liverpudlian Beatle voice.

Once they picked up their small suitcases, Morty and Doris led them outside into the humid Florida night. There was a slight breeze and the palm trees around the airport swayed gently, bringing back memories to T.J. of their previous summer in Bermuda. The group crossed the parking lot area at a good clip—the Barretts were exceptionally spry for their age—and came upon a rather large, well-maintained, cream colored four-door sedan. "You know what this is, T.J.?" asked Morty, with a sweep of his hand. Bortnicker groaned, as he'd obviously been through this line of questioning before.

T.J. eyed the car's badging. "A Mercury Marquis?" he asked.

"No, son, it's more than that," replied Morty, popping open the spacious trunk with his remote. "This is a 2004 *Grand* Marquis, the top of the line. It's what I call the quintessential Florida Cruiser. Hop in!"

Doris took her place up front with Morty and the boys slid into the plush rear leather seats. Morty turned the key and car's V8 engine sprang to life, as did the blessed air-conditioning. Doris immediately said, "Morty, it's too cold in here," but her husband shushed her.

"The boys need to get acclimated," he said as they pulled out of the parking lot. "Okay, now let me tell you about Florida Cruisers. You've got your Lincoln Town Car, your Caddy Eldorado and Coupe De Ville, your Buick Park Avenue. But for my money, the Grand Marquis has it all. Maximum comfort, handles good, and it looks sharp—for way less than a Lincoln or a Caddy."

"Don't forget to mention the gas mileage is lousy," cut in Doris.

"Like we need it? So where do we go that we require good mileage?"

"You've got a good point there," she shot back. Over her shoulder she said, "We bought this new, eight years ago. Know how many miles we've put on it? Under 20,000!"

"So where do you want to go, Miss Hotshot Traveler? Disney World? Key West? Where?"

"Somewhere outside the Boca city limits would be nice."

"What's wrong with Boca? Suddenly it's not good enough for you?"

"Forget it! It's fine! Just shut up and drive!" she yelled as the boys looked on in horrified amusement. Then Doris turned around in her seat and winked at her grandson, who shook his head.

Soon they were tooling along at 50 mph on the highway to Boca Raton. T.J., comfy as could be in the plush seat, was about to nod off when Morty boomed, "So, Sammy, have you filled your friend in about the ins and outs of Boca Vista Royale?"

"Kinda," he replied, "but I don't know if I covered everything."

"Well, here are the basics," answered the old man. "Boca Vista Royale is a pretty expansive gated community with over 100 condo buildings, 14 units to a building, two floors each. There are roads that wind through the complex, as well as a golf course. And there are four clubhouses, including the main one, Palm Pointe, where the restaurant and ballroom is. The one we go to is called Royal Palm. It's within walking distance. Anyway, when you go out, there aren't any sidewalks, so you walk on the road, which is barely wide enough for two cars. Always walk against traffic, but if you're riding a bike, go with traffic. And never walk on the golf cart paths. You with me so far?"

"Yessir," said T.J.

"And always make sure you have your visitor pass on you at all times. Someone might ask to see it. I got both your temporary passes at the apartment. And whenever somebody passes you on a bike, in a car, whatever, make sure you give a friendly wave. You don't want them think you're a crab."

"Morty, enough with the rules," admonished Doris. "You're making it sound like Stalag 17 already. Tell them about the fun things we've got lined up for them this weekend!"

"I was gonna get to that. Well, besides going to the pool, we'll be going out a lot, because if my grandson hasn't told you, Doris isn't exactly Julia Child. You know what she makes for dinner? Reservations!"

Bortnicker did a drumroll sound effect while Doris promptly smacked Morty on the shoulder.

"Ow! That hurts, you know. Anyway, we'll be going out for breakfast tomorrow—the McDonald's nearby has a great dollar menu—and then again for dinner tomorrow night. And how could I forget? After dinner, it's Bingo Night at Palm Pointe!"

"Woo-hoo," whispered Bortnicker to T.J., who could barely contain himself.

"Then on Sunday we've got a shuffleboard tournament, and a big surprise for that night."

"Sounds great," said T.J., whose greatest aspiration was to veg out at the pool and sleep.

"And here we are!" proclaimed Morty, turning into a grand entrance where a huge tan stucco marquee with inlaid tile and an American flag surrounded by a stand of Palm trees and bougainvillea announced they were entering the grounds of Boca Vista Royale. Morty gave a wave to the security guard in a small stucco booth, who offered a breezy salute in return. The Florida Cruiser, after passing a large sign informing those who entered that pickup trucks, motorcycles, any forms of solicitation, and speeds over 15 mph were strictly forbidden, prowled the empty road that meandered past one tan stucco, red tiled roof condo building after another. Many were dark at this late hour. As if reading the boys' minds, Morty said, "The high season is January through the end of April. That's when all the snowbirds come down. Then the place kind of empties out, except for year-rounders like us. But there's still plenty to do."

"Morty plays shuffleboard and bocce, and I do water aerobics, computer club, and arts and crafts," said Doris. "It's really pretty active."

"Define 'active'," whispered Bortnicker sideways as T.J. tried to keep a straight face.

They finally arrived at building 62 and made their way to the Barretts' spacious two-bedroom/two bath apartment. The boys, who were pretty tuckered out, bid the elderly couple good night, quickly unpacked, and washed up for bed. Thankfully, the guest bedroom had separate single beds, though T.J. would have to deal with his buddy's maddening snoring yet again.

"So why is it we're down here again?" asked T.J. after snapping off the light.

"Just a little R&R for the holiday weekend. Plus, my grandfather's been bugging me to come down for months. I think he gets a little lonely at times."

"Is that all?"

"Well, the last time we talked, right after I got back from Cooperstown in April, I told him I wanted to try and find out where my dad is. Maybe he has some new info, or at least some leads."

"You sure you want to know?"

There was a long pause in the darkness, and then Bortnicker, the slightest tremor in his voice, replied, "Yeah, I think so. I want to know why he's basically blown me off the past few years. What memories I have of him are getting pretty hazy."

"I take it your mom doesn't talk about him much."

"Not unless I bring him up…which is like, never."

"Well, okay then. Let me know if I can help out."

"Glad you offered, 'cause I might need you to distract my grandma to give us some time alone."

T.J. sighed. "The things I do for you," he said.

* * * *

The next morning, as always it seemed, T.J.'s eyes snapped open at 6 AM. Figuring there would be just about another hour of Bortnicker's snoring to endure, he quietly put on a T-shirt, shorts and his running sneakers and slipped out the apartment door, but not before grabbing his visitor pass and hanging it around his neck. His Bridgefield High baseball cap completed the ensemble, and then he was off for a jog around Boca Vista Royale.

Almost immediately, he was struck by the humidity, which was about two months ahead of Connecticut's. The sun was barely up, but it promised a warm day. Surprisingly, he was not alone—some old timers on two and three wheeled bikes, as well as walkers, alone or in pairs, were already out. He made sure to wave to each and every one. And every single one's eyes checked out his visitor pass. He even managed to see a 6-foot gator, sunning itself near a pond on the ninth fairway, which he thought was pretty cool.

By the time he got back, everyone was up. "Did you have a good run, Sweetheart?" asked Doris, who was already dolled up.

"Yeah," he replied, "it was great. Very scenic."

"Fantastic. Well then, grab a quick shower and we'll be off to breakfast."

"It's all yours," said Bortnicker, emerging from the guest bathroom with his curly locks sopping. T.J. showered and dried his hair, which fell into its Beatle cut naturally. Within minutes, they were in the Florida Cruiser and on the way to Mickey D's. T.J. wondered how Bortnicker, who had a ravenous appetite, was going to be satisfied with just the dollar menu offerings. But they were guests and had to act accordingly.

Upon entering, T.J. was awestruck. The fairly large fast food restaurant was literally packed with seniors, all of them ordering dollar menu items—and some had two-for-one coupons as well. Doris went to stake out a table after giving her order to Morty, who went to the counter with the boys. The girl behind it seemed relieved to see some young people, because everywhere T.J. bent an ear the seniors were grousing—either the coffee was too cold or too hot, or the McMuffins were too small. As if reading his mind, Morty said, "These old people, they have to complain about something, T.J. It's like a hobby for them." Then he said sweetly to the counter girl, "Please make sure my egg and cheese biscuit is hot, honey. Last time it was horribly undercooked."

T.J. ordered an orange juice with his breakfast, but Bortnicker succeeded in requesting a coffee without getting reprimanded by his grandfather. "Come with me while I get some cream and sugar," he whispered to T.J., who followed him innocently.

"What do you need me for?" he asked as Bortnicker removed the plastic lid from his cup.

"To keep an eye out, that's what," he replied, and started grabbing handfuls of pink, blue, and white packets from the bins, which he deftly stuck in the pockets of his cargo shorts.

"What are you doing?" asked T.J., embarrassed.

"My grandma recruited me to restock her sweeteners for home," he replied. "She said nobody here leaves without a fistful. But I think they have her under surveillance."

Their stealth mission complete, the boys joined the Barretts at the table, where Bortnicker gave his grandmother a wink. "Good boy," she said, munching on an English muffin.

"You guys ready for some pool time?" asked Morty through a mouthful of scrambled eggs.

"Can't wait," replied T.J. "Are there any rules for the pool I should know about?" At that, the Barretts laughed uproariously.

"Big Mon, you have so much to learn," said Bortnicker with mock seriousness. "The list of pool rules is too long and involved to recite here. But they are posted in rather large red letters on a rather large sign at the pool for your convenience."

"Just remember to put on a lot of sunscreen," advised Doris, who looked like a blonde chocolate Easter bunny. "The sun is not your friend."

* * * *

The Royal Palm clubhouse and pool were hopping as the Barrett entourage arrived at around 10 AM, building 62 being only a short walk away. (The boys were told that for the sake of decorum, T-shirts must be worn outside the pool area.) They strolled through the single floor clubhouse, past ping pong tables and a glass door leading to the complex library, and emerged on the pool deck, which, like the pool itself, was large and rectangular. Adjustable white lounge chairs were arranged facing the pool from every side. In each corner was a round umbrella-covered table with four sturdy plastic chairs. Only one long side of the pool offered any shade, provided by low hanging palm trees. T.J. surmised these would be primo afternoon spots. But Morty waved them toward a set of four loungers near one of the far corner tables. "This is our spot," he said nonchalantly as he offered waves to the pool goers who were already gawking at the boys. Bortnicker and T.J. laid oversized towels on their loungers (so as not to stain the plastic with tanning oils—it was a rule) and walked over to the huge rule board to have a read while Doris slipped into the pool to join her water aerobics group and Morty settled into his lounger for a snooze.

"Well, this sure is comprehensive," said Bortnicker sarcastically. "Any strike you as particularly interesting?"

"Let's see," said T.J. "How about *Swimmers MUST shower before entering pool?*"

"I like *No scuba equipment or flotation devices of any kind allowed except noodles.* I believe these multicolored things in the bin over there are the noodles."

"Speaking of which, *Noodle use is limited to one per person.*"

"Don't forget *No running, eating or drinking on the deck or in the pool.*"

"Or that *People with diseases or diarrhea are not permitted in the pool.*"

"And in case you didn't notice the six-inch letters, *NO DIVING* !"

They dissolved in laughter, rinsed off in the shower stall adjacent to the clubhouse, grabbed a noodle each and eased into the pool's deep end, so as not to disturb Doris's water aerobics group of ten or so matronly ladies, which she stopped in mid-routine to point out the boys. They smiled and weakly waved.

After floating aimlessly for a while, the teens returned their noodles and eased back in the lounge chairs after liberally applying more sunscreen. Then T.J. put on his sunglasses and lay back to get some sleep, but not before asking Morty where the piped-in music he was hearing was coming from.

"Oh, that," he said, his eyes still closed. "Every clubhouse and pool in the complex is tuned in to this station, Seabreeze 107.5, from seven in the morning to ten at night. They play the real classics, not the garbage people listen to nowadays."

"Like who, for instance?" asked Bortnicker.

"Sinatra, Perry Como, Johnny Mathis—you know, the real masters."

Indeed, 'Ol Blue Eyes was crooning "Fly Me to the Moon" at that moment.

"All day long?"

"I told ya, seven to ten."

"The perfect background music to our day," whispered Bortnicker to T.J., who smiled behind his shades and shortly thereafter drifted off to "Chances Are." When he awakened an hour or so later Bortnicker's lounger was vacant, as he was again noodling in the pool, this time surrounded by Doris and her crew, who seemed to be peppering him with questions.

"Look at those magpies," said Morty, sitting up in his lounger as Engelbert Humperdinck sang "After the Loving." "Doris is the ringleader, but that lady next to her with the flaming red hair, that's Mrs. Greenblatt, who's probably trying to fix up Sammy with her granddaughter, who by the way is no Ava Gardner." He chuckled, as Dean Martin was next with "That's Amore."

T.J. just nodded, figuring Ava Gardner must've been some hot actress or singer back in the day.

"Hey, T.J.," said Morty conspiratorially, "my grandson, he does okay with the girls?"

T.J. felt himself redden but kept his cool, despite the fact that Bortnicker's entire catalog of middle school romantic train wrecks were flashing before his eyes. "Uh, yeah, he does okay," he replied. "He, uh, met a really nice girl last summer in Bermuda, and they kind of hit it off."

"That's good to hear. His father was so awkward with girls it was pathetic. I'm surprised Pippa ever married him."

T.J. saw an opening and jumped in. "Mr. Barrett, he really needs to talk to you about his father. Something happened to him up in Cooperstown—nothing bad—but it got him thinking about trying to reconnect with his dad."

Morty gave a derisive snort. "Good luck with that," he said. "I don't even know where he is most of the time, and I'm his father. I'm lucky if I get a Hallmark on my birthday. What I'm saying is, if Sammy does catch up with my son, he might be disappointed in what he finds."

"Well," said T.J., "I get that, but I think it's still something he feels he has to do."

Morty turned to him and flipped up his oversized sunglasses. "You look out for him a lot, don't you," he said matter-of-factly.

"We look out for each other."

"His mom told me you guys have been like brothers since you were little."

"Yeah, that's about right, I guess."

"But I would suspect that you do pretty well in that area?"

"What area?"

"Girls," he said, as Andy Williams sang "Moon River."

"Oh, that." T.J. paused a few seconds. "I, uh, guess I do okay."

"Good boy. And I hope the TV thing hasn't gone to your heads?"

"We're trying not to let it."

"That's commendable. Some boys would take advantage of it."

Just then, Bortnicker caught T.J.'s eye from the pool. *Help me* he mouthed as the old women fussed around him.

"Man, it's getting hot," he said to Morty. "Time for a dip." In a flash he had grabbed a noodle and was paddling to rescue his friend yet again.

* * * *

At precisely 3:00 PM Morty announced it was time to go. Groggy from a few hours in the sun, the boys sat up. Indeed, the pool seemed to be emptying out. "Why do we have to go, Grampy?" said Bortnicker. It's only midafternoon."

"You want to go to dinner, boys?"

"Now that you mention it, I was getting kind of hungry," said T.J.

"Well, the early bird special at Capt. Bobby's Crab Shanty begins at four, and if you want to get a table we gotta go."

"What? Who eats dinner at four o'clock in the afternoon?" cried Bortnicker.

"Everybody in this complex, that's who," shot back Doris. "Besides, we've got to be back by seven for bingo, so let's get moving!"

Doris was right about Capt. Bobby's. The Barretts arrived around 4:15 PM and were lucky to get seated within 20 minutes. Fortunately, both the boys found something they liked on the limited early bird menu—Cajun catfish for Bortnicker and seafood Alfredo over pasta for

T.J.—which was augmented by a copious salad bar.

"And we get coffee and dessert!" crowed Morty. "You can't beat the value!"

Once again, the teens were treated to the griping of customers at the adjoining tables (Doris chimed in by sending her after dinner coffee back because it wasn't hot enough) but the late afternoon meal was for the most part pleasant, the boys answering endless questions about school and the TV show, which they carefully steered away from any unsettling topics. The only anxious moment came when Doris asked T.J., "So tell me about your other partner, this LouAnne. She's your cousin, right?"

"Kinda," said Bortnicker, nobly stepping in. "Actually, LouAnne's adopted, so she's not really a blood relative."

"Forgive me for saying, but she's quite a tomato," said Morty.

"Don't be a dirty old man," scolded Doris, administering another trademark punch to his shoulder, "you're old enough to be her grandfather."

"You keep doing that, you're gonna give me a hematoma in that spot," he snapped, rubbing the area gingerly.

"Serves you right. Eat your bread pudding; bingo starts in a half hour."

On the way back, Morty said, "Capt. Bobby's puts out a good spread, but sometimes we'll get some Chinese takeout and then go for dessert at Sonic. After eight o'clock all their shakes are half price."

"We usually split a medium," added Doris, who had purloined a few more sugar packets from the restaurant, "unless your grandfather feels like making a pig of himself."

"It's not that—it's the strange flavors you like. Who orders a coconut cream pie shake?"

"It's good!"

"Me, I like chocolate mint chip."

"The chips get stuck in the straw, Morty. It's aggravating."

Bortnicker just rolled his eyes.

* * * *

Bingo Night turned out to be a huge bore. First of all, two thirds of the 70 or so people who showed up seemed to be women in a bad mood.

49

Then, Morty took it upon himself to offer a few weak jokes every now and then between numbers (Doris was in charge of turning the crank on the hopper) and those who were enduring streaks of bad luck started grousing.

"Just call the numbers already!" yelled one octogenarian from her table in the back. The boys excused themselves and went into the next room to shoot a little pool.

They were well into their second game when a trim, silver-haired gentleman in white deck pants, top siders and blue golf shirt sashayed in with what appeared to be his cosmetically enhanced, much younger wife.

"Let's play a round, Babs," he said, uncovering the table next to the boys. He handed her a stick and they chalked up. As the older man lined up his first shot Babs looked in T.J.'s direction with an appraising glance that gave him the creeps, causing him to miss an incredibly easy shot.

"I can only take so much of Barrett," the man said as he broke. Immediately the boys' ears perked up and they exchanged glances. "He actually thinks he's funny with his lame jokes."

"Don't get worked up, Sweetheart," she soothed. "It's not good for your ulcer."

"Still and all, why can't he just call the numbers? Self-important big shot. Well, he'll get his soon enough. He and his wife are playing in the shuffleboard tournament tomorrow, aren't they?"

"They always do, and we always beat them," said Babs positively. "So why stress about it?"

"You're right," he said, sinking a ball in the corner pocket. "I'm so glad I have you to keep me grounded."

T.J. and Bortnicker fled the room before they laughed out loud.

Back at the apartment, Bortnicker asked his grandfather how the night had gone. "It was a lot of fun," he answered brightly. "I really had them going. You shoulda stuck around."

"We felt like playing a little pool, Grampy. But I have a question. This guy blew in with his wife, looked like he'd just stepped off a yacht—"

"Oh, you must mean Greg Burrell," growled Morty. "Made a lot of dough as a plastic surgeon. We despise each other."

"And his wife, too," threw in Doris. "She's had more work done than the Interstate between here and Miami."

"Why, did he say something? Was he nasty to you boys? Because I'll go over to his place right now and—"

"No, no, Grampy, nothing like that," assured Bortnicker. "But, ah, he was saying something to his wife about a…shuffleboard tournament tomorrow?"

"Yeah, he's the shuffleboard king around here. He cheats, of course. But he's just sneaky enough to get away with it."

"We've never beaten them in doubles," complained Doris. "Just once I'd like to see them lose."

"Hmm, interesting," was Bortnicker's reply.

Before they turned out the lights, T.J. asked what was up with his buddy.

"What do you mean, Big Mon?"

"C'mon, man, I know you were cheesed off in the pool room. What's the deal?"

Bortnicker removed his glasses and gave them a final polish for the day. "Remember that dorky sleepaway camp my mom sent me to one summer?"

"Yeah, like around fifth grade. What was it called again?"

"Camp Hohotonka, up in Maine," he replied. "Boy, did I hate it. Basically, I got tormented the whole time, which is another story, but there was one bright spot. Yeah, they had baseball and basketball and archery, which I was terrible at, but there was one thing I got *very* good at up there."

"Don't tell me."

"All I can say, Big Mon, is that tomorrow afternoon, Greggie Boy and Babs are *going down*."

Chapter Six

Day two of the Memorial Day weekend started much differently, as T.J. almost never ran on Sunday mornings. But he couldn't just lay there, so he borrowed the key to Morty's three wheeled bike, which was locked up to the bike stand outside building 62, and pedaled out of the complex and down the road a mile or so to the local Winn-Dixie, where he bought some cinnamon buns and suspect Florida bagels for breakfast, tossing his purchases in the bike's huge handlebar basket.

After some heartfelt thank you's, Doris brewed some coffee and they sat down to breakfast. As always, she began the day by telling Morty the apartment was too cold, which he ignored. "So, gentlemen, another day at the pool?" he asked as he slathered cream cheese on his bagel.

"Sounds fine to me," said T.J., sipping his orange juice. "But I have a question, Mr. Barrett. When I was in the water yesterday I saw this lady walking around with a clipboard—"

"Oh, you mean the Pool Nazi," he snapped.

"Morty, that's not nice in front of the boys," scolded Doris, followed by a shoulder smack.

Morty shook her off. "You see, boys, in a place like this, even a little power is a dangerous thing. This woman, whose name believe it or not is Tootsie Zaza, volunteered for the board and was given the job of pool warden. So, what she does every day is, she goes to each clubhouse and checks the passes of anyone who's not a year-rounder to see if anybody sneaked in. I showed her your pass, which was on your towel. By the way, T.J., she thinks you're cute."

"Thanks."

"I'm sure that means a lot to him, Grampy," cracked Bortnicker, who was on his third cinnamon bun. "These are good, Big Mon," he wuffed. "Not as good as the ones in Cooperstown, but they'll do. By the way, Grampy, what's on for tonight? Another early bird deal?"

The grandparents looked at each other. "You tell him, Morty."

"No, you."

"C'mon, you've been dying to."

"All right already! Sheesh!" He looked at his grandson with a devilish smile. "Sam-ela, your crazy mother tells me that you're a pretty big fan of the Beatles, no?"

"He's a mega-fan," said T.J.

"Well, my friend, it just so happens that this year's Memorial Day dinner dance is a Beatles extravaganza!" Morty was clearly excited, but his words hung in the air as the stunned boys considered the possibilities.

"You mean, they're going to turn off Seabreeze 107.5 and play Beatles stuff?" asked Bortnicker.

"Better than that. We've hired a band that plays nothing *but*. They call themselves The Beatle Boys, and their manager says they can do any song the Beatles ever sang!"

"Plus, there will be a buffet dinner and dancing," added Doris. "So what do you guys think? Sound exciting?"

"I...uh...yeah," said Bortnicker finally.

"Great!" said Morty, clapping his hands with glee. "Can't wait to cut the rug tonight, even if it isn't exactly my kind of music."

"You know, T.J.," said Doris, lowering her glasses, "you actually look like one of them, when he was young, anyway. What's his name, the cute one."

"That would be Paul McCartney," intoned Bortnicker in his Beatle voice.

"That's very good, Sammy," she said. "Is he alive or dead? Paul, I mean."

"He's still with us," answered Bortnicker, enjoying his friend's embarrassment.

"Well, then we're set for tonight. Should be quite a soirée. Ready to go to the pool?"

"Uh, Grampy," said Bortnicker, "before we head over there, I'd like to talk to you two about something."

Doris dramatically put her hand to her heart. "Not anything bad, I hope."

"Oh no, Grammie. Just a little proposition."

* * * *

The Royal Palm clubhouse pool was even more active than the previous day. There was not a cloud in the sky, and the humidity was down a few ticks. After laying out their towels and showering, the boys quickly eased into the deep end, away from gossiping clutches of half-submerged old ladies. It was near the pool's center that they came upon a hilarious scene. A couple, who had to be at least in their mid-70s, was floating together on their noodles, almost nose to nose, and treading water as they whispered sweet nothings to each other. But as they were obviously hard of hearing, it ended up being broadcast to their general area, and the boys nonchalantly edged to within earshot to get the dirt. As Nat King Cole sang "Mona Lisa" on Seabreeze 107.5, the portly, orange-haired woman, whose name was apparently Eve, looked into the eyes of the man, who was almost bald with tremendously bushy eyebrows, and said something like, "But I'm so lucky I have you, Alan. Why is it you treat me so good?"

From behind saucer shaped sunglasses the dashing Alan replied, in a distinctly Brooklyn accent, "You know why? Because you're like a *spidah*. You pull people into your web of love, and they can't geddout."

"And do you know what you are?" she countered. "You, my love, are a *cougah*."

"A *cougah*? What's this *cougah*?"

She burst into peals of laughter, at which point the boys took a breath and then sank to the bottom of the pool, holding their sides in mock hysteria.

After a quick noonday snack in the clubhouse the boys drifted off on their loungers as Morty and Doris kibitzed in the pool with their friends. They'd only been asleep a few minutes when T.J. felt someone standing over him. Or rather, he was assaulted by the overpowering scent of perfume. Cracking one eye open, he was met with the visage of the dreaded clipboard-toting Pool Nazi. "May I see your pass?" she barked.

T.J. fumbled around a bit for it, found it on the concrete under his lounger, and held it up. She nodded, then turned to Bortnicker. "And yours?"

Bortnicker smiled slyly, then said, "Passes? We don't need no stinking passes!"

The Pool Nazi's mouth dropped open as Morty called from the water, "Jeez, Tootsie, you saw their passes yesterday. And Sammy, don't be a wise guy. Apologize."

"Sorry, Ms. Zuzu," he muttered.

"It's Zaza!"

"Oops. Sorry again." She marched off, the boys biting their lips to keep from laughing.

Around 2 PM Morty and Doris exited the pool and toweled off. "You sure you want to do this?" Morty said to his grandson.

"Oh yeah."

"Okay then, let's go back to the apartment and change."

T.J. stayed put with Doris, who said, "I hope they know what they're doing. I swear, Morty's like a little boy sometimes."

Within minutes, grandfather and grandson had returned, decked out in shorts, T-shirts and sneakers. Doris and T.J. got up and accompanied them to the adjacent shuffleboard courts, which were green painted concrete with yellow numbered pyramids on each end of the five 39'x 6' rectangles. The courts were alive with action, seniors shoving the red and black plastic discs back and forth and tallying numbers, which were recorded for the ongoing complex standings. A perusal of the current leaderboard found the Barretts in second place behind Mr. and Mrs. Greg Burrell, who awaited them eagerly. As usual, Dr. Greg was dressed impeccably, with tan dress shorts and a pink Izod golf shirt. Babs had chosen to go with a mini tennis skirt ensemble that accentuated her shapely legs. Again, she smiled at T.J.; again he was creeped out.

"Bad news, Burrell," opened Morty. "We gotta cancel the match today."

"Whatever for, Morty?" replied the doctor in a smarmy tone.

"Doris hurt her wrist. She can't play."

"What's the matter, hon?" asked Babs with mock sincerity, "that big bracelet causing some pain?"

"Hey, Babs," she shot back, "looks like you missed a spot with the crack filler near your right eye. S'matter, the paint roller broken or something?"

The boys exchanged sideways glances as Babs inadvertently put a hand halfway to her face before stopping herself.

"However," continued Morty, "my grandson here has graciously agreed to stand in for my wife…if that's not a problem."

"A problem?" Burrell nervously flicked his eyes to the grinning Bortnicker for a moment, then regained his composure and flashed a pearly white faux smile. "No problem at all, Morty. You do realize, however, that this game will still count in the standings, and that, well, last night I happened upon these boys shooting pool and…how can I say this delicately…it doesn't seem as if hand/eye coordination runs in the family."

Before Morty could blow his stack, Bortnicker got dramatic. Dropping to one knee, he bowed his head and said, "Oh Great One, please deem that I am worthy of doing battle with you here on this field of honor."

T.J. turned away and put his hand over his mouth, but Bortnicker's histrionics had brought the tournament to a screeching halt. Suddenly, the other courts emptied and gathered within earshot.

Burrell had no choice. "Well, *of course* you can substitute for your grandmother," he said gallantly for all to hear. Then he whispered, "And enough with the kneeling, okay?"

Bortnicker, beaming, sprang to his feet. Turning to T.J., he said, "Pick me a good stick, Big Mon. It's game on."

Standing under one of the canvas overhangs that provided shade to the court players as they awaited their turn, T.J. asked Doris how the game worked.

"Well, as you can see, on each end of the court of play you've got this big triangle, with the tips facing in toward each other. The scoring grid itself is divided into sections. The smallest is a triangle at the top; if you push the disc into that space without touching any of the border, it's 10 points. Then you have three horizontal zones below that. The second zone behind the triangle is eight points and the third is seven. Both of these are divided down the middle, which makes it harder to score. But if you land in the last and widest zone, which is called 'the kitchen', you *lose* 10 points. The two teams alternate shots. If you are 'sending the biscuit' as it's called, you want to have it land cleanly in one of the plus zones without touching any borders or dividers. But you can also try to knock your opponent's disk out of a scoring zone. First team to 75 points wins. Get it?"

"Got it. Uh, if you don't mind me asking, is Mr. Barrett a good player?"

Doris sighed. "He has his good days and bad days. The reflexes aren't as sharp as they used to be. Plus, he always wants to beat Burrell so badly he tenses up. I hope this is a good idea."

By now the two teams were set; Morty and Bortnicker went with the red pucks, and the Burrells chose black. "You first," politely offered Bortnicker, and Dr. Greg stepped up for his first shot, but not before planting a good luck kiss on Babs's cheek.

"Yecch," whispered Doris.

But that smooch would turn out to be the high point of the Burrells' afternoon. Bortnicker, who had purposely allowed Greg to go first, thus putting his team into a defensive position with the last shot in every round, time after time knocked them out of scoring position with expertly placed shots that left team Barrett's discs nestled in the 8 and 7 zones, and a few times in the 10-point triangle. It wasn't even close.

Of course, Bortnicker being Bortnicker, his pre-shot routines became more and more elaborate and dramatic with each success. At times, he would even wet his index finger and hold it aloft to check for wind currents. Morty, clearly enjoying the experience, merely grinned from ear to ear as the gathering of old-timers laughed uproariously and cheered their shots. As for the Burrells, their mutual support turned to whispered sniping and eye rolling as the score mounted against them. By the time Bortnicker landed his last shot—holding the stick behind him and shooting from between his legs to seal the 75-51 win, the doctor and his wife could barely muster the strength to shake hands with their conquerors and stalk off the courts, to the tune of Sammy Davis Jr. singing "I've Gotta be Me." T.J. figured that if the crowd could have lifted Morty and Bortnicker onto their shoulders, they would have.

T.J., applauding with the rest of them, could make out tears of joy behind Doris's sunglasses as her grandson took a deep, dramatic bow.

* * * *

"I've got to hand it to you, man, that was some performance," said T.J. as he slipped into his tropical shirt back at the apartment.

"Yeah," said Bortnicker, who lounged on his bed, towel drying his scraggly curls. "The good doctor and Babalicious got more than they bargained for. It's all in the strategy, Big Mon. And, tell you what, Grampy's not so bad a player himself. I think all my fooling around took the pressure off, and he raised his game."

T.J. brushed his hair and regarded his friend through the mirror. "So, uh, have you gotten a chance to talk to him?"

"Yeah, we kind of hashed things out on the way to the pool, when we were alone. He's gonna try to help me locate my dad."

"Good deal."

There was a knock at the door, and Morty, still beaming, poked his head inside. "Ready for some Beatlemania?"

"Always," said his grandson.

For this big event on the social calendar, the Barretts had really dressed up. Morty sported a tropical shirt and golf slacks with white shoes and matching belt, while Doris wore a blue sundress. For a couple in their late 80s they didn't look too bad. The foursome piled into the Florida Cruiser for the short drive to the Palm Pointe clubhouse. Upon entering, Morty was afforded the reception of a conquering hero; word of his stunning defeat of the Burrells had spread beyond the Royal Palm clubhouse. And the place was packed.

"Wow, there has to be over 150 people here," said Bortnicker.

"I told you this was a big deal," said Morty. "See that guy at the bar having a soda? The guy with the cameras? He's from the *Boca Herald* newspaper. I guess they sent him over to cover the event." The group made their way to a reserved table not far from the slightly raised bandstand, where the Beatle Boys' guitars, amps, keyboard and drum kit were set up and ready to go.

A waitress came around and took their drink order. Morty grandly ordered a bottle of champagne for himself and Doris. "A whole bottle? Morty, are you nuts?" she warned.

"Hey, we had a good day," he replied. "Let's enjoy ourselves."

"If you say so," she said with a shrug that sent her jewelry tinkling.

"So, Big Mon, has this weekend been restful enough for you?" asked Bortnicker, sipping some ice water.

"Really, it has. Just vegging out for two days has been neat. Then, tomorrow we fly back, I have a couple more baseball games, we take final exams, and bam, sophomore year's over."

"And then, on to our summer at Tasteefreez."

T.J. shook his head. "Man, I don't know how you talked me into that one." The Tasteefreez ice cream shop in town center was in direct competition with the Dairy Queen farther down Boston Post Road toward Southport. Its owner, Rocco DiPalermo, had known the boys for years, and his establishment was a quick bike ride from their homes near the beach. But when word got out that they were minor TV celebrities, he'd immediately recruited them for summer employment. Rocco was even putting up a framed 8 x 10 glossy still photo from the show and a sign reading *Here to serve you—our own local TV stars, T.J. and Bortnicker!* He had also purchased copies of the *Bermuda Case* DVD, which he planned to resell for a modest profit. The boys were all set to start the week after school let out in late June. It beat mowing lawns, which is what they'd done up until now with their summers—when they weren't ghost hunting, that is.

"I can't believe how everyone here is so decked out," chuckled Bortnicker. "Looks like this group is ready to party!"

"Hey," said T.J. "There's the Burrells, back in the corner with some other people. Dr. Greg looks like he's still fuming, man."

"Well isn't that wonderful," replied Bortnicker in his best Beatlese.

Just then the Beatle Boys took the stage. Thankfully, they weren't going to try to pull off the look-alike deal—there were five of them, anyway—but when they launched into a rocking rendition of "I Saw Her Standing There" it was clear they knew what they were doing. They followed up with "Please Please Me" before introducing themselves and announcing they'd be doing four sets of almost an hour apiece, with a Beatles trivia contest before the last set. Bortnicker, who with T.J. was loading his plate at the buffet table, wiggled his eyebrows and smiled.

They returned to their seats to find Morty and Doris gone; they were boogying on the dance floor. In fact, for a throng of old-timers the action was pretty lively. But then, 1964 was nearly 50 years ago, so why wouldn't this crowd be familiar with the Beatles? By the third song, "This Boy," it seemed that 90% of the audience was up and dancing. Even the Burrells—who appeared to have made up after their shameful display that afternoon—were slow dancing to that romantic tune. Fortunately, none of the older ladies asked the boys to dance, which would have mortified them.

And so the evening went. As the Beatle Boys transitioned from set to set, the patrons—who had never stopped imbibing cocktails—became more bold and less inhibited in their gyrations. "There's gonna be some sore people tomorrow," observed Morty during one of the breaks.

Finally, before the last set, the "John" member of the band called for participants for the trivia contest. A few people got up, somewhat wobbly from the drink and dancing, as did Dr. Greg Burrell, who was probably looking to atone for his humiliation of that afternoon. But upon seeing him approach the stage, Bortnicker rose, shot T.J. and his grandparents a wink, and stepped forward to join the lineup.

"Uh-oh," said T.J.

"Okay, then," said Beatle Boy John, whose gray hair, what was left of it, was pulled back in a ponytail. "We have seven entrants. The grand prize is a dinner for two, with drinks, at Capt. Bobby's Crab Shanty. Let's start with our first round. I'll ask each of you a question. If you get it, you move on to the next round. If you're wrong, you sit down. Understood?"

The seven contestants nodded, including Burrell and Bortnicker, who stood at the end of the line. Before the questions began, Dr. Greg half turned to his young adversary and said, "This is *my* era, son. Sit down while you can."

"Well you're quite the doubter, aren't you?" replied the boy in his best John Lennon twang, which he hoped gave the doctor pause for thought.

Difficulty-wise, the questions were cream puffs (What city were the Beatles from?) and yet the first five contestants went down in order. Then it was Burrell's turn. Beatle Boy John asked, "What is Ringo Starr's real name?"

"That's easy," he replied, "Richard Starkey."

"You're right!" There was mild applause in the ballroom, and Babs gave her husband a thumbs-up.

The musician turned to Bortnicker. "Where did the Beatles record their records?"

Bortnicker looked stumped. "You mean, like, the name of the studio?" he stammered.

"That's what I mean," smiled Beatle Boy John.

"Well, I would think it's...it's... Abbey Road?"

"That's correct!" crowed the musician, and the crowd applauded.

"Okay, we've got one round left," said Beatle Boy John, shuffling the index cards that held the questions. Burrell looked supremely confident, while Bortnicker appeared strangely uneasy. That first question had nearly thrown him for a loop, or so it seemed. "Since we've got such a big prize on the line, let's go best of ten." The crowd oohed and ahhed.

"No problem," said Burrell suavely.

"I guess so," agreed Bortnicker.

"Age before beauty," said Beatle Boy John, drawing some guffaws from the mildly intoxicated crowd. He proceeded to throw questions at the doctor, who managed to field eight of ten. As the audience clapped he said, "Beat that, Junior," out the side of his smiling mouth.

Beatle Boy John became serious. "Okay, son," he began, "question one: Who was the Beatles' producer on most of their records?"

Bortnicker mopped his brow.

"I need an answer, son."

"Um, Ed Sullivan?"

"That's incorrect," said the musician as the audience groaned. "You've got to get the next nine right to win."

Suddenly Morty stood up. "Hey Greg, a hundred bucks says he does it!" The audience—those who could hear him—gasped. The others buzzed. "What did he say? A hundred dollars? He said a *hundred*?"

Doris tugged at the back of Morty's shirt. "I knew the champagne would hit you," she hissed. "Sit down before you make a scene, you idiot!"

"What about it, Greg?" pressed Morty.

"It's your money," said the doctor with a nonchalant shrug.

Beatle Boy John reshuffled the deck, a little shakily. This definitely wasn't in the script for the evening. He faced Bortnicker with a piteous look. "All right, son. Here we go: Who was the Beatles' drummer before Ringo Starr?"

"Pete Best," he shot back.

"Right!" The audience offered mild applause.

"Next question: A week after their appearance on the Ed Sullivan Show in February 1964, the Beatles were on the show again. Where was that show filmed?"

"Miami Beach."

"Right!" More applause.

"Where were the beach scenes in the movie *Help* filmed?"

"Nassau, Bahamas."

"Correct!" The clamor was building.

"Who were the dastardly cartoon characters in *Yellow Submarine*?"

"The Blue Meanies, of course." Now Bortnicker was using his John Lennon voice to answer.

"Right! That's four in a row. Five to go!" He plucked a card. "In what famous hangout were the Beatles discovered by future manager Brian Epstein?"

"That would be The Cavern Club," he intoned. "A bit damp, it was."

"Right again!" Now Burrell was squirming.

"Who came up with the movie title *A Hard Day's Night*?"

"Me good mate Richie, whom you might know as Ringo."

"Correct!" Some people in the audience were standing now.

"Where was the Beatles' last US concert held?"

"Candlestick Park in San Francisco," he replied, "but our last actual live performance was on a rooftop in London."

"Right!"

Now Morty got a rhythmic chant going: *Bort-nicker! Bort-nicker! Bort-nicker!*

"Two more," said Beatle Boy John. "Here's a tough one. What Indian guru did the Beatles learn transcendental meditation from?"

"That would be the somewhat shady Maharishi Mahesh Yogi. Personally, I thought it was all a load of bollocks."

"You're right again! One more!" The crowd was now standing as one (except for Babs) and stomping their feet. The musician waited for silence and plucked a card, then blanched as he read it to himself.

This one must be a humdinger thought T.J.

"Okay, for the grand prize—"

"And a hundred bucks!" cried Morty.

"And a hundred dollars, your final question: Which of the Beatles could not read sheet music?"

A hush fell over the crowd. Burrell, who actually had no clue on half the questions Bortnicker had answered, turned and looked at his young adversary, who closed his eyes and lifted his arms to the heavens, as if channeling some divine spirit.

"Uh, I need an answer," said Beatle Boy John.

Bortnicker opened his eyes. "It's a trick question," he replied. "The fact is, mate, *none* of us could read sheet music."

"That's... *right!*" announced the amazed musician, and the room exploded. He handed the Capt. Bobby's gift certificate to the boy, who waved it under the doctor's nose and said, "And a splendid time is guaranteed for all," before returning in triumph to his seat beside T.J.

"I guess all those trivia contests with your cousin are paying off, Big Mon," he told his friend as Burrell dropped a hundred dollar bill on Morty's dessert plate and kept right on going.

* * * *

The crowd, still revved up from Bortnicker's dramatic come-from-behind victory, threw itself into the Beatle Boys' final set, which was all by audience request. One would think as the night wound down that the calls would be for slower numbers, but the songs were decidedly up-tempo. Even Morty, the hundy self-stuck to his forehead, gave it a go.

Bortnicker was just finishing T.J.'s blueberry pie a la mode when someone screamed and the music screeched to a halt. An old lady had suddenly crumpled to the floor in the middle of "Back in the USSR."

"Omigod!" a woman screamed. "It's Mrs. Rynderman! Someone help her!"

Someone else yelled, "Does anyone here know CPR!"

The boys looked at each other. One thing Rocco DiPalermo had required when hiring them on for the summer at Tasteefreez was that they take a CPR/choking course at the local Red Cross office. A few years before a man had nearly died when he'd swallowed a maraschino cherry whole, and Rocco wanted no part of a tragedy on the premises. He'd paid for the boys, who'd passed the half-day course, which included a written test and practical application on a dummy, with flying colors.

"I've got this one," said T.J. quietly. "Go call 911." As Bortnicker bolted from the clubhouse to the parking lot where he could get reception on his cell phone, T.J. pushed his way through to the stricken woman, who lay flat on her back with her eyes closed. "Mr. and Mrs. Barrett, get everyone back!" he said sternly. Immediately Morty and Doris sprang into crowd control mode. T.J. began by asking the victim, "Are you okay?" There was no response. He leaned in close to her nose and mouth to check for breathing. There was none. But she had a faint pulse.

"She's dead!" someone cried.

"Not yet, she isn't," he said to himself. Mrs. Rynderman, who'd been whooping it up all night, was a big woman; this wasn't going to be easy. First, kneeling by her head, he tilted her chin back to open an air passage. He pinched her nostrils and blew a preliminary breath into her mouth, which thankfully was mostly filled with real teeth. Still, he tasted the chicken Cordon Bleu the woman had feasted on, and it almost made him gag. After the first breath he checked to see if her chest rose; when it did, slightly, he realized the airway probably wasn't blocked and she had no obstruction in her throat, which was a good thing. He gave a second breath. Then, he quickly transitioned to a straddling position above her blocky thighs and placed the heel of his right hand slightly below the centerline beneath her ample bosom. T.J. laid his left hand over his right. Hoping that he wouldn't crack any ribs, he performed 30 2-inch depth compressions, counting out "andone-andtwo-andthree" as he went along. After the 30th compression, he administered two more rescue breaths.

"She's gone!" someone wailed, and then others joined in.

Morty turned toward the stage. "Hey, you! Beatle Boys!" he yelled. "Play something. Anything!" At that, the band began an instrumental rendition of "Yesterday."

After the breaths failed, T.J. went back to another round of compressions. And then it happened. A voice—or maybe it was his inner consciousness, he couldn't tell—said, *It's not her time*. This gave him a shot of adrenaline, and he began muttering, "notyourtime-notyourtime-notyourtime" with each feverish compression. After the set, he gave a breath.

Mrs. Rynderman's eyes fluttered, then opened, all glassy. Some onlookers in the front shrieked, "She's alive!"

And Myrna Rynderman, with the strains of "Yesterday" wafting overhead, peered up at T.J. Jackson and said, *"Paul McCartney?"* as paramedics burst through the doors of the Palm Pointe ballroom.

* * * *

What happened in the ensuing minutes was a blur. The now-conscious Mrs. Rynderman was hefted onto a gurney and whisked away to the hospital, but not until the *Herald* reporter had finished photographing the entire episode for a next-day exclusive. T.J., who had only wanted a weekend of quiet and relaxation, was totally wrung out; it was Bortnicker, whose call had brought the paramedics, who spoke briefly to the reporter as the ballroom emptied out, many of the patrons offering words of praise and shoulder rubs to T.J. as he sat slumped in his seat, flanked by Morty and Doris. The Beatle Boys packed up and left, and then—at last—it was quiet.

"Proud of you, Big Mon," said Bortnicker finally.

"You would've done the same," replied T.J. wearily.

"Are you serious? I could barely dial the cell phone."

Then Doris spoke up. "It's been a long, long day," she said brightly. "Anyone for Sonic? It's after eight o'clock."

* * * *

The next day, Memorial Day, everyone was up early to get the boys to the airport for their 10:00 AM flight home to Connecticut. Nobody said much; T.J. had even failed to mention "the voice" to his friend, because he wasn't sure if it was a figment of his imagination. But he *had* heard it. They stopped at McDonald's for a breakfast-to-go and made it to the airport easily on this national holiday morning.

"Thanks for everything, Mr. and Mrs. Barrett," said T.J. as he hugged the old people goodbye.

"No, T.J., thank *you*," said Morty. "You literally livened up Boca Vista Royale. Take good care of Sammy here, will ya?"

"Sure thing."

Bortnicker had a few private moments with his grandparents, and then the boys passed through security and trudged to the departure gate to sit. But as they were passing the airport newsstand store Bortnicker said, "Oh-oh."

"What?"

"Put on your Bridgefield cap and your shades right now," he instructed gently. "Then go find us a couple seats away from everyone." This T.J. did, and sat quietly until his friend returned with the newspaper. "Well, Mr. Low-key," he said with a chuckle, "looks like you made the front page of the *Boca Raton Herald*."

"No way."

"Yes way. Check it out."

The headline read **Young TV Star Saves Senior Citizen**. The story, accompanied by photos of T.J. performing CPR and Mrs. Rynderman being carted away, was compelling:

Boca Vista Royale: This usually sedate retirement community was rocked—literally—last night when TV reality star T.J. Jackson, 16, dove in to resuscitate a woman who had collapsed from cardiac arrest during a Beatles-themed dance. Jackson, visiting the complex with costar Bortnicker of the paranormal series *Junior Gonzo Ghost Chasers* (Adventure Channel) intervened when Myrna Rynderman, aged 78, suddenly collapsed to the dance floor. Using CPR techniques learned in a Red Cross training course, Jackson was able to revive the stricken woman, who had stopped breathing. She was then rushed to Boca General Hospital by paramedics, where she is resting comfortably and is out of danger. Jackson, the handsome young leader of the show's ghost hunting team, was not available for comment afterwards. The show's next episode, which features an investigation in Cooperstown, New York, is set to air in mid-July.

To view further photos from this event, as well as exclusive video, visit our website at www.bocahearald.com.

A "Jeez Louise" was all T.J. could manage.

Then Bortnicker's cell phone rang. He checked the caller ID. "It's your cousin," he said.

T.J. took the phone and spoke quietly. "LouAnne?"

"Cuz," she said, her voice quivering, "are you okay? What the heck's going on down there?"

"Yeah," he said, "I'm okay. What's up?"

"What's *up*? You mean, why am I calling you in Florida at nine in the morning on Memorial Day? Because our phone's been ringing since like 6 AM!"

"From who?"

"Hmmm, let me read you the list. I've been contacted by my local paper, *USA Today, Entertainment Weekly, People Magazine, and CNN*!"

"About *me*?"

"Yes, about you. Some reporter at that Beatles dance you were at took a video on his phone of you saving that lady and it's gone viral! It's already on *YouTube* and *TMZ*!"

"You've got to be kidding me."

"Cuz, wake up," she said. "This isn't Civil War times—it's 2012, and you're all over the place. Oh yeah, and Mike Weinstein called to say congrats. He told me The Adventure Channel's issuing a statement about how proud they are of you, blah blah blah. Can you imagine what this is going to do to the Cooperstown ratings in July?"

T.J., a little woozy, pinched the bridge of his nose and closed his eyes to compose himself.

"You there, Cuz?"

"I'm here."

"So I ask you again: are you okay?"

"Yeah, I guess so. Bortnicker's here with me at the airport. We're waiting to leave for home."

"Well, just hang loose. Wish I was there to help. Be ready for an onslaught when you get home."

"I wish you were here, too. I guess all I can do is lay low till this all blows over. Or try to."

His cousin turned serious. "I've got to ask you, though: was the woman really on her way out?"

T.J. thought again of the eerie voice. "I think so. Guess I was lucky."

"You're too much. Hey, call me when you get back to Connecticut. Love ya."

He put his hand over the phone and whispered, "Love you, too."

Bortnicker, who had been feigning non-attention, asked if LouAnne had heard of his exploits. "You've got no idea," he groaned. "It's all over the place, man. What next?"

Bortnicker's phone rang again, and he checked the caller ID. "Well, looky here," he said with a wry smile. "It's our friend Ronnie from Bermuda. Wonder what *she* wants to talk about at this early hour?"

Chapter Seven

July, 1662

Charity Blessing lay in bed, fully dressed and wide-awake, waiting until she was sure her mother and stepfather were sound asleep. Outside her window, crickets chirped and there were rustling sounds as the occasional nocturnal animal made its way across the property in search of food. When the girl was sure the coast was clear, she gathered her skirts and, holding her clog shoes so as not to be noisy, tiptoed over the floor boards and eased open the front door. Slipping outside, she put on her shoes while drinking in the fresh night air, which was invigorating despite its midsummer humidity. Outside of a few chores performed in the immediate area of the dwelling, she had more or less been under house arrest, awaiting her trial for witchcraft. Now she was blessedly removed from the judgmental stares of passersby and the pointing of curious children. After a quick scan of her surroundings, she headed south.

At this time of night, a young lady was taking a chance traveling alone. For one thing, despite the town's environs being laid out in an orderly fashion, with parcels of farmland divided among the townsmen, there was still the threat of wild animals such as bears and wolves intruding in search of chickens or livestock; there was also continued unease over the inhabitation of local Indians. Supposedly, the colonists' war with the Pequot nation had ended in 1637 with a great battle to the south of town, but small tribes such as the Sasqua and Pequannock still lived in the area in what appeared to be a peaceful fashion. They fished in canoes in Long Island Sound for shad and hunted within their

69

territorial boundaries, wearing animal skins as clothing. There had been some attempts by the white settlers to Christianize them, but for the most part, they kept to themselves, which fostered a general air of distrust in the colonists.

Charity made her way across the village, past the residences of men who earned their living as carpenters, masons, wheelwrights, smiths and coopers, into the fields toward Sasco Neck, where a dam had been built to drain a portion of Pine Creek and create salt meadows. Particular attention had been paid to the building and maintenance of fences that sectioned off people's properties. In fact, inspectors were chosen to check on the settlers' fences each month. If they found defects in the fences, the guilty party had to pay for the viewer's time. Of course, at midnight the appointed fence viewers were tucked into bed, as was everyone else. It seemed fitting to her that the townspeople were so preoccupied with the setting of boundaries, because it was she who had been accused of overstepping hers.

Finally, her skirt bottom pocked with nettles, Charity Blessing reached her destination—the cottage of the family of her beau, Trevor. His father was the proud owner of a choice parcel of salt meadow; Trevor, the only male child, was in line to inherit the property upon his father's demise. Boyishly handsome, with dark, wavy hair and big brown eyes, Trevor was considered among Fairfield's young women to be quite the catch. He was serious, hard-working and God-fearing. Even better, his heart belonged to Charity.

Or so she wanted to believe. He had told her such during clandestine meetings in the salt meadow bordering Long Island Sound, during which he had even been so bold as to kiss her. Tonight she would determine the depth of his ardor.

Charity approached the modest dwelling slowly, careful not to awaken the family's old hound dog, Isaac, who was thankfully hard of hearing. She sneaked around to the back window opening and whispered his name twice before receiving a response. "It's me," she hissed. "Meet me in five minutes at the big rock."

"All right," he whispered back from the blackness of his tiny room.

When the boy arrived at their predetermined meeting place near Pine Creek, Charity immediately threw her arms around him and buried her face in his chest. "Oh, Trevor, Trevor, what's to be done about all this?" she moaned, her words muffled in his coarse shirt. But she immediately sensed something amiss. His arms had instinctively gone around her as well, but they seemed limp and noncommittal, not the strong but tender embrace she was used to. She pulled back and looked into his doe eyes. "What's wrong?" she said, her own eyes searching.

"Why are you here?" he asked in turn. "Do you know how dangerous it is to be away from your home, Charity? To be seen here, with me? I cannot fathom your recklessness."

"Recklessness? I thought you would be pleased to see me. We could discuss our plans—"

"What plans?"

"To leave this place, and spend our lives together. Was that not what you told me you wanted?"

Trevor took a deep breath, then looked out toward the rippling waters of the Sound. "Things have changed, Charity," he said with the slightest tremor in his voice.

"How so?"

"You have been confined to your house for these many days, but the entire town has been thrown into an uproar. Rumors and accusations have been flying about you. Do you realize that people in this community are attributing every negative occurrence in their daily lives to your powers of sorcery? From the death of livestock to crops drying up to food going bad—"

"This is ridiculous, Trevor!" she fumed. "While it is true that I have no love for these people, I do not spend my days conjuring spells to lay upon them and their families. Surely you have spoken out in my defense?"

The boy looked down and shook his head. "Charity," he said evenly, "my father is a respected man in this community. As his only son, it is the expectation that I will carry on his good name and take over the farm. I cannot, and *will not*, simply run off and shirk my responsibilities to my family and my community. What I am trying to say is, our pairing from this point forward would be ill-advised, to say the least."

She regarded him as if he were a stranger. "You did not think that while holding me in your embrace in private," she said sarcastically. "Or do you forget that?"

"I was weak," was his pained reply. "And now, perhaps, I have an idea of what made me act so."

"Are you implying that I bewitched you?" she asked, her voice rising. "What have you ever seen in me that would suggest I practice the Devil's worship?"

He thought for a few seconds, choosing his words carefully. "I know that you had speaks with the African slave woman called Clarisse when she was quartered here with the Nelson family a few years back. She might have disappeared, but I am beginning to think you were versed on the black arts before she left. Can you attest that this was not so?"

Charity looked away and thought.

* * * *

It had all begun innocently enough. The Nelson family, one of the more well-to-do clans in town, had come from Barbados two years earlier, their patriarch a doctor, which was a valued occupation in so primitive a time. Dr. Nelson was known throughout Fairfield as a man who would give freely of his time and expertise, limited as it was, to help the townspeople deal with the multitude of ailments that poor hygiene and their surrounding harsh elements engendered. Ironically, his wife was frail due to an almost fatal miscarriage some years before, and could do little in the way of household chores. It was also determined that the hot, humid climate of Barbados was not conducive to her health, so he had packed up his family of two young boys and his practice and sailed for Connecticut, where his brother, also a physician, had settled in nearby Stratford.

One day Charity was asked by her mother, who was taking in washing, to deliver a bundle of clothes to the Nelson home. When she arrived the woman of the house was out, accompanying her husband on a visit to a pregnant neighbor who was having difficulty in the delivery. She walked into the dwelling to find Clarisse, the Nelsons' slave, sitting at the table, putting dried herbs in different small bottles. She was a broad woman, dressed plainly, her skin jet black. For Charity, who had never been around a person of color, the woman was both exotic and mysterious.

"Yes, child?" she said with a lilt native to her island.

"I've…come to deliver Mrs. Nelson's wash," she replied timidly.

Clarisse put down her herbs. "Come sit," she said, nodding to the chair across the table from her. Charity placed the bundle to the side and faced the slave. "And aren't you the pretty one," she said, breaking into a gap-toothed grin. "What is your name, child?"

"Charity. Charity Blessing," she answered.

"Charity Blessing," repeated the black woman. "Such a meaningful name. Give me your hands, child."

With some trepidation, the girl slid her hands toward the center of the table. Clarisse took them, her touch warm, the skin calloused from years of labor. "Hmmm…" murmured the woman, closing her eyes. She smiled to herself. "Yesss…you're an unhappy one, you are…you like to scheme on things, too—"

Charity jerked her hands away in alarm. "How can you tell this?" she spluttered in fear.

"I know things," replied the slave impassively. "I see things. You see, I, too, am on the outside of society. Your home, it is a loveless one?"

"Yes," she whispered. "My father, whom I did love, was a drunkard. He died, and my mother, a good woman, married the minister, Reverend Melrose."

"Is that so? But it seems the love of God has not found its way to you, girl dear. Has it?"

"No," she confessed. "In fact, I am resented, and cannot wait to marry and leave his household."

"And you have a boy in mind?"

"Yes," she whispered.

"This boy, does he feel as you do?"

"I'm not sure."

There was a pause as the slave woman studied her face. Then she said, "Child, the place from where I come is a beautiful one. But in that place, the same as here, people of color like myself are put upon by white masters such as Dr. Nelson. Our lot in life is not pleasant. And so, we turn to measures beyond what is viewed by our people as 'normal' religion in order to cope with the forces of evil and hatred that hold us down. Do you understand what I am telling you?"

73

"Yes," said Charity. "Could you verse me in such knowledge?"

"I could," she replied, her voice steady, her eyes betraying no emotion. "But this would have to be kept secret. Not even your dear mother would be allowed to know."

"I won't tell," the girl replied, her heart hammering.

"But you must realize," continued Clarisse, "that what you will learn must not be used to do bad, only to protect yourself."

"Is it that powerful?" asked the girl, with a hint of excitement.

"It could be, and therein lies the danger. When would you like to begin?"

"As soon as possible," said Charity, barely able to contain her eagerness.

"Very well, then," said the slave, again picking up the herbs to continue her work. "I will let you know where and when we will next meet. This house is not safe. But again, you are sure this is what you want?"

"I have never been more sure in my life," said Charity.

For the next six months, stealthy meetings were held at various sites in and around the town. Charity had little trouble slipping away from her mother, especially because laundry deliveries gave her reason for daily excursions. Clarisse was a patient teacher, and Charity a sharp and inquisitive student, always wanting to ascend to the next level of enlightenment. Some of Clarisse's instruction involved the mixing of herbs and other ingredients to create preventative or restorative elixirs; at other times, the harnessing of the Earth's forces were discussed and, after a while, practiced. And though she promised repeatedly to never use her abilities for negative purposes, the acquisition of this knowledge was both intoxicating and empowering. Although Charity was hesitant to put her newfound knowledge to practical use, she couldn't help but consider the myriad ways it could be implemented, from combating the plain-looking, jealous girls her age who considered her haughty, to punishing the older men who leered at her when she did see fit to attend Sunday services. There was also the matter of Trevor, whom she would attempt to bring under her romantic spell.

Of course, the infusion of self-confidence that she received was picked up upon by her stepfather, who felt even more determined to bring this recalcitrant child under control. The fact that this girl, whose notoriety was spreading, was allowed to exist under the roof of a man of God and community leader, was embarrassing and unnerving to him. When screaming at her brought only a smirk of loathing, he resorted to physical abuse, either by imposing total seclusion—sometimes accompanied by a diet of bread and water—or outright beatings. But still the girl, drawing strength from some unnatural reservoir, would not bend an inch.

And then, one day Charity arrived at the Nelson house, again to deliver laundry, only to find that her mentor was gone. According to Mrs. Nelson, the slave had "vanished into thin air," and she was not pleased. "My husband spent good money to acquire that woman legally," she complained aloud as Charity listened politely, trying mightily not to betray her disappointment. "We brought her here to this new country and a new beginning, put a roof over her head and clothes on her back, and how does she repay us? By running away like the heathen she is."

"Perhaps what she had here was not enough for her—ma'am," said the girl, immediately realizing she'd made a horrible mistake.

Goody Nelson's eyes widened in amazement. "Not… enough!" she blustered. "Are you suggesting that this…slave…was somehow *justified* in her actions?"

"No, ma'am," replied Charity, backtracking, "I just—"

"There are rumors about that you two were keeping company, you know," said the woman, her eyes slitted. "And that Clarisse had the power to leave here *without* running away. What say you to this?"

"I wouldn't know about any of that, ma'am," she replied, her head down. "I must go now, if you please. My mother will be expecting me."

"Fine," said Goody Nelson with a vengeful tone, "and you may inform Mary Blessing I am no longer in need of her laundry services."

"Yes ma'am," muttered Charity.

"And one more thing, young lady."

"Yes?"

"I'll be watching you."

* * * *

She snapped out of her reverie to the sound of Trevor's accusatory tone. "Is it true, then?" he was saying, more forcefully than he had ever spoken to her. "Do you have capability in this area?"

"Trevor," she replied, "believe me when I promise that I would never do anything to hurt you. I will only want for us to be happy."

"Then it is as I suspected," he said coldly. "I have no choice, then, but to implore you to return to your home and be done with me. And I, in turn, will pray to Almighty God for the salvation of your soul."

At these words, her catlike green eyes flared. "And so it is, then. Even you, the boy I love, have turned your back on me." She placed her hands on her hips and thrust out her chin. "Whether it is that I am a witch or not will be determined by our fair townspeople," she declared, "but no matter the outcome, I'd keep a weather eye out for danger if I were you. I won't be as easy to get rid of as you might think, Trevor Jackson."

Chapter Eight

LouAnne was right on the mark. T.J. walked into a media maelstrom upon his return to Fairfield. "Thank goodness you're home," said a concerned Tom Jackson after he hugged his son and helped remove his suitcase from the airport limo. "The phone's been ringing nonstop, and I frankly don't know what to tell people. It seems a lot of them want a few minutes of your time."

"Did they leave their numbers?" asked the weary boy.

"Yes. But I told them you have to be back in school tomorrow. Of course, that wouldn't stop *Entertainment Nightly* from possibly knocking on our door later this afternoon. I'm sure they got your flight info and gauged when you'd be back—"

As if on cue, a large black SUV screeched to a halt behind the departing airport shuttle van and an attractive blonde leaped out of the side door, followed closely by a cameraman. "T.J.?" she asked with a pearly smile. "Hi, I'm Lisa Hunter from *Entertainment Nightly*. Could I have a minute of your time?"

"For what?"

"Don't be so modest. The video of you saving that woman's life has gone viral. We'd like to be the first ones to get a sound bite from you."

T.J.'s gaze darted first toward his father, who shrugged his shoulders, then to Bortnicker's picture window across the street, where the boy and his mother were checking out the commotion. He signaled for his friend to come over. "Only if Bortnicker gets to be here with me," he said firmly.

"Sure, whatever," sang Lisa merrily. "Could we perhaps go inside and talk?"

"I think that would be best," said Tom, hustling the boys and Lisa's film crew inside to the living room before the neighborhood was disrupted.

The boys took a seat on the sofa and were mic'd; in no time some temporary lights had been set up and a makeup assistant had even "pouffed" them, which Bortnicker found completely amusing. "I'm ready for my close-up," he joked.

But Lisa Hunter was in no mood for frivolity; *Entertainment Nightly* wanted this feature on screen tonight, and they had to get right to business. The newswoman stared into the camera. "I'm here with T.J. Jackson and Bortnicker, two of the stars of the *Junior Gonzo Ghost Chasers* specials that air on The Adventure Channel. Less than 24 hours ago T.J. saved an elderly woman who had gone into cardiac arrest at a senior citizens dance by administering CPR, which included mouth to mouth resuscitation. The video from which the clip we just showed you is all over the Internet, and we're here at T.J.'s house for an *Entertainment Nightly* exclusive." She turned to the boys and flashed thousands of dollars' worth of gleaming dental work. "T.J.," she began, "tell our audience how this all came about, if you will." Then she whispered, "Don't worry, we'll edit it down later."

"Okay," he said warily. "Well, Bortnicker and I were down in Boca Raton visiting his grandparents, and there was this Beatles-themed dinner dance, so we showed up with them."

"It was really hopping," interjected Bortnicker. Hunter frowned at him and motioned to T.J. to continue.

"It was near the end of the night and I guess this one lady got over exerted, and—"

"Boom!" said Bortnicker. "She went down like a sack of potatoes!"

"Would you please let T.J. tell the story?" said the irritated reporter.

"Oh, sure," said Bortnicker. "Just trying to help, Lisa."

"So anyway," continued T.J., "both of us got trained in CPR for our summer job—"

"At Tasteefreez in Fairfield," cut in Bortnicker, who caught Hunter's quick shaking of the head as a signal to shut up.

"And," said T.J., "it's a good thing we were, because there wasn't really anyone else there to help the lady. So, while Bortnicker called 911,

I started CPR on her, and kinda got her back breathing."

"So you saved her life, then?" asked Lisa with a leading expression.

"Yeah, I guess I did," said T.J. "It all happened so fast, I just kinda reacted. I'm glad I was there to help her."

"So are we," said Hunter, who then turned to the cameras once again. "So there you have it, folks. The Adventure Channel has already issued a statement commending T.J. for his quick thinking, and remind fans of the show that the next *Junior Gonzo Ghost Chasers* special will air opposite the Major League All-Star Game this July."

"And… cut!" barked the crew chief.

"Do we have enough?" asked Hunter.

"Sure," he answered. "We can always edit out the interruptions."

"Hey!" said Bortnicker, obviously wounded. And then, as quickly as they'd blown into the house, the *Entertainment Nightly* crew thanked T.J. and Tom and were on their way. "Did that just happen?" asked Bortnicker as the SUV sped away.

"Yes, indeed," said Tom. "With the speed at which news travels today, it's a real race to get the scoop on stuff like this."

"You going to school tomorrow, Big Mon?" asked Bortnicker from the kitchen as he was rooting through the refrigerator. "I mean, if you want to hide out here—"

"No," he said. "We've got a paper due tomorrow in biology, and we're starting an English project in class. I'm not staying home."

"I'll phone the principal first thing," said Tom, "and request that no media people be allowed on campus. Is that okay with you, Son?"

"Definitely," said T.J., running his hand tiredly through his Beatle cut. "I just want to have a normal, quiet end of the year."

"That's what you said about our weekend in Boca," replied Bortnicker, peeling a banana.

* * * *

Later on, both Bortnicker and his mother came over to watch the show. T.J. in the meantime had politely returned the dozen or so calls Tom had received, mostly from the local papers, and patiently answered the same questions over and over. However, not all the calls were from media outlets. Two were from entertainment agents looking to sign him to a contract, and a couple were from star struck teenaged girls posing as reporters, who wanted to date him.

The *Entertainment Nightly* feature, which ran all of two minutes, wasn't bad, although Bortnicker was miffed that they'd virtually excluded him from the interview. When the video from the dance was shown, T.J. leaned forward in his seat, trying to identify the instant he'd heard the voice by the look on his face. There was a moment when his eyes seemed to widen a bit, but he couldn't be sure. He still hadn't told anyone of the voice.

* * * *

LouAnne called shortly after the Bortnickers went home. "So, what'd you think, Cuz?" she asked playfully. "Did *Entertainment Nightly* capture the essence of T.J. Jackson?"

"I guess," he said. "I almost wish it didn't happen, but that would be selfish."

"Hey, without you the lady's dead," said the girl. "This'll all calm down. Tomorrow there'll be another headline, another story. You'll be old news."

"Good."

"But I'm proud of you, Cuz. Mom and Dad were practically crying watching the show."

"*Your* dad? The ex-college linebacker?"

"Oh, yeah. Your uncle Mike's a sucker for that kind of stuff."

He sighed. "Can I change the subject?" he asked.

"Sure."

"Are you gonna come visit me this summer, or what?"

LouAnne thought for a few seconds. "I'll tell you what," she said. "After Reenactment Week's done and over with and Gettysburg calms down, I'm sure my parents won't mind me coming up there for a week or so. We're probably looking at the end of July. Sound good?"

"But that means we won't get to watch The Cooperstown Special together," said T.J. "The All-Star Game's the 10th."

"Sorry, Cuz, it's the best I can do. Gotta make the dinero for college. But if I do decide to come up there, will you promise me it'll be the total opposite of that craziness down in Florida?"

"That I can guarantee," said a beaming T.J., who was over the moon at the thought of spending time with the love of his life. "Tell you the truth, I'm afraid you'll be bored. Fairfield's a pretty dead place in the summer."

"No worries," she said. "I'm sure you and your buddy will cook up something interesting."

Chapter Nine

The Saturday of the Jaguar Club of Southern New England's annual concours was always circled on the Jackson calendar. Scheduled for late July to assure good weather, it was a forum for like-minded auto enthusiasts to gather in good fellowship and engage in a little friendly competition.

The car club, which had over 100 active members, was the local branch of JCNA, the Jaguar Clubs of North America, which included the United States and Canada. Although Tom Jackson's profession as a sought-after architect took him all over the world, he always blocked off the date for his club's concours. It was an opportunity to show his beloved 1993 oyster metallic XJS coupe and, hopefully, add to his trophy collection. But it wouldn't be easy—it never was. The judging team for his club was notoriously picky.

There were two categories of competition for the concours, Driven and Championship. Cars being judged in the Driven division were gone over with a fine tooth comb for any defects in the outer fit and finish, the tires and wheels, the electricals, and the interior components. An itemized score sheet three pages long was filled out, with deductions as small as a 10th of a point possible out of 100, and those tenths could make or break a car's score and separate a first-place finish from the runners-up. The Champion division, Tom's, was even more demanding, as it also entailed a stringent inspection of both the automobile's engine compartment and trunk, or "boot," according to British terminology.

It was a glorious day at Lyman Orchards in central Connecticut, the site of the club's concours. The show field upon which the cars would be parked according to year and category were freshly mowed and dry; the registration tent, which included a hospitality table, was buzzing with activity as volunteers readied scoring clipboards for the judges and "goody bags" containing sample sizes of car detailing products for registered entrants.

As Tom, T.J., and Bortnicker, who was wedged into the sportscar's back seat, pulled into the greeting area at 9:00 AM, it was clear from the signposts designating the various classifications that the turnout would be good. Just about every model of Jaguars would be represented multiple times, from sleek 120s, 140s and 150s open roadsters of the 1950s to stately sedans or "saloons" and timeless convertible and hardtop XKEs of the 1960s. The XJS, Tom's model, had replaced the wildly popular XKE in the mid-70s and was produced until 1996, when Jaguar went with a more aerodynamic style that, in his opinion, had somewhat homogenized the marque. But that was a matter of taste. Whatever, it was a fine day to display one's car—which was why, upon exiting the vehicle once it had taken its place in the XJS row, the boys were immediately handed brand-new microfiber cloths and bottles of detailing spray.

"Okay, fellas," said Tom with great seriousness, "I gave the car a good hand-washing and waxing earlier this week, but there's some stuff we still have to do, and I need your help."

"Righto, Mr. J.," joked Bortnicker in his best John Lennon voice while snapping a smart salute. "We'll bring home the gold, we will."

"Stop fooling around," cautioned T.J. "He's serious."

"Thank you," said Tom. "Anyway, I'm going to clean up the inside of the engine bay. T.J., I want you to get the inside of the windows and then go over the seats and the dashboard with the Armor All. Try not to get any grass on the carpets, okay? And then, we'll switch out the everyday car mats with the special ones I have in the trunk. Got it?"

"I'm on it, Dad."

"Now, Bortnicker, I need you to really concentrate on your job. After wiping down the body and checking the rubber bumpers and windshield for bug splatters and whatnot we might've gotten on our way over here, you are going to take this box of Q-tips and some Armor All and get inside every nook and cranny of these latticed wheels."

"Looks like there's 100 holes in each one," the boy muttered.

"Yeah, probably," said Tom with a grin. "But I just know you're the man for the job. And then, wipe down the tires with the rubber dressing and you're done."

"Sounds great," he said with a forced smile.

"He'll *love* doing it, Dad," said T.J. with a hint of sarcasm. "After dragging me down to Boca Vista Royale, it's the least he can do for payback."

"Fantastic," said the senior Jackson. "Well, it's a little after nine right now, and they'll announce 'rags down' at noon. That'll give us more than enough time to make this baby shine. Let's get to work!"

The boys immediately fell to their tasks as Tom popped the "bonnet" and began searching for specks of dirt and grease. T.J. made sure to inspect the body as he wiped it down, section by section, from different angles to make sure there were no smudges. Then it was on to the interior, where he contorted himself into various positions to get at all the corners of the back seat and rear window. Meanwhile, Bortnicker, singing a succession of Beatles tunes beginning with "Drive My Car," laid out on the grass next to each wheel and methodically cleaned the honeycombed metalwork before moving on to the blackwall tires. By the time the three were finished it was 10:30 AM and everyone was tired out. Afterwards they made their way to the hospitality tent for cold drinks and conversation with other JCSNE members trying to escape the July sun. Most of the club members, it seemed, were middle-aged couples, and T.J. felt a pang of sadness for his dad, who had bought the car as a diversion after the passing of his wife. Of course, those few unattached females in the group eventually gravitated to the dapper Mr. Jackson.

The boys also attracted a fair amount of attention from the Jaguar club members as the Cooperstown Special, which had aired opposite the Major League All-Star Game a few nights earlier, had garnered respectable ratings. Bortnicker and Pippa had come over to watch the program in the Jacksons' spacious rec room, and Tom had served up a huge bowl of popcorn to his guests.

T.J., who was always uncomfortable watching himself on TV, had to admit the bits and pieces they'd sent along to Mike Weinstein had been blended into a fast-paced, exciting feature. Of course, LouAnne had been on a conference call with the boys the entire time, and the numerous commercial breaks afforded them ample time to comment and answer questions from the adults on both ends. Uncle Mike and Aunt Terri, in particular, were impressed, and at the same time inwardly relieved that their daughter had returned to Gettysburg with the positive outlook that they were accustomed to. They realized that the girl's friends, particularly T.J., must have worked some magic to bring her back from the depths of despair over her attack at the hands of the football hero of her high school the previous December. They were also aware of what appeared to be her deepening affection for her cousin, though at the moment they were completely stumped—as was Tom Jackson—about how to deal with it. But, at the end of the day, their daughter was happy, the show was a hit, and life was good again.

As the Lyman Orchards Park also featured a huge farmer's market and children's playground, a steady stream of people turned up to mill around and admire the automobiles arrayed on the show field. And Tom's XJS, though not the oldest or the most expensive model in the show, got its share of onlookers and photographers, who were clearly digging its distinctive color and whimsical "SHAGWA" license plate, which Tom had based on the *Austin Powers* movies.

At precisely noon, "rags down" was announced and the boys looked on as a judging team shook hands with Tom and began their earnest task. First, they had him activate his headlights, blinkers, and horn to see if they were in good working order; then, he had to step away from the car so they could visually take it apart. It was nerve-racking to watch them pause and confer in whispers after one of them pointed out some minute imperfection. The minutes passed at an agonizing pace as the clipboard forms were filled out. Then, their judging completed, the four-man team thanked Tom and moved on to the next victim. With obvious relief, the senior Jackson then treated the boys to a grand lunch on the back porch of the farmer's market building, which overlooked a small man-made pond.

"When do they announce the winners, Mr. J.?" asked Bortnicker through a mouthful of chicken salad sandwich.

"Awards are at three o'clock," he replied, sipping an iced tea. "Everybody gathers at the tent for the results. But, listen, guys, no matter what happens, we all did our best, and my baby has never looked better."

They were cleaning up their table when Tom's cell phone beeped. He appeared puzzled as he checked the caller ID. "It's Reverend Stirling over at First Community Church. Hope nothing happened to the building; I personally oversaw the renovations." He clicked on and said hello. Then the boys watched the blood drain from his face as he listened. "I see," he said, finally. "I'm so sorry, Stephen." There was another long pause before he said, "Sure thing. We'll see you after the eleven o'clock service tomorrow morning. No, it's no imposition, believe me. See you then. Goodbye." He clicked off and frowned. "Bad news, T.J.," he said. "As you know, Reverend Melrose fell into a coma shortly after they found him last December, and Reverend Stirling took over for him. Well, Melrose just died."

"That's too bad," said T.J. "I didn't know him that well; he was kinda too serious for me, but he seemed like an okay guy."

"He was all right," said the elder Jackson. "Reverend Melrose was passionate about his church. I learned that while we were renovating the building. Everything had to be just so."

"And you did a great job," said his son.

"Thanks, but there's more. I don't know what it's about, but Stephen Stirling wants to see you after the morning service tomorrow."

"Me? What for? Am I in trouble or something?"

"No, Son, I'm sure it's nothing bad. But the man did seem worried. So listen, let's just enjoy the rest of the afternoon and tomorrow we'll see what it's all about."

"Anyone feel like dessert? I saw homemade apple pies in the farmer's market," said Bortnicker.

* * * *

Thunderstorms had raged over Fairfield County most of the night, and Sunday morning was soggy and humid. For the most part, father and son were still on a positive note from the previous afternoon, when the SHAGWA had scored a 99.982, edging out a black XJS convertible for first place by a point. At the announcement, the boys had shared a high-five, proud of the fruits of their labor. Tom's score would be coupled with that of another concours he would attend in Sturbridge,

Massachusetts in late August; having two scores would qualify him for a Northeast regional award. The Jackson contingent's victory was celebrated at the Fairfield Dairy Queen, Tom's favorite cruising destination, despite the fact that the boys were working for the competition, namely Tasteefreez, a few blocks away. But the festivities were tempered by the impending meeting with Reverend Stirling. There had been something disquieting in his tone that gave Tom the impression his son's services might be required. And though Tom was immensely proud of T.J.—as well as Bortnicker and his niece—for all they had accomplished, he secretly feared for the boy's mental well-being. These experiences had to be taking a toll on his psyche; what normal high school boy, whose waking hours should be filled with thoughts of school, girls, and sports, had time to contemplate all these otherworldly problems? He marveled that his son had been able to strike a balance without any outside consultation—his meeting with Jill Rogere notwithstanding. But as he watched T.J. and Bortnicker goof around as they worked on their Blizzards, he concluded that all he could do, as always, was to be there in a supporting role.

* * * *

"Thank you for coming, so nice to see you this morning," said Stephen Stirling over and over as he greeted his parishioners after Sunday service. The day was as gloomy weather-wise as the previous one was glorious. But, in a way, it was fitting. Although the official funeral mass and burial of his predecessor, Daniel Melrose, was not until Tuesday, Stirling had dedicated most of his sermon to paying tribute to the man who had brought him in as an eventual successor a couple years earlier. They had been opposites in many ways; Melrose was middle-aged, portly and taciturn in his approach when leading his congregation, while Stirling was tall and lithe, almost gaunt in appearance from a Spartan regimen of exercise and healthy eating, and projected an energy and enthusiasm that was helping to attract a new generation of parishioners on Sundays. But when he sat down with Tom Jackson and his son in the wood paneled study of First Community Church he seemed hollow-cheeked and exhausted, and there were dark circles under his eyes as well. "Thank you so much for coming on such short notice," he began, pouring himself a glass of ice water from a pitcher; both Jacksons accepted one as well.

"Good speech, Reverend Stirling," said T.J.

"Yes, Stephen," agreed Tom, "Reverend Melrose would've been happy."

"Thank you," said the pastor after a sip of water. "I almost felt like he was standing right behind me the entire time. Even in life, he always looked over my shoulder, but in a good way. Daniel was such a perfectionist that it was hard for him to cede responsibility to anyone."

"Don't I know," joked Tom. "Remember, I had him as a 'consultant' during the renovations to this place."

"Which turned out wonderful, and our congregation is eternally grateful, Tom. But today, I'm afraid it's T.J. whom I need to consult." He turned his gaze upon the expectant teen. "T.J.," he began quietly, "I know you don't consider yourself the most dedicated of parishioners to the church. But you've got a good heart, and I perceive you to be a true believer; is that not so?"

Harkening back to his meeting with Jill, T.J. nodded. "Yes, I believe," he replied.

"Good. Because what I may have to ask you to undertake is not for the faint of heart. I think it's going to take some spiritual fortitude."

Tom glanced sideways at his son, who nodded in assent.

"All right, then," said Stirling, "I'll continue. But if at any point this becomes too overwhelming, just say the word and we'll end it with no hard feelings. Okay?"

"Sure," said T.J.

Stirling took another drink of ice water. "I have to go back to last December," he began. "As you know, Reverend Melrose was found in the Old Cemetery one morning by a couple of youngsters. He was half frozen and barely alive, sprawled across the marble slab of his ancestor, Jonathan Melrose, the first pastor of First Community.

"The nanny of the children immediately called 911, and paramedics rushed to the scene. By the time I was contacted by Mrs. Moose, the church secretary, he was already in intensive care at St. Vincent's Hospital in Bridgeport. I was in Hartford at the time attending a theological conference of Connecticut clergy when I got the call. Of course, I expressed my regrets and took off for St. Vincent's. But with traffic and all, it was some two hours before I made it to his room. In retrospect, those two hours were critical.

"When I came upon him it was a pretty shocking scene. Reverend Melrose had suffered a stroke, and lying there throughout the frigid night had only made the situation worse. He was hooked up to an IV and oxygen, and his skin was the color of cardboard—a ghastly sight. He was in and out of consciousness, but sensed my presence. I sat at his bedside and took his hand, which was quite cool."

The clergyman took a deep breath and looked at the ceiling for a few moments, thinking back to that painful day. Then he returned his gaze to T.J.

"I asked, softly, if he could hear me, and I felt in response the slightest pressure from his hand. So I leaned in, inches from his face, and asked what happened. He uttered three words that I could understand, T.J.: 'curse', 'Fairfield', and 'blessing', or at least that's how it sounded, because his pronunciation was slurred. And when I asked him if Fairfield was in danger, a tear rolled down his cheek—" Stirling took out a handkerchief, excused himself, and blew his nose— "and then he slipped into the coma from which he would never emerge."

"Do you have any idea as to his meaning?" asked Tom.

"I've turned over those words time and again in my head, and I always come up empty. But what I do feel strongly is that Daniel saw something—or someone—in the graveyard that night that frightened him beyond belief; I had also heard from Mrs. Moose—who always seems to have her ears open, if you know what I mean—that there was an incident somewhere in the church beforehand that might have paranormal implications."

"So, Reverend," said T.J. respectfully, "what exactly is it that you want from me?"

"Well, son, it seems that I require someone with expertise in this field to get to the bottom of what happened to Reverend Melrose in that graveyard, and if there is indeed something horrible hanging over our heads that we need to know about."

"Of course I'd like to help you, Reverend," said T.J., "but I wouldn't know where to even begin."

"Well," he replied somewhat embarrassedly, "I was hoping that would be your response, so I took the liberty of preparing a reply. I think your best approach would be to start with some serious research of this immediate area, including First Community Church. For that, your contact person would be Mr. Robert Sherwood, who for years has been regarded as Fairfield's leading historian and now serves as the president and historian-in-residence at the Fairfield Museum and History Center, which, as you might know, was relocated to the modern facility between the Old Cemetery and the Village Green. He's always been a good friend of our church, and I'm sure he'd lend a hand in any investigation you'd want to conduct. Speaking of which, do you think you'll be calling together your crack team for another go-round?"

"That depends," T.J. replied carefully. "My buddy Bortnicker will be all in, I'm sure. I mean, all we've really been doing so far this summer is working at Tasteefreez on Boston Post Road. And my cousin LouAnne is supposed to come up for a visit, anyway, in a week or so. This would sure give us something to do.

"But here's the thing, Reverend. In order for us to really conduct an investigation—that is, if there's paranormal activity in the mix—then we'll need all the ghost hunting equipment that involves. And the only way to get our hands on all that stuff fairly quickly is by asking my friend Mike Weinstein at The Adventure Channel. They're pretty much open to anything we want to do, within reason, but they'd have to get a TV show out of it. Are you ready to let the world in on whatever's happening here in Fairfield?"

Stirling took another sip from his glass and replied, "I'm afraid I have no choice, T.J. It seems to me Reverend Melrose had every intention of taking care of whatever problem there is out there when he recovered. But he didn't, and I fear we've lost valuable time waiting for a miracle. I just get the feeling the clock is ticking, so to speak. Therefore, without being melodramatic, I'm giving you full authorization to do your best to reveal what we're up against. And I pray to God we aren't too late."

Chapter Ten

"Well, so much for lounging on the beach in Fairfield," said LouAnne on the phone with a sigh after T.J. had filled her in on his meeting with Stirling. "But I can tell from your voice that this is really worrying you, Cuz."

"Yeah," he admitted. "See, in the past we've been dealing with other people's problems, kinda. But this is my town, LouAnne. It's where I grew up. And trust me, if you saw Reverend Stirling this morning, you'd be worried, too. He's got the notion that something really nasty could go down." He paused. "But, hey, that doesn't mean we won't be able to work in a little downtime. We always manage to do that."

"And will you promise that we'll be able to get our running in? I really have to gear up for cross-country this fall. A college scholarship might be riding on it."

"Don't worry. We'll run every single morning if you want to."

"But aren't you playing American Legion baseball this summer?"

"Yeah, but we're done practicing, and there's only one or two games a week. Coach Pisseri from school is my manager, and he'll understand if I have to miss a night or two. I mean, after he saw what happened in Cooperstown—"

"Is he still freaked out from meeting Clemente's ghost?"

"We don't talk about it, but yeah."

"Have you told Bortnicker about our new adventure?"

"He's on his way over right now. I'm sure he'll be psyched about it; then we'll call Mike Weinstein and order up the equipment."

"But where's our base of operations going to be? The Hall of Fame let us set up a command post in their Halper Gallery. What are you thinking? The church, maybe?"

"No, I want to get closer to that cemetery. Reverend Stirling gave me the name of a guy who's the head historian at our Fairfield Museum, which is right next to the cemetery. Hopefully he'll be able to provide us a space to set up."

LouAnne went silent on the other end of the line for a few seconds. "So the question is, my dear cousin, when do you want me up there?"

"I guess, as soon as possible."

"Give me twenty-four hours. I'll text you a time to meet me at the train station. Just let me get things squared away down here."

"Thanks, Cuz, you're the best."

"Don't you forget it! Talk to you tomorrow."

"Oh, and one more thing—"

"There can't possibly be more."

"But there is; I just forgot to mention it. The Cooperstown Special was such a success that the Red Sox would like us to come up to Fenway Park and throw out the first pitch at a game."

"*Really*? When?"

"Well, I told them I had to wait until I knew when you were coming."

"So now you do. It sounds really cool."

"Great. Then I'll call Mike *and* the Red Sox. See you tomorrow night, hopefully."

"Can't wait."

* * * *

"Dude, this sounds ominous," said Mike Weinstein on the phone to T.J. Mike was on location in Las Vegas where he and the *Gonzo Ghost Chasers* were based while exploring an abandoned mining town in the nearby California desert. "Too bad about the minister, man."

"Yeah," said T.J. "Something happened to him in that graveyard that nobody can explain. So, I guess we'll need cameras and stuff for an outdoor investigation."

"With all the usual doodads," added Bortnicker, who was at his side, munching a PB&J. "Handhelds, EVP recorders, a computer or two. You know the drill, Mike."

"No problemo," Mike said. "I'll have The Adventure Channel ship the stuff tonight. But to where?"

T.J. thought. "I don't want to be, like, presumptuous, but I think if you have it sent to the Fairfield Museum on Beach Road, we'll be okay. We're going to meet someone over there to ask about some space. If that's a no-go, we'll just reroute the equipment to First Community Church a block away."

"Sounds like a plan. Hey, dudes, the suits were *really* happy with the Cooperstown Special. Hope you can serve up another winner."

"Mike," said T.J., "that's kind of secondary at the moment, if you want the truth. I think we have a real situation here. If we get a TV show out of it, fine."

Weinstein, ever the publicity hound, laughed out loud. "You're too much, dude. The reluctant celebrity. Except you keep getting your name in the papers!"

"It's not like he's trying," said Bortnicker with mock defensiveness, "it just happens!"

T.J. shot him a disapproving look.

* * * *

True to her word, LouAnne Darcy stepped from the Metro-North train onto the Fairfield train station platform at 8:05 the next evening. There were still the last strains of the sunset above and her beauty, as always, made her stand out, though she was dressed down in her Beatles *Abbey Road* T-shirt and cutoff jeans. It was quite a change from her last entrance on the same platform some three months earlier. The trauma and heartache of the previous winter behind her, LouAnne was radiant and feisty as ever. "Jeez, I was hoping it'd be cooler up here than Gettysburg," she joked as the boys engulfed her in a team hug.

"Don't worry, hon, the guest room's air-conditioned," said Tom, giving her a welcoming kiss. "And if one bed gets too warm you can switch to the other."

"What's the make of Paul McCartney's famous bass guitar?" asked Bortnicker, resuming their ongoing Beatles trivia contest immediately.

"Hofner," she replied airily, handing him her suitcase. "And Ringo's drums were Ludwig."

"Right again."

"I heard about your triumphant trivia victory in Florida," she said. "Don't think I'm a pushover like that doofus that you beat."

"I bow to you, my queen," he replied with mock reverence and his crooked grin.

"Hey, Dad," said T.J. as they made their way to Tom's SUV, "could we cruise by the church and the graveyard on the way home? I just want LouAnne to get an idea of where they are."

"No problem," said Tom, starting up the car. "We've still got a couple minutes of light left."

They followed Boston Post Road south, turned on Beach Road and drove toward the Sound.

"There's First Community Church on the right," said T.J. as they passed the turreted red building before crossing Old Post Road. "That's Town Hall and the Village Green...here's the entrance to the Fairfield Museum parking lot, and, right after it, the Old Cemetery." They pulled up to the curb, which was situated no more than ten feet from the low outer wall. One of the black wrought iron entrance gates was slightly ajar.

"Let's go in," said LouAnne.

"We'll just be a minute, Dad," said T.J. "I want LouAnne to check it out."

"Sure, Son. I'll keep the car running."

"And if we see something, *we'll* be running," joked Bortnicker, opening the passenger door.

T.J., leading the way, pushed open the gate with a rusty creak.

"Wow," LouAnne said, "this reminds me of the cemetery in Cooperstown. You know, the leaning, crooked headstones with the skulls and angel wings on them... how old's this place?"

"The 1630s," said Bortnicker.

"Well, you've got Gettysburg beat," she admitted, "although this is a whole lot smaller. It can't be more than a couple hundred feet square." She squinted in the deepening dusk. "What's out there beyond that far wall?"

"Marshland," said T.J. "Last August, during the hurricane, it was pretty flooded out—"

"Owww!" cried Bortnicker suddenly, slapping his neck. "Oops, sorry," he said to his alarmed friends. "Mosquito. We *are* near a marsh, you know, and it *is* the height of summer. We'd better bring gallons of repellent if we're gonna spend any amount of time in this place."

"You've got a point," said T.J., "but I think mosquitoes will be the least of our worries. C'mon, let's go."

They turned and picked their way among the headstones through the gathering darkness. When they were almost to the gate LouAnne whispered, "Hey, Cuz, is it just me, or do you feel like someone's watching us?"

"Uh-huh. Since the moment we got here."

Chapter Eleven

T.J. emerged from his second-floor bedroom the next morning to see his cousin sitting atop the staircase, lacing on her Nikes.

"'Bout time, sleepyhead," she quipped, pulling the laces tight before double knotting them. "Where to today?"

"Well," he replied with a yawn, "my idea is to go a block up to Oldfield Road, then down that steep hill to the Historical District and run around the side streets. That way you can see all the area points of interest in broad daylight."

"What about breakfast afterwards? I didn't realize how hungry I was till I woke up. Mom packed a sandwich and snacks for me, but between the Amtrak and Metro-North rides I wiped them out."

"We've got it covered. Chef Bortnicker is in charge and will be serving breakfast at his house. His mom should be around, too. You remember her, don't you?"

"How could I forget? We met her at the premiere party in New York City for the Bermuda Special. She's kinda interesting."

"You think?"

They descended the steps and exited the front door, immediately enveloped by the oppressive midsummer humidity.

"Yuck," said LouAnne as they executed some quick stretches. "Where's the ocean breeze I expected? This is as bad as Gettysburg, and we're landlocked!"

"Sorry," said T.J. as he leaned into a hamstring stretch. "First of all, it's not an ocean breeze we get here; technically it's off Long Island Sound. But even so, the only way you're gonna feel it on a day like this is by running down on the beach, which we can do next time, if you want. The sand gets pretty packed down when the tide goes out."

"And it's long enough for a good run?"

"Yeah; we could do Sasco Beach all the way down to the Southport Yacht Club and back, but only at low tide. Or, we could do Jennings and Penfield Beaches, which are only separated by the Fairfield Beach Club, but nobody cares if we'd run across that stretch."

"Sounds picturesque, almost like Bermuda," she said, recalling their early-morning jaunts on the island a year ago.

"Well, in a way," he replied. "Remember, in Bermuda we mostly trained on the old Railway Trail. We never really saw the water until that 5K race, when—"

"When I got the charley horse in my calf and had to drop out, thanks for reminding me."

"Oops," he said with a mischievous smile.

LouAnne straightened up. "Enough talk, wise guy. Let's hit it." And off they went.

The cousins hung a left out of Tide Mill Terrace and climbed a quarter-mile to the crest of Sasco Hill, where they turned left again on Oldfield and began their steep descent to the Historical District.

"This hill should be fun later," LouAnne grunted as they pounded downwards. Finally Oldfield Road flattened out and they were running freely, through the intersection of Oldfield and Reef near the 7-Eleven and then towards where Oldfield became Old Post Road, which featured the most venerable houses in Fairfield. Stately colonial mansions, some dating back to Revolutionary War times, graced the thoroughfare. All had immaculate yards dotted with ancient trees that provided a prodigious canopy.

Soon the Village Green came up on their right, with Town Hall nearby.

"What're those old buildings on the Green?" asked LouAnne.

"I think they were either original to the area or brought in from other towns around here and completely restored," huffed T.J., who was having a hard time keeping up with his athletically superior cousin. "There's a tavern, a schoolhouse, and a few others." He pointed to his left. "Up ahead is First Community, the church I go to, where Reverend Stirling is the pastor."

"Looks like a fort," she observed, which was the usual architectural appraisal.

"Yup, it's built to last. Dad helped out on some interior renovations and upgrades a couple years back, and boy, it wasn't easy. In the Historical District, you can't put any stuff on or around your house that isn't historically accurate. Even when they replaced a part of the church's roof that had suffered wind damage, they could only use a specific kind of shingle that my dad said was super expensive."

The duo turned right on Beach Road and passed the graveyard they'd visited the previous night. "Looks a lot less creepy in daylight," said LouAnne.

"Doesn't everything?"

After a few blocks, they reached Fairfield Beach Road, which they followed all the way to Reef before turning up towards Oldfield again.

"Quite a variety of homes," said LouAnne as they breezed along. "You've got tiny cottages and some huge houses."

"Yeah," said T.J. "The cottages, obviously, are the older ones. They took a real beating during Hurricane Irene last August; some ended up being flooded so bad they had to be demolished. My dad says at one time this was kind of a blue-collar area, but what's happening now is that people are buying the houses for the property, knocking down the structures, and building what he calls 'McMansions', houses that are huge vertically 'cause the land plots are so small. There's one right over there that they're working on. See how it's raised off the ground? That's in case the beach area floods again. And when we do run on the beach, you'll see the beachfront houses that got really pulverized."

"So why would anyone want to live there?"

"Some people just rent the houses to students from Fairfield U. It must be pretty sweet sharing a beach house while you're going to college. Of course, there are some really wild parties from time to time where the police have to come out.

"And of course, the other reason people build—and rebuild—here is because they can afford it. Houses near the water are primo. The beach area isn't blue-collar anymore."

About halfway up Reef Road, LouAnne wrinkled her nose. "What's that smell, Cuz?" she asked.

"Oh, that. We just passed the entrance of the town dump. Depending on tides or the wind, it can be kinda stinky."

The cousins turned left on Oldfield to begin the last leg of their run. T.J. was laboring; baseball was a game of stops and starts and quickness, quite different in its physical demands from cross-country. But he knew that although he was playing summer ball, fall track season was looming, and LouAnne's visit marked the beginning of his preseason running program. And if this first test was any indication, he had a lot of work to do. When they reached the base of the big hill they'd so breezily come down before he asked, "Hey, Cuz, think we can slow-jog it up?"

Surprisingly, she replied, "I was hoping you'd say that. This humidity is getting to me." Methodically, they worked their way back up to the crest of Sasco Hill, then coasted back to Tide Mill Terrace.

"I need a shower," moaned a soaked LouAnne.

"I need *oxygen*," wheezed T.J.

* * * *

"Welcome to the International House of Bortnicker," said the scruffy teen as he waved T.J. and LouAnne inside. The decor of the home, oddly, contrasted with the Bohemian appearance of its owner. Pippa Bortnicker was known to favor peasant blouses and stonewashed jeans; her son just threw on any old thing, as long as it was clean. But the furnishings were Scandinavian Modern, with everything aligned just so. This came as no surprise to T.J., and not just because he was a frequent visitor. Pippa had carved out an apparently necessary—and lucrative— niche in lower Connecticut as a Feng Shui advisor to wealthy homeowners desiring perfect harmony in their dwellings. The kitchen was the same—functional yet welcoming, with artistically weathered light blue cabinetry and a formidable butcher block island. The appliances were all of a creamy yellow hue, including the stove, at which Bortnicker was whipping up a marvelous first breakfast.

"Pull up a stool to the counter," he said while dipping slices of Challah bread in a spiced egg batter to begin his French toast. "I've got fresh strawberries and powdered sugar to top it off, and syrup, of course," he added, while laying the first slices on the griddle.

"I've got to say, you certainly took this cooking thing and ran with it," observed LouAnne while helping herself to a generous glass of orange juice. "Who knew that cooking with my mom two years ago would change your life?"

"Not I, my dear," he said, turning down the flame beneath the griddle a smidge. "Besides becoming an expert ghost hunter, my trip to Gettysburg led me to discover the joys of the culinary arts—and it was all because of your mom, bless her heart."

"Yeah," said T.J., "if only Aunt Terri could see the monster she's created!"

"Shush," said his cousin. "A guy who can cook—and look cute doing it—is a rare thing."

"How are your accommodations at the Jackson Hilton?" he asked. "Up to your four-star standards?"

"Are you kidding? I had my choice of beds and central air conditioning. It's better than my bedroom at home!"

At that moment, Pippa sashayed into the room, wearing a tie died T-shirt, peasant skirt and matching beret. After greeting T.J. and LouAnne with hugs, she began pouring herself some nasty looking green liquid from a bottle she'd retrieved from the fridge.

"What on earth is *that*," Mrs. B.?" asked T.J. with a grimace.

"Let's see...alfalfa, carrot, tomato, and a bunch of other veggies. Totally healthy and not bad tasting. Want a sip?"

"No thanks," he replied with a cautionary wave.

"I guess you're saying I can't tempt you with some French toast and bacon, Mom?" teased Bortnicker.

"Not for me," she chirped. "Totally unhealthy. But you kids enjoy yourselves. Just make sure to clean up. I've got a consultation in Darien this morning, and one in Weston later on, so I'll be out most of the day. Where are you kids off to?"

"We've got a ten o'clock appointment this morning over at the Fairfield Museum," said T.J., forking a slab of French toast onto his plate. "Then Bortnicker and I are working from noon to five."

Pippa drained her veggie cocktail and daintily wiped her mouth. "You know, it creates a real moral dilemma with me, knowing that my son is pushing all those empty calories onto the innocent youngsters of this town." She turned to LouAnne. "Young lady, I don't allow any junk food in this house whatsoever—never have. My son has to go across the street to get his fix."

T.J., blushing, shrugged his shoulders apologetically. Bortnicker was renowned for whipping up huge Tex-Mex party buffets for the Jackson men, which were usually consumed in the rec room during baseball or football watching. "Yeah, Mrs. B.," he reasoned, "but Mr. DiPalermo does allow him to create his own healthy flavors with the ice cream mixer. He actually uses a lot of fresh fruit in them—"

"As well as bubblegum, Sweet Tarts and gummy bears," she shot back. "Don't think I don't pass by from time to time to check the 'flavors of the day'."

"Busted!" cried LouAnne merrily.

"Well, have to run," said Pippa. "Please stay out of trouble and don't bring any ghosts home with you. It's bad Feng Shui." She slung a leather tote bag over her shoulder and rushed out, her long frizzy hair trailing behind her.

"Your mom's too much," said LouAnne. "Great French toast, by the way. And you crisped the bacon just right."

"Thanks," said Bortnicker. "Here's a good one: What do the French words in 'Michelle' mean in English?"

"The same as in French: 'These are words that go together well'. Duh!"

"So, how are we getting down to the Fairfield Museum today?" asked Bortnicker, rinsing their plates in the sink.

"I was thinking that both you and I have our bikes," said T.J., "and LouAnne could use your mom's if it's okay."

"Sure, if she doesn't mind the Day-Glo paint and flowers my mom's covered it with."

"As long as it gets me there," said the girl with a smile.

* * * *

The Fairfield Museum and History Center, accessed through a paved entrance on Beach Road between Town Hall and the Old Cemetery, was opened to the general public in September of 2007. Its architecture, inspired by that of old time warehouses which lined neighboring Southport Harbor, housed a totally modern facility with both traditional and interactive exhibits, as well as a comprehensive research library. Both T.J. and Bortnicker had visited the building while in middle school with their social studies classes, as well as the restored Colonial structures on the adjacent Village Green. As they chained their bikes to the rack outside the front entrance, LouAnne said, "Nice place. Not as huge as the Visitors Center in Gettysburg, but it'll do."

"The best thing," said T.J., "is that the graveyard's right next door." Indeed, its low outer wall was a stone's throw from the parking lot; the vast marsh lay beyond.

The teens, who had all worn their black *Junior Gonzo Ghost Chasers* golf shirts to make a good impression, gave their name to a senior volunteer manning the front desk. "Ah, yes, Mr. Jackson," said the pleasant septuagenarian. "Mr. Sherwood is awaiting your group in the research center."

"Thanks, ma'am," he replied politely. They strolled down a carpeted hallway past the current exhibit on local baseball history and entered the impressive room. A high vaulted ceiling with a huge chandelier capped tall built-in bookshelves that encircled the room. Rolling ladders were needed to access the upper shelves, and many of the volumes therein seemed old and valuable. A large picture window looking out on the Village Green buildings gave the space a splash of sunlight. At the far end sat a white-haired man at a desk pouring over an old ledger, his glasses pushed down to the tip of his angular nose. He waved the teens over. "Pull up a chair, folks," he said softly. Then, looking at LouAnne, he added, "Pardon me if I don't get up, miss." It was then they noticed that Robert Sherwood was confined to a wheelchair.

Sherwood gently closed the ledger he'd been reading, removed his glasses, and leaned back as much as the wheelchair would allow. The teens, despite their smart matching outfits, felt the tension that the inception of an investigation always entailed. Whether it was Gettysburg, Bermuda or Cooperstown, the time and effort invested in preliminary research had been a great help. Of course, not every resource tapped by the ghost hunters had yielded valuable information; in fact, an official at the Bermuda National Trust had tried to thwart their efforts to uncover the dark truth about their local pirate/patriot, Sir William Tarver. But mostly, the adults they encountered at the various museums and historical societies had proven both sympathetic and invaluable. It was their hope that the esteemed Robert Sherwood would help configure their search into a manageable time frame.

The historian, whose pale complexion reflected a lifetime of indoor study, pushed back an unruly lock of iron gray hair and shot them an appraising look. T.J. noticed his bowtie was perfectly knotted and that he wore a button down shirt and cufflinks, despite the dripping humidity outside. This guy looked *organized*. But any fears the threesome had of being rebuffed or discounted were allayed immediately by the affable academic who said, "When my friend Stephen Stirling contacted me and told me about your adventures as paranormal investigators, I was initially dubious. First of all, I believe those television programs to be mostly comprised of pseudoscientific, overly dramatized claptrap. However, it did prompt me to watch both of your Adventure Channel specials. And I must say, your preliminary research methods in both cases are to be commended. It has been my experience with today's younger crowd that they regard research as a colossal bore.

"Furthermore, I considered Daniel Melrose a fine man, and would like nothing more than to uncover the cause of his demise. As you can see, I am somewhat limited in my ability to access places and things, but I'm here to tell you that the Fairfield Museum will assist you in any way necessary. Now, how about some introductions?"

"I'm T.J. Jackson," said the leader, reaching across the desk for a handshake. He was followed closely by Bortnicker and then LouAnne.

"And you boys are lifelong residents of Fairfield, correct? T.J., your father's an architect, I believe."

"Yes, sir."

"Miss Darcy, am I correct in what I've learned that you hail from Gettysburg, Pennsylvania?"

"Yes, Mr. Sherwood," she replied. "And my father's a Park Ranger at the National Battlefield. The three of us came together as a team on our first investigation there."

"Splendid. So, for all of you, there is an appreciation of history. You'll need that to conduct this investigation. Now, tell me how I can be of assistance."

"Before we begin, sir, may we film you for the TV show?" asked

LouAnne politely.

"Yes, certainly, if we can out of respect omit any references to Reverend Melrose."

"They'll be edited. You have my promise," she said, and her mates nodded.

"Very well," said the historian.

"Mr. Sherwood," began T.J., "we have no clue what happened to Reverend Melrose in the graveyard. What we do know is that he said three words to Reverend Stirling before he went into that coma: 'Fairfield', 'curse', and 'blessing'. That's about it. In our other cases we either knew who or what we were dealing with; this time we don't know where to begin."

Sherwood nodded towards LouAnne, who aimed and pressed RECORD. "Then you begin at the beginning—when this town we call Fairfield came to be. How much of what you were taught in elementary school have you retained? Be honest, now."

"Truthfully? Not much," admitted Bortnicker. "The field trips we took to the Village Green and stuff were just a day away from school."

"Understood. Thank you for your candor. So we'll have to delve into 1600s Fairfield." He scribbled some notes on a pad. "I'll pull all the necessary books and materials and have them for you by tomorrow. What else would you need?"

"Well," said T.J., "at the Hall of Fame we were given a room to use as kind of a command post, to set up our computer and other equipment. Since the Old Cemetery's right outside, this would be the logical place."

"I totally agree, and so this is what we'll do. There's a room off this one, much smaller, that we use as a lecture place for local elementary educators who will be bringing their classes here. There's a conference table and Wi-Fi access, and a door that opens onto the parking lot. In fact, from the door you can see the right rear corner of the Old Cemetery wall less than one hundred feet away. Sound good?"

"It's perfect, Mr. Sherwood," said LouAnne, batting her eyelashes.

"Fine," he concluded. "This afternoon I'll have some volunteers remove any clutter that might be in there. When do you anticipate this equipment arriving?"

"Actually," said T.J. sheepishly, "we've already ordered it to be sent here."

Sherwood chuckled. "Well played, Mr. Jackson. Then why don't we start bright and early tomorrow, same time?"

"Sounds great. Hey, we really appreciate this, Mr. Sherwood," said T.J., rising to his feet to shake hands again with the man.

"It's the least I can do for a descendent of one of Fairfield's founding fathers," replied Sherwood as he grasped the boy's hand.

T.J. stopped in mid-shake and cocked his head. "Excuse me?"

"You do know that your family was here in the 1600s, don't you, T.J.?"

The boy blushed, then gently released Sherwood's hand and sat back down. "I don't mean to be disrespectful, sir," he said haltingly, "but according to my dad, our ancestors lived in New Canaan. In fact, if you go to their oldest graveyard, you'll see tombstones for our family going back to, like, 1680."

"And that would be Jedediah Jackson, correct?" asked the historian.

T.J. was stunned. "How did you know that?"

"Well," said Sherwood with a chuckle, "if you don't mind me sounding too pompous, it's what I do. When Reverend Stirling told me about you, the name rang a bell. So I traced your family tree, combining the Internet with old town ledgers. The family of Jedediah Jackson, a farmer, lived down near what is today Pine Creek—"

"We passed that on the way here," observed LouAnne.

"Exactly. Anyway, for some unexplained reason, the Jackson family disappears from all Fairfield records as of late 1662. That is, until your father bought the house where you now live, in 1995—"

"When my parents were married," finished T.J. "This is pretty wild, Mr. Sherwood. The accepted family history is that we helped settle New Canaan, not Fairfield."

"It seems like Jedediah had a hand in both," he replied. "And who knows? Maybe his exit plays into this whole mystery. Whatever the case, we'll start digging tomorrow."

* * * *

As the teens emerged into the hazy sunshine, T.J. seemed to be in a funk.

"Whatcha thinking, Big Mon?" asked Bortnicker as he unlocked his bike.

"Yeah, Cuz," added LouAnne. "You got this weird look on your face in there. Personally, I don't think where this Jedediah guy lived has anything to do with what happened to Melrose. So what if he moved to New Canaan? People move all the time, right?"

"Listen, you guys," he replied quietly, wrapping the bike chain around the seat riser before snapping the hasp shut. "I'll be honest. Since I was a little kid, every time I pass Pine Creek I get a strange feeling, kinda like I've been there before. One time last year, I went to play par-3 golf with my dad at the course there, just for a goof, and the whole time on the course I couldn't concentrate. Know why? I was trying to picture the area like it was before there were houses or cars, when it was just the colonists and Indians. Why would I do that?"

"You got me, my brother," replied Bortnicker, but not before he'd exchanged a furtive look with LouAnne.

* * * *

The ghost hunters were so immersed in their mission that they hardly noticed the woman who held the door open for them on their way out of the research library. Within seconds, Detective Susan Morosko was sitting in the very seat T.J. had occupied; in fact, it was still warm. "Thanks for your time, Mr. Sherwood," she began.

"Glad to help, Detective," he replied. "I like being busy, and it's been a busy day."

"Did you just finish meeting with those kids?" she asked.

"That I did. Why, is there something wrong?"

"No...they just look familiar."

"Well," he reasoned, "the boys are local residents, and all three of them have been on television lately."

"That's it," she said, snapping her finger. "T.J. Jackson's the cute one. He was just in the papers for resuscitating some woman who was dying. And his group is called the *Junior Gonzo Ghost Chasers*."

"You get an 'A'. The girl, LouAnne Darcy, lives in Gettysburg where, according to Reverend Stirling over at First Community, they solved their first mystery...something about a ghost terrorizing trespassers on the National Battlefield."

"Hmmm," said Morosko, jotting names in her notepad. "Interesting."

"So what brings you here? Do you need me to research someone or something for you?"

"I'm not sure," she said, "but let me run a few stories by you, and then you can tell me if I'm crazy."

Chapter Twelve

"Jonathan," said Mary Melrose, "I implore you. Does my daughter actually have to endure the embarrassment and public humiliation of an ordeal by water? Has she not suffered enough?"

He replied, "I will explain this one more time to you, wife. The girl has been subjected to only one test so far to determine her guilt or innocence regarding the accusations of witchcraft: that of examination for the Mark of Satan. As that result did not go in her favor, I would think you would welcome the chance for vindication in this second test."

"I've heard of similar events in other towns, and it sounds ghastly. How exactly will you conduct this so-called test?"

"It's quite simple," said the minister matter-of-factly. "She'll be taken to Edwards Pond in the town center and a rope will be secured around her waist, to be held by one of the Town Council on shore. Her hands and feet will be bound, and she will be thrown in."

Mary covered her face in horror. "To what end?"

"The belief is that if she is innocent, she will promptly sink to the bottom. If she floats..." He raised his hands in a show of resignation.

"My God," she said, the blood rising in her face. "So what you are saying is that she is doomed either way. It's Goody Knapp all over again!"

The tragic tale of Goodwife Knapp had begun in 1651 in Stratford, which lay some eight miles to the north of Fairfield, when a woman named Goody Bassett was executed after making a confession, probably under duress, that she knew of the existence of witches within many of the neighboring communities. Most, if not all, were single women. One was named Goody Knapp, a woman thought to be simpleminded, and for whom the citizens of Fairfield felt a measure of contempt. Goody Knapp's trial had been held in the church, which also served as the town's meeting place and courtroom, presided over by the Council—which had included Melrose—and the highly regarded Roger Ludlowe, one of the founders of the Connecticut colony.

During the proceedings, testimony was given against her, claiming she had exhibited strange behaviors and had generally disregarded "her place" in the community as a single woman. This occurred after the Mark of Satan had supposedly been found upon her, much the same as with Charity Blessing.

As a result, Goody Knapp was led to a gallows constructed just outside the northern part of town in Try's field, and hanged by the neck until she was good and dead.

"Be thankful that I have arranged for a second prerequisite of evidence before we go to trial," said Melrose. "There are some who maintained that the witch's mark was enough." At that moment, a knock on the front door reverberated through the otherwise silent dwelling. "It's time," said the clergyman solemnly. "Go fetch her." He rose to answer the door as his wife shuffled off to Charity's room.

And so it was on this dreary, overcast July day that Charity Blessing was led through town to the ducking pond. A few townspeople preferred to stay indoors as the procession, which began with only Melrose and his fellow councilmen, passed by, watching from behind drawn curtains so as not to make eye contact with the accused. But others—many others, including women and children—ended up trailing behind, forming a macabre parade.

As for Charity Blessing, she walked smoothly, her head held high, revealing no traces of emotion, determined not to give anyone the satisfaction of seeing her cry or lose control. Even as the contingent spread itself around the 50-foot diameter pond and her hands and feet were bound, the girl did not utter a sound.

The tow rope was securely fastened around her trim waist by a councilman; he nodded to Melrose, who nodded in return. Then, without any further ado, two of the more burly men in attendance stepped forward and grasped the girl by her hands and feet. Swinging her back and forth three times, mostly for dramatic effect, they heaved her some ten feet out over the pond as the crowd let out a collective scream.

When Charity, who was fully clothed except for a skull cap, hit the brackish water, she was immediately chilled despite the water's tepid temperature. Quickly sinking beneath the surface, she kept still, refraining from opening her eyes—it would have been pointless, anyway, so clouded was the pond with algae and other matter—and held her breath, fighting back the panic rising inside her. Fueling her determination was the white-hot hatred she felt for the townspeople, whom she could hear buzzing above her. But even so, she was running out of time; after a minute red spots began blooming behind her eyelids.

And then, amazingly, she started to rise.

When Charity broke the surface of the water, gulping air, a collective gasp was let out by the crowd.

"She floats!" cried a woman.

"Witch! Witch! Witch!" screeched a child.

There followed a cacophony of voices, but she could identify only one: that of her stepfather. "Pull her in," ordered Reverend Melrose, who sounded none too pleased. There was a quick huddle of the Town Council on a grassy hummock above the pond as Charity's mother and a boy—who most certainly was *not* Trevor Jackson, who was watching impassively alongside his father across Edwards Pond—untied her bonds and released her, a soaked, crumpled figure in the mud. The townspeople, who had come for a show, had been thus entertained. Their curiosity sated, they drifted away, gossiping in twos and threes, returning to their daily chores, many looking back over their shoulder as they went.

Finally, the councilmen, including Melrose, approached the prostrate girl and her mother, who knelt in abject humiliation beside her. One of the men stepped forward. "Charity Blessing," he said sternly, "as you have twice now given cause of proof to be considered a witch, you will stand trial one week from today before the Town Council to determine your fate. Until then, you will be confined to your residence in custody of Reverend Melrose." The men turned as one—except for the minister—and retreated.

"Let's get you home and out of those filthy clothes," whispered Charity's mother, helping her up. When Melrose attempted to take her arm in assistance the girl shook him off and glared hotly before setting out the way she had come, her long hair plastered to her skull, green tendrils of vegetation trailing from the bottom of her skirts.

Chapter Thirteen

"I can't believe it! All the *Junior Gonzo Ghost Chasers!*" crowed Rocco DiPalermo as he extended a meaty paw to LouAnne. "What brings you to Fairfield?"

"Just visiting T.J.," she replied coyly, avoiding mention of their upcoming investigation.

"What do you think of our little *Junior Gonzo* display?" he asked proudly, pointing to the framed photos—one each of the boys, and a group picture taken in Bermuda—that were prominently displayed over the back counter, along with DVDs of the Bermuda Special, which were for sale.

"Impressive," she said with a chuckle.

"Yeah, we're proud of the guys," said Rocco, "and our little establishment in general." The Fairfield Tasteefreez was located on Boston Post Road in the center of town, flanked by the Fairfield University Bookstore, Banana Republic, Victoria's Secret, trendy smaller shops and upscale restaurants. As the local Dairy Queen's chief competitor, Rocco had wisely adopted an inventory of designer hand-packed ice cream flavors, some of which that he'd given Bortnicker free reign to concoct. There was also a toppings bar built into the front counter that featured just about anything one would desire to put on ice cream.

For his decor, Rocco had eschewed the fast food look and gone with a retro style featuring small red leatherette booths and freestanding, marble-topped tables accentuated by chrome bistro chairs with red bottoms. The pale yellow walls were festooned with vintage Coca-Cola ads and signs. Antique-looking ceiling fans lazily hummed overhead. All of the fixtures behind the counter were kept meticulously polished, either by the staff or Rocco himself, and the black and white checkered floor was spotless. Instead of Muzak, Rocco allowed the staff to play the 60s satellite radio station nonstop.

Rocco, a former bodybuilder and shot putter at UConn, was always in and out, sometimes helping to scoop ice cream and schmoozing with Fairfield mothers who found his dark Italian features and Fabio-like mane of black hair tantalizing. He was a good boss, too, permitting the boys to flex their hours and—of course—eat all the ice cream their hearts desired. Overall, Tasteefreez had a work staff of ten kids, mostly from Bridgefield High, but also from the local colleges around Fairfield. Today the boys were supposed to be working with Abby, a sophomore at Sacred Heart, but she'd called in sick, which gave Rocco a brilliant idea.

"Hey, LouAnne," he said with a crafty smile, "you familiar at all with the restaurant business?"

"Are you kidding?" replied Bortnicker, tying on his apron, which he wore in conjunction with a mandatory navy blue Tasteefreez T-shirt. "She's been working at an inn in Gettysburg since she was a kid."

"Super. Are you up for slinging some ice cream with the guys? I'd pay you, of course."

She thought for a second. "Is there a T-shirt in it for me?"

"Coming right up." He hustled into the back room, which housed the mixers and storage rooms just as T.J. was emerging in his Tasteefreez regalia. "Your cousin's workin' your shift with you!" he sang out excitedly.

"The more the merrier."

After LouAnne had suited up, DiPalermo called them together. "Okay, gang, we open up in fifteen minutes. And I got a call yesterday that a fairly large group from the Stratfield School day camp will be hitting us on the way back from the beach between one and three. So it's gonna get crazy, just don't know when. Now, I've gotta go to Norwalk and pick up more fruit. Let's have fun and make a lot of money!" He bounded out the front entrance.

"Wow, he's high-octane," observed LouAnne.

"And he doesn't even eat the ice cream!" said Bortnicker.

"Tell me the truth," she said, "don't you get sick of being around it all the time?"

"Not me," confessed T.J., wiping the counter. "We've been working a couple months and I still crave a scoop of chocolate chip mint here and there—"

"With hot fudge topping," cracked Bortnicker. "And mini marshmallows, strange as that sounds."

"Guilty as charged." The boys exchanged high-fives.

Shortly after their opening people started to stream in, hoping to escape the noonday sun. As with their ghost hunting endeavors, the trio quickly established a rhythm. Cones, shakes and sundaes were assembled and dispatched with speed and a smile. A couple younger kids even had the teens pose with them for iPhone photos, and a few adults purchased autographed DVDs. The old-fashioned, nickel plated cash register was singing Rocco's favorite song.

Shortly before 2 PM the day campers invaded, a crew of over 50 rugrats in flip-flops and still-dripping bathing suits shepherded by harried middle-aged female chaperones. T.J., Bortnicker and LouAnne increased their pace to keep up with the mostly screaming youngsters. A formidable din reverberated through the establishment, drowning out the 60s tunes. "Big Mon, we're low on a few toppings," called out Bortnicker as he peeled a banana. "Can you get some shredded coconut, rainbow sprinkles and Reese's Pieces?"

"I'm on it," he called back, mopping his brow with a napkin, and disappeared into the back room.

And that's where things went south.

Because next to make a grand appearance on this sunny day was a specter from T.J.'s past. Bortnicker's eyes got very wide, and he said to LouAnne, who was mightily scooping some rocky road, "Hey, my dear, remember that Katie Vickers girl T.J. told you about back in Gettysburg? The one he claimed was his girlfriend?"

"Yeah, what of it?"

"Well," he answered, pointing a dripping scooper across the room, "thar she blows."

Indeed, the raven-haired Katie, object of T.J.'s pre-LouAnne affections, had paraded into the Tasteefreez with a retinue of admirers and sycophants, dramatically fanning herself with her hand. Katie was this day sporting a clingy white tank top and super short cutoff jeans that didn't leave much to the imagination. Her entourage included a couple of Katie clones who were attempting to pull off the same look with limited success, and what appeared to be the entire football team's defensive line from her exclusive prep school in Greenwich. They were loud, obnoxious and self-entitled, the very things the *Junior Gonzos* were not, and LouAnne regarded them with a wary squint.

Finally, after staking out a booth and sliding a table and chairs over alongside it, one of the girls motioned to Bortnicker. "Hey, would you be a dear and wipe down this table?" she requested in a smarmy voice. "It's a bit sticky."

"Sure. Be there in a sec," he replied, grabbing a washrag and a spray bottle of Windex.

"Uh-oh," whispered LouAnne to herself. "Hurry up, Cuz."

As Bortnicker, a forced smile plastered on his face, bent to wipe the table Katie said, "Hey, don't I know you?"

Biting back a response, he mumbled, "Probably not. Okay, we're all cleaned up."

But as he turned to walk away he heard her whisper all-too-loudly, "I know who he is. That guy was the ultimate nerd of my middle school in Fairfield." Bortnicker paused for a moment, his face impassive, but beet red. His eyes, obscured by his thick glasses but full of hurt, met LouAnne's, and her intuition told her that her dear friend had just been forced to revisit his traumatic past. And all the TV shows in the world weren't going to erase those memories.

It was at that moment that one of the crewcut football players, muscles rippling under his Greenwich Academy Varsity T-shirt, approached the counter and blithely ordered ten hot fudge sundaes, nine with nuts, and all with a cherry on top. LouAnne blankly took the order as the football player, the bridge of his nose lumpy with scar tissue, looked first at her, then up at the *Junior Gonzo* photo, then back down at her. She could see him putting two and two together, and then he clomped off to report back to his posse, who seemed to be snickering as they cast glances her way. *Hurry up, T.J.,* she thought.

When she and Bortnicker had finished the sundaes assembly-line style, they were loaded on two trays, which they brought to the Vickers booth/table, gingerly maneuvering around tables of antsy campers with ice cream-smeared faces. One by one, Bortnicker and LouAnne set them down in front of the party; luckily, nothing was spilled, and everything was fine until LouAnne turned to go and one of the football players grabbed her arm. "Hey, Sweetie," he barked, "I wanted mine with chopped al—"

He never got to finish the "monds" part because the girl, still damaged from the attack on her by the star quarterback of her high school football team the previous December, reacted instinctively, scooping up the gooey sundae bowl from underneath and smashing it into his face just as her cousin emerged from the back room toting containers of toppings.

T.J. managed a "What the—" before he saw Bortnicker block Katie Vickers' wrist as she lifted her bowl to retaliate. It was at that precise moment that one of the startled campers stood on his chair and screamed "FOOD FIGHT!" and ice cream in every color, flavor and form began to fly. Within seconds the Tasteefreez walls, floors, fixtures, and patrons were covered in ice cream and toppings. T.J. tried to wade into the melee, but everyone was so slippery that he couldn't wrestle the football players out of the way to get to his cousin. At one point his feet flew out from under him and he ended up nose to nose on the floor with none other than his former crush. She managed a "Hey, aren't you T.J. Jackson?" before one of the football players flopped on top of him. Seconds later, two police cruisers screeched to a halt—apparently, one of the mortified camp counselors had called 911—and four of Fairfield's finest burst in and screamed for everyone to freeze. Within a few seconds, all that could be heard was the laughing—and crying—of the campers, who had more excitement this day than any other of the summer. Everyone was ordered out of the ice cream palace as a stunned Rocco DiPalermo shouldered his way past the logjam near the door to find his two employees and their deputized helper sitting at a small table, flecked with ice cream and other matter, staring vacantly. After the owner assured the cops that the crime scene was secure, they returned to their vehicles, shaking their heads while repressing smiles.

"So, uh, what's the haps, guys?" he asked, scanning the devastation.

"This Cro-Magnon football player from Greenwich grabbed

LouAnne and she just snapped," explained Bortnicker with a shrug as LouAnne, embarrassed, stared straight ahead.

"That burns my butt," seethed DiPalermo. "There's no excuse for any man to ever, *ever* put his hands on a woman. I'm sorry this had to happen when you're visiting my establishment in my town. My apologies, LouAnne."

"No big deal, Rocco," she whispered.

"You okay, Cuz?" attempted T.J., wincing as he plucked a maraschino cherry from her ponytail.

"Yeah. And, you know what? Truthfully? It felt *good*." She gave him a heart-melting smile.

Rocco nodded, then clapped his hand on T.J.'s shoulder. "Looks like we've got some cleaning up to do, gang," he said. "And since this fiasco is at least going to make the police blotter in the local papers—that is, unless somebody had their cell phone video going, which I don't want to even think about—then I think a few days off for you all might be just what the doctor ordered."

"Okay, Rocco," sighed T.J. "Hand me a mop and let's get after it."

* * * *

Just about the time that LouAnne was smooshing a hot fudge sundae into the football player's face, Susan Morosko was put through to the desk of the Gettysburg Police Department.

"Sergeant Rudy Herzog speaking," came the gruff response.

"Sergeant Herzog? Good afternoon. This is Detective Susan Morosko from Fairfield, Connecticut, PD. Would it be possible to speak with your chief of police?"

"Sorry, Detective," he replied, his voice softening. "Chief Warren is finishing up his vacation out West in Colorado. He always takes the end of July or the beginning of August, after we're done with our battle reenactment week. We all need a bit of a breather after that—and next year's the 150th commemoration—"

"I don't mean to cut you off, Sergeant," she said firmly, "but I need some information from you all, and I figured I'd start with the Chief."

"Well, maybe I can help you, ma'am."

"Maybe you can. Were you with the force two years ago?"

Paul Ferrante

"Sure was. I was just an officer then."

"Okay...so are you familiar with some strange goings-on at the National Battlefield Park that summer?"

Herzog almost dropped the phone. He'd had a front row seat—literally—for the haunting of the Gettysburg battlefield by the ghost of a Confederate cavalier, at one point chasing him at breakneck speed in his cruiser in the dead of night, rolling the vehicle, and nearly dropping off the crest of Little Round Top. Herzog had later stood side-by-side with the stunned Warren as the ghost had inserted himself into that year's reenactment of Pickett's Charge and been blown from the saddle in an explosion of fire by a bullet fired from the Sharps carbine of one of the reenactors, who just happened to also be a Park Ranger at the battlefield. But because the Ranger, Mike Darcy, had been Herzog's high school football coach and valued friend, and because there had been no tangible evidence or video of the shooting, the whole thing had been purposely swept under the rug and forgotten. Or so he thought.

"Sergeant? Are you there?" persisted Morosko.

"Oh, uh, sorry, Detective," he stammered. "Yes, I remember the incidents."

"That's great. What I'm calling about specifically are the kids who were involved in the situation."

"I see. Well, there's LouAnne Darcy, a local girl whose father is a Park Ranger here—"

"I was thinking more about the two boys who were involved, especially one named T.J. Jackson?"

"Oh yeah, sure. Nice kid. Good looking, as I recall. Pretty serious. Not your typical teenager. He and his buddy, I can't remember the name offhand—"

"It's Bortnicker."

"That's it, Bortnicker. Quirky kid. Well, T.J., Bortnicker and LouAnne Darcy, who's kind of Jackson's step-cousin, somehow managed to help get rid of this ghost. And, from what I've seen, they've gone on to have success as paranormal investigators. I think they've done a couple cable TV specials."

"That they have. But what I have to ask you, Sergeant Herzog, is this: are these kids legit?"

118

Rudy Herzog thought hard, making sure to choose his words carefully. Then he said, "Detective Morosko, before the summer of 2010, if you asked me whether I believed in ghosts—even though I work in what's reputed to be one of the most haunted places in our country—I would have laughed in your face. But I saw things I can't explain, and those kids are not only *legit*, they're some of the bravest young people I've ever encountered."

"That's all I need to know, Sergeant," she replied. "Thank you for your time."

"But wait a second, Detective," he said. "Before I let you go, answer *me* this: are you having a...*problem* up there?"

"I hope not," was her honest reply.

* * * *

Early that evening Tom gave the kids a lift to the American Legion ball field on the other side of town, where his son was about to cap a tumultuous day with a twilight ballgame. Tom had been working from home on a project when the trio had turned up on their bikes, covered in various confections. "What on earth happened to you?" he'd said, aghast.

"Long story, Mr. J.," Bortnicker had replied. "But the good guys won...I think."

"Bottom line, Dad, is that we now have some time off work to concentrate on the case," said T.J. "so I guess it's all for the best. Which reminds me, guys. In all the excitement, I never got to tell you why I took so long in the back room at Tasteefreez. I got a call from the head of public relations with the Red Sox asking if this Thursday was okay to do the first pitch thing. They've got a one o'clock day game and I figured we could do it and still get back by nightfall, so I said that sounded good."

"How do we get up there?" asked Bortnicker.

"The Sox will send a limo for us and drive us home, too. Dad, you and Mrs. B. are invited as well. Sound like fun?"

"You bet," said Tom. "A day off from work won't kill me. I've been mostly working from home on this current project, anyway. And I'm sure Pippa will be excited to do a road trip with her illustrious son." He made the mistake of mussing Bortnicker's permanently mussed hair, coming away with a handful of liquid caramel, which sent everyone into gales of laughter.

"If you'll excuse me," said LouAnne primly, "I think I'll take a shower. I'm sticking to everything."

"I'll be right behind you," said T.J. "Even though I have a game later I've gotta wash this goop off me."

"Well, I'm happy none of you got hurt today," said Tom. "You sure you still want to play tonight?"

"Why not?" said his son. "If we really get into this investigation, I might have to miss a game or two, anyway."

"Suit yourself," Tom had said with a shrug.

* * * *

After exchanging hellos and hugs with Coach Pisseri and catching up a bit, LouAnne and Bortnicker retreated to the bleachers while T.J. joined his American Legion teammates for pregame stretching before their game with Trumbull. There was the faintest hint of a breeze, and the first of the twilight lightning bugs began to dance in the trees behind the stands.

"Well, wasn't that a wonderful first day in our fair town," intoned Bortnicker in his nasally best John Lennon voice.

"Never a dull moment with you guys," observed LouAnne, all the time concentrating on T.J.'s warm-up tosses. "So that was the great Katie Vickers, eh?" she added with a raised eyebrow.

"Yup. And, c'mon, you've gotta admit, she's pretty hot looking. Or are girls not supposed to acknowledge stuff like that?"

"No, you're right, she's okay. I can see why T.J. liked her."

"Yeah, but it never went anywhere. She was like this unattainable dream girl to him. The thing about T.J., he's got his romantic notions— or *had* them, anyway—where it seemed like he was falling in love every ten seconds in middle school. But that's kinda done with."

"Done with? Why?"

"Why? Because he met *you*, that's why."

She blushed. "The game's starting," she said, ending the train of the conversation.

"Listen, my dear," he countered, "you don't want to talk about it, that's cool. So let's switch to something more relevant. Like maybe his weird behavior over the ancestor news at the Fairfield Museum today."

"Yeah," she agreed, "that was strange. And that whole golf course story? Bizarre."

"Which is what I was trying to tell you up in Cooperstown. I think T.J. taps into stuff sometimes, and it kinda scares him. I don't know if he even suspects that *we* know. I think it's time you two had a heart-to-heart."

"Think he'll open up to me?"

"Listen, LouAnne," he said, removing his glasses for a polish. "You told him about...the stuff that happened to you at school while we were up in Cooperstown, right? That couldn't have been easy."

She nodded. "It was one of the hardest things I ever had to do. But I felt so much better when it was over. Are you mad I didn't tell you, too?"

"Nah. I know you guys have a special understanding or whatever...besides, he told me about your whole deal later on. The point is, I think you're the only one who can reach him on this. I think you need to give it a shot."

She leaned over and gave him a peck on the cheek. "You're a good friend," she said.

"Hey, cut that out," he joked. "People will talk."

Chapter Fourteen

"One-for-three with a walk—not horrible," chided LouAnne as the cousins laced up their sneakers the next morning. "And I liked that sacrifice bunt you laid down in the third inning. The base runner eventually came around to score."

"Yeah," said T.J., pleased that his cousin was actually paying attention. "That's why Coach P. has me batting second, just like on our JV team. I'm pretty good at moving the runner."

"And you did a Clemente-style basket catch out in center. Was that for my benefit?" she teased, remembering their midnight workout at Doubleday Field in April when the Hall of Fame outfielder's ghost had taught T.J. the technique.

"Nah, I wasn't showboating or anything. I actually used it in my JV games if the situation was right. Coach P. didn't mind."

"After what he saw that night, why would he?"

"Good point."

"So, what do you think, Cuz? I'm dying to try that beach run."

"You got it. We done stretching?"

"I'm loose. Lead the way."

They hung a left onto Sasco Hill Road as they had the previous day, but instead of making another left onto Oldfield, they proceeded along the crest of Sasco Hill, passing majestic mansions and private clubs. "Lifestyles of the rich and famous, eh?" huffed LouAnne.

"Uh-huh," T.J. replied, "but my dad told me some of these people lost their shirts in the economy downturn a couple years back. There's still a 'For Sale' sign or two along this stretch." They reached the end and then turned right down a steep incline to Sasco Beach, which was bordered on the right by an exclusive golf club.

"Sweet!" cried LouAnne as they cut across the narrow parking lot to the beach.

"No pink sand, but it'll do," said T.J., referring to their idyllic stay on the South Shore of Bermuda. The cousins found a ribbon of flat sand just below the high tide line and started running toward Southport. It was still somewhat cool, with a light breeze, and the salt air made for a delightful workout.

"So, you excited about Fenway Park tomorrow?" she asked.

"Yeah, it should be cool. I mean, I feel funny doing stuff like that, but if they really want us up there, why not? Bortnicker's totally psyched up about it. He loves the Sox."

"What do you think of Mr. Sherwood?"

"Seems like a really smart guy. At least he's not like that crabby Mrs. Tilbury in Bermuda, who thought the paranormal stuff was all a bunch of baloney. But we know better."

"You got that right." She saw her opportunity. "Since we're on the topic, can I ask you something?"

"Sure. What?"

"I'm gonna just come right out and say it, so don't get mad, okay?"

"Just say it, Cuz."

"All right. It's just that, well, both Bortnicker and I are getting the impression that you're a little more tuned in to this ghost stuff than you're letting on. Am I right?"

T.J. sighed. It was stupid to think that he could ever keep this from the two people who cared most about him. "Actually, I've been having these feelings for a while now, so you two are on the money. And, well, I was gonna tell you eventually, but I went to see someone about it a couple months ago."

"Like a psychiatrist?"

"No, nothing like that. A woman who calls herself a 'sensitive'. I got her name from Mike Weinstein, actually."

"Was she pretty…you know…normal?"

T.J. laughed. "Yes, Cuz, she was normal. But she's definitely dialed in to the paranormal. She told me some interesting stories, to say the least."

"And did you tell her *yours*?"

"Yup."

"And?"

He abruptly stopped running and they stood facing each other, hands on hips, panting from their exertion. "Yeah," he said, "she thinks I have some ability in that area. I hope you don't think I'm weird because of it."

She leaned over and kissed him gently on the lips. "Not any weirder than you were before," she smiled, and took off running up the beach. He exhaled, happy to have it over with, and gave chase.

* * * *

"So you ran the beach to Southport, huh?" asked Bortnicker while sliding a spinach and feta cheese omelette onto LouAnne's plate. "How romantic."

"Yeah, if you call getting your butt kicked 'romantic'," replied T.J. "When she turned on the jets I just couldn't catch her."

"Don't feel bad, Big Mon," he replied. "I'd like to see our fair maiden get around on a fastball."

"Betcha I could," she countered.

"Yeah, right."

"Enough, you two," said T.J. as he buttered a slice of wheat toast. "Let's concentrate on today's meeting. I just got a text from the Museum that the equipment's there, ready to go. Bortnicker, why don't you set up the command post while LouAnne and I hit the books with Mr. Sherwood?"

"No problem, Big Mon," he replied, sipping his coffee. "Wish I still had my assistant from Cooperstown." He was referring to Fiona Bright, the cantankerous niece of the Hall of Fame's president who had inserted herself into the Cooperstown investigation as Bortnicker's tech assistant and ardent admirer. "She still emails and texts me all the time, you know," he said proudly. "And LouAnne, you helped her a lot with getting over the usual middle school stuff. She always asks for you."

The girl waved him off, her mouth full of eggs. "No pwobwom. Gwad to hewp."

"Hey, where's your mom?" asked T.J.

"Sleeping in this morning. See, when you do what she does for a living, you kinda make your own schedule. But she's looking forward to Fenway tomorrow."

T.J. glanced at his cousin, who nodded. "Listen, Bortnicker," he began, "before we head over to the Fairfield Museum, I've gotta share something with you."

"Fire away."

He proceeded to tell both of them the entire story of his sit-down with Jill Rogere, including her warnings of misusing his sensitivity.

"So I guess it's a good thing you've got us, then," Bortnicker said in his John Lennon voice.

"Uh-huh," he admitted sheepishly. "But listen, guys, do me a favor. If it ever seems like I'm kinda...you know, going overboard, smack me in the head or something, okay?"

"We can do that," assured LouAnne.

* * * *

"Welcome, welcome!" said Robert Sherwood with exuberance as the teens entered the Fairfield Museum's research library. "I've pulled all the necessary files and books, I think, and we'll get to them in a minute. Your equipment has been placed in the auxiliary room. It was delivered in a black trunk with JUNIOR GONZO GHOST CHASERS stenciled in white on the sides—"

"*Junior* Gonzo Ghost Chasers!" cut in Bortnicker. He turned to his mates. "You mean, we rate our own equipment now?"

"Guess so," said T.J. with a grin.

"And we *should*," added LouAnne smartly. "After all, we *are* making money for The Adventure Channel."

"Have a seat, folks," said Sherwood, who seemed eager to begin. "First, let me say that this endeavor is all very exciting to me, but that's because it's what I do. So, what I should start with is to ask you boys just how much you know about your town. It will give me a baseline, so to speak."

Both T.J. and Bortnicker reddened. Although they were lifelong residents of Fairfield, their knowledge of its history was spotty. Even Bortnicker, whose addiction to the History Channel was one of his quirks—which had served them well, especially in Gettysburg—had only a rudimentary understanding of his hometown's roots. LouAnne chuckled at their embarrassment. "You'd better start at square one, Mr. Sherwood," she advised.

"All right, then. From the beginning, people have been attracted to our town because of its coastal location and plentiful natural resources. The Native American tribes who came here first, including the Sasquas, Uncowas, Maxumux, and Pequannocks—all derived from the Paugussetts—saw that the area was abundant with game, fish, fresh water, and productive soil.

"Of course, the Europeans had to crash the party, so to speak, and they brought with them not only the desire to acquire land, but a variety of contagious diseases for which the Indians had no immunity, thus wiping them out in great numbers. The last vestiges of Native resistance ended in 1637 with what was called the Great Swamp Fight, where the English colonists, amongst them Roger Ludlowe, the town's founder, defeated the Pequots in an area which today is our town's border with Southport.

"Which brings us to the actual settlement of our town. Ludlowe, who came from Windsor, Connecticut, decided to develop this 'fair field' and received a commission to do just that."

"There's a school named after him in town," observed T.J.

"The fact is," said Sherwood, "a majority of the names of streets, schools, et cetera in this town came from the founders, who were also notable landowners. Getting back to Ludlowe, he really initiated the permanent settlement of Fairfield by laying out four squares of land, divided by five roadways, which became the center of the Old Town; this included First Community Church, the Village Green, and the Old Cemetery. Ludlowe has been described as a stubborn, sometimes arrogant man, extremely self-confident. He saw the world as a hostile place, where one had to fight for what he had and always strive to achieve more.

"The neighborhood rose and then branched out from this center as Ludlowe purchased more tracts of land from the Indians, who had done much of the original clearing of the land. Home lots were located within the four squares, and the land farther out was used for pasture, meadow, and crops. T.J., your ancestor, Jedediah Jackson, farmed the land near

Pine Creek, a fairly choice area. During this time neighboring towns such as Stratford, Greenwich, and Norwalk were founded as well.

"Most people in the settlement were, of course, farmers, although you did have blacksmiths, weavers, and the like. The first houses were situated fairly close together surrounding the meeting places such as the church, mostly for defense against attack, but also so these people could keep an eye on each other."

"Why were they so paranoid about each other?" asked Bortnicker.

"I'll get to that in a minute, if you'll bear with me," said Sherwood gently. "I hope I'm not boring you with all this."

"No, sir," said T.J., ever the diplomat, "what you're doing is saving us a lot of time; and I feel that you're leading up to something."

"You're quite perceptive, T.J. So let me continue a bit, and I'll try to be brief. The early colonists lived fairly simply, growing their own vegetables and manufacturing the goods they needed for daily life— including their furniture and what they wore. The men and boys worked the fields while the women folk made cloth, butter and candles, and tended chickens and vegetable gardens. Everyone—even children—was expected to contribute. If you were a boy, you looked forward to inheriting or being awarded land to farm. Girls hoped to bring household items with them when they married. LouAnne, at that time in American history there was no such concept as 'women's rights'."

"Yuck," she said.

"Well put. Now, on to the workings of the town. From its inception, Fairfield was tightly knit. This was due, in part, to the close proximity of the dwellings—but there were other factors as well.

"These people had very similar backgrounds and religious values. They brought with them from England their Puritan beliefs, which were, to say the least, restrictive. They were required to attend services and strictly adhere to the teachings of the Bible, which were blended with traditional English law. And since, as I stated before, people could keep an eye on each other, they were not above getting into other people's business and turning them in to the authorities—whether religious or governmental—if they perceived any transgressions."

"Who exactly enforced the law?" asked Bortnicker.

"There were town meetings run by the Council, or Selectmen. At these meetings, decisions were made regarding taxes, boundary disputes, and conflicts between the citizens. They also meted out justice for those who broke the law. For example, you could be fined five shillings for not going to church. If you disrespected the minister, the payment was five pounds, and you were made to stand on a block in the town square for all to see."

"Wow," said LouAnne, who was filming Sherwood's entire lecture on her cell phone.

"Oh, that's mild compared to some other offenses."

"Like what?" asked T.J.

"For burglary, you could have the letter B branded into your forehead," said Sherwood. "Do it again, and you were in for a public whipping. Probably the worst thing a man could do was go off to live with the Indians. That could get you a few years of prison time.

"What I can't stress enough is the role of the church in all this, specifically First Community. Probably no real church existed in Fairfield until Reverend Jonathan Melrose arrived in the early 1640s."

"Was he related to the Reverend Melrose who just died?" asked Bortnicker.

"Oh yes. He and his large group of followers had come down from Massachusetts, mostly because of overcrowding in their area and burdensome taxes. The lure of wide open spaces for farming proved irresistible. The arrival of his group of fifty or so families nearly doubled the town of Fairfield's size, to four hundred or so. Melrose was, of course, an Anglican, well respected by his peers in the clergy. He oversaw the construction of the town's first formal meeting house for services and gatherings of the Town Council. Keep in mind that most residents of the town at that time lived in crude dwellings; only the wealthy, such as Ludlowe, had more upscale homes.

"As pastor of First Community, Jonathan Melrose wielded great power within the community, and was of course a pillar of the Town Council. As such, he had a hand in the hearing of local trials and the meting out of punishments, with an eye toward those whose offenses were in violation of religious doctrine.

"This brings us to why I believe we are here. You see, outside of murder, which would obviously be punished by execution, the most heinous crime to be accused of was witchcraft. And that, my young friends, is what I believe we're dealing with."

"Oh, brother," said Bortnicker.

Sherwood raised an eyebrow. "Does that mean you don't believe in witchcraft, or that you doubt it happened here?"

"Neither, sir," he said apologetically. "What I meant is, 'Oh, brother, we've never had to deal with something where the ghost might have—you know—evil powers'."

"What makes you think we're dealing with a witch here?" asked T.J.

"A couple things," said Sherwood. "First, the people we're talking about were in a precarious position. You had diseases, Indian attacks, livestock dying, crops failing, and other natural disasters. People would tend to read into these calamities and, as is true of human nature, look for scapegoats. So if there was anyone in their midst who wasn't fervent enough religiously, or rubbed people the wrong way, or was just plain strange, they might be in line for an accusation. That may seem outrageous in today's society, but back then, without the benefit of modern science to explain most natural phenomena, people turned to things like religion and superstition to explain away their troubles and hardships."

"I thought this all happened up in Salem, Massachusetts," said LouAnne.

"The Salem witchcraft trials of 1692 are the most publicized—and notorious—but Connecticut had its share of witch hunts, and they predate Salem's by many years."

"Someone recently told me about witches in Wethersfield," said T.J., thinking back to his conversation with Jill Rogere. "You mean, Fairfield had them, too?"

"Indeed," said Sherwood, "and that is what you fine young folks are about to research today. I've pulled all relevant materials—some going back to 1662, when the minutes of town meetings were first recorded—to see if we can uncover a connection of some sort."

"What kind of connection?" asked T.J.

"Well, Daniel Melrose was found in the Old Cemetery sprawled across the tomb of his ancestor, Jonathan Melrose, for one thing. And—"

"I'll take it from here, Robert," said a voice from behind the teens,

Paul Ferrante

whose heads snapped around to find the woman who had held the door for them the previous day. They had been so engrossed in Sherwood's history lesson that they'd failed to hear her slip inside the room. "Kids, I'm Detective Susan Morosko of the Fairfield PD, and we have to talk."

"Is this about the brawl at Tasteefreez?" asked Bortnicker nervously.

"No," chuckled Morosko, "though news of your epic food fight did trickle back to headquarters. Robert, could we all move to the conference table?"

"Surely," replied the historian, putting his wheelchair in motion.

When they were seated with Sherwood and Morosko facing the teens across the book-strewn table, the detective began: "Okay, I apologize for my sneaky entrance, but to tell you the truth, I'm late. I got caught in traffic on Post Road."

"Did you put your flashers on?" asked Bortnicker, breaking the tension as always.

"Yes, I did, as a matter of fact," she replied, repressing a smile. "Robert here knew I was coming; he and I had a long talk yesterday, and he's on board with my being here." She looked directly at T.J. with dark brown eyes.

I wouldn't want to get interrogated by her, he thought.

"Here are the facts, kids; because as a policewoman, I deal in facts, not fantasy. There have been three occurrences over the past few months in the vicinity of this museum where a woman, dressed in what appears to be seventeenth-century attire, has been spotted. Since the sites were, specifically, the marsh formerly called Wolves Swamp alongside the Old Cemetery and the Village Green near the historical buildings, I am assuming some connection."

"So you *do* think it's a ghost?" asked LouAnne.

"I didn't say that. I said that the people who filed the reports described a woman, approximately twenty years of age, in period attire."

"Did she interact with any of these people?" asked T.J.

"No. In two of the instances, however, she did acknowledge the presence of the witness with a look."

"If I may, Detective," interrupted Sherwood gently. "When Susan came to me yesterday she inquired as to who you young people were. When I told her, she immediately recognized the names; you do have a

130

knack for getting into the papers—"

"And social media," said Morosko. "Anyway, after Robert filled me in as to the nature of your visit—to conduct an investigation into a possible haunting of the area and its connection to the death of Reverend Melrose—I did a little back-checking on you guys. First, Robert was kind enough to lend me the DVD of your Bermuda Special, which gave me an insight into your method of operations. I also spoke to a Sergeant Herzog at Gettysburg PD—"

"Rudy Herzog?" asked LouAnne.

"One and the same. He had nothing but good things to say about you, although the story he told me regarding your exploits on the battlefield was a little out there."

"That's putting it mildly," observed Bortnicker.

"Well, guys, I want to make it clear that when it comes to this ghost stuff, I'm a dyed-in-the-wool skeptic. As I said, I deal in facts, and hard evidence. But I'm also here to tell you that, if need be, you'll have the full cooperation of the Fairfield Police Department. Here's my card with my cell phone number. Don't hesitate to call, at any time. Or just stop by HQ on Reef Road and ask for me."

"We really appreciate your support, Detective Morosko," said T.J. in his role as team leader.

"Yeah," added Bortnicker, "and sorry about the Tasteefreez thing."

"Are you kidding?" she replied, finally breaking into a broad grin. "We laughed about it for *hours*. Take care, and stay in touch." She shook hands with each of them and strode out.

"Well, my friends," said Sherwood, "are you ready to hit the books?"

"If you don't mind, guys, I'll go in the other room and start assembling the command center," said Bortnicker. "You can fill me in on stuff later."

"Good deal," said T.J. as Bortnicker left. "So, Mr. Sherwood, what exactly are LouAnne and I looking for today?"

"Anything and everything relating to witchcraft in and around the immediate area in the mid-1600s," he replied. "If your investigation dovetails with Detective Morosko's reports, we are specifically looking for a younger woman who might have been a witch, or at least who was tried as such. In a few minutes, I have a board meeting with our contributors upstairs. Give a call if you need me, but I think you'll have enough here to keep you occupied for a while." He swept his hand over the cluttered conference table. "Good hunting." He backed away from the table and wheeled himself out, T.J. holding the door open for his exit.

"We've got a ton of stuff to go through," moaned LouAnne as he reseated himself.

"You're not kidding, but from what Mr. Sherwood said, we can narrow our focus to the mid-1600s. Man, some of these books are really old. I guess that's what this box of cotton gloves is for," he said, tugging on a pair. "The ledgers he pulled are the town meeting minutes, starting with 1662. I'll hit these and you can scan the history books."

"Sounds like a plan," she said. She paused and looked dreamily out the window; a slight breeze was rippling the leaves of nearby trees and the cattails in the marsh beyond. "I could be on the beach right now working on my tan," she sighed.

"We'll get there when this is over," promised T.J. They bumped fists and got to work.

* * * *

Sometime later, LouAnne looked up from her reference book. "I think I've got something," she said.

"Let's hear it."

"Okay, in 1651 this woman named Goody Bassett—I think that's short for 'goodwife'—was executed in Stratford for witchcraft. It seems like she was determined to take others down with her, so she started naming names from the area. To be a prime candidate for these allegations, it looks like you had to be female, preferably single, and maybe not too well-liked.

"So anyway, she accused a Fairfield woman named Goody Knapp. The Town Council had this woman named Lucy Pell examine her for witch's marks, whatever they are, and she claimed Knapp was sporting a few of these. And, based on that, they found her guilty and condemned her to death. Are you kidding me?"

"Did Knapp ever make a confession?"

"According to this account, she told them she had nothing to confess, and got hysterical. They hanged her in a place called Try's field, in what is today the Black Rock section of Bridgeport."

"That's near Captain's Cove, where Bortnicker and I did our SCUBA certification water test."

"Think she's our ghost?"

"No," he said. "Sounds too old. Let's keep looking."

* * * *

Around 12:30 PM Bortnicker staggered in. "I'm almost there," he said wearily, "but I've gotta take a break, and my stomach's talking to me. How about we bike over to Subway on Post Road?" Subway was the boys' go-to sandwich shop before trips to Sasco Beach.

"Nah, I'm not feeling it," said T.J. "Actually, I was kinda in the mood for wings—"

"Archie Moore's!" crowed Bortnicker, and the boys high-fived.

"And what, might I ask, is Archie Moore's?" questioned LouAnne.

"Only the place with the best Buffalo chicken wings in Fairfield," answered Bortnicker. "And other good eats, too. It's near the train station. We can bike there in five minutes."

"Archie Moore's it is," declared LouAnne. T.J. left a note on Sherwood's desk telling him they'd return in an hour or so, and they pedaled off to the eatery. The teens arrived during the height of the midday crush, and the town's popular sports bar/casual restaurant was buzzing. Overhead TVs were tuned in to ESPN or YES, the New York Yankees network, and the wait staff was hustling from table to table. The famished ghost hunters ordered the twenty-eight piece wing platter (medium spice), the Nachos Grande, and a pitcher of iced tea.

"Ummm, you're so right about the wings," said LouAnne as she licked orange Buffalo sauce off her fingers. "Just spicy enough."

"What kind of electronics did they send us?" asked T.J., dipping his wing into a bowl of bleu cheese.

"A pretty good variety," said Bortnicker, crunching a celery stalk between wings. "We've got one computer terminal, which we can go split-screen with; hand-held EVP recorders and camcorders; and remote film recorders we can set up around the graveyard and the Village Green. There's also three walkie-talkies and packs of extra batteries if the entity drains our power."

"Good idea," said LouAnne, remembering how the ghosts in Bermuda and Cooperstown had rendered their equipment useless by sucking dry their energy source while trying to manifest themselves.

"Hey, what'd you think of our fine Inspector Morosko?" asked Bortnicker in his Beatle voice.

"It's *Detective* Morosko," corrected T.J., "and I'd watch my mouth around her if I was you. She looks like a pretty tough customer."

"And thorough," observed LouAnne. "She even contacted the cops in Gettysburg."

They were just polishing off the last of the wings when the Nachos Grande, a heaping helping of tortilla chips topped with salsa, melted cheese, spiced beef, refried beans, onions, olives and jalapenos, was brought bubbling to their table. "Round two!" called Bortnicker, eagerly rubbing his hands together.

"My goodness," marveled LouAnne. "I've never seen anybody pack it away like you, but you never gain a pound."

"It's the metabolism, my dear," he replied, pulling a cheesy chip from the mound in front of them.

"It's gotta be," agreed T.J., "'cause he's not exactly killing himself working out."

"Hey, not fair, Big Mon," Bortnicker smiled, popping a chip into his mouth. "I've already biked twice today, with two more trips ahead. I've got to build up my strength!"

* * * *

Shortly after they had returned to their respective chores at the Museum, T.J. hit pay dirt. "Hey, Cuz, listen to this," he said excitedly. "These ledgers are nearly impossible to make out, between the faint ink and the old-fashioned English, but I think I have a lead."

"What is it?"

"There's mention of a girl here in the town meeting of July 19, 1662 who is under suspicion for witchcraft. Let me get a name…" He traced his gloved index finger over the page, squinting hard to make sense of the ornate calligraphy of the recorder. "I think it says…Jeez Louise!"

"What?" asked LouAnne. "What's the name?"

He sat back in his seat. "What were the three words Daniel Melrose said to Reverend Stirling before he went into his coma?" he asked.

"They were, uh, 'blessing', 'curse', and 'Fairfield', right?"

"Uh-huh. And the girl's name is Charity Blessing."

"I think we just narrowed our search," said LouAnne. "You'd better get Mr. Sherwood down here."

* * * *

"Splendid!" cried Sherwood as he looked upon the passage T.J. had bookmarked in the town meeting ledger. The teens, who were now joined by their tech expert, beamed with pride. "Charity Blessing. How very ironic."

"It says that she was accused by various townspeople of witchcraft," said T.J., "but it doesn't get specific."

"Then we must keep searching," said the historian earnestly.

"As Ringo said in *Help!*, 'There's more here than meets the eye,'" intoned Bortnicker.

"Agreed," said LouAnne after playfully punching her friend in the shoulder. "Let's get after it."

Almost an hour later, it was she who called, "Got it! And it's a doozy. It would appear that our Ms. Blessing was not just anybody."

"What?" asked Bortnicker. "Was she wealthy or something?"

"No, better. Charity Blessing was the stepdaughter of—wait for it—Reverend Jonathan Melrose."

"Jeez Louise," said T.J.

"Extraordinary," remarked Sherwood with a shake of his head. "Imagine it...the religious leader of Fairfield having an accused witch under his roof!"

"What next?" asked Bortnicker. "I mean, what happened to her?"

LouAnne shrugged. "This book just says she was 'suspected' and leaves it at that."

"Wait a minute," said T.J., flipping forward through the 1662 ledger. "Okay...in July of that year the Town Council orders an examination of her body for 'witch's marks'. What's the deal with that, Mr. Sherwood?"

"Well," he said, "forgive me if I am indelicate, LouAnne, but one of the determining factors that could be used to prove one was a witch was strange marks on the body, even in the most discreet of places. What they were looking for, actually, was a third teat on a woman; however, this was later expanded—depending upon just how much they wanted to find someone guilty, it would seem—to any marks or blotches that seemed irregular."

"That's crazy," spat LouAnne. "Everybody has birthmarks or stuff like that. I even have one on my thigh that looks like a scrunched-up butterfly—"

"It's more like a moth, actually," reported Bortnicker. When all heads swiveled to him, he embarrassedly explained, "Hey, in Bermuda we were all in our bathing suits half the time. Give me a break!"

They turned back to Sherwood, who continued: "As I was saying, if they really had it in for someone, any kind of mark—even a rash or a case of Lyme disease from a deer tick bite—could be interpreted as a mark of the devil. Apparently, they gave Miss Blessing a going-over. The question is, did they find anything?"

T.J. flipped ahead a couple pages. "That would be a 'yes', Mr. Sherwood. Three women all attested that she had the markings."

"Oh dear."

"But wait, there's more," he said, trying not to sound like a TV infomercial. "Next, they made her go through a 'ducking'. What's that?"

"Another dubious test of witchery that was used in different countries, in various forms, going all the way back to the Roman Empire. In some places, they'd tie the accused person to a chair called a ducking stool, which was at the end of a large lever. They'd plunge the person into whatever body of water was nearby and try to coax a confession out of her. Sometimes it worked, and sometimes it didn't."

"Meaning she drowned."

"Precisely. Now, in the colonies, there was sometimes a variation on the theme where the accused would be bound hand and foot and tossed into a lake or pond. If she floated, she was a witch, albeit a live one. If she sank—"

"An innocent corpse," finished Bortnicker.

"Were these people serious?" gasped LouAnne, who was becoming more and more exasperated with her forefathers.

"How did Charity Blessing do?" asked Bortnicker.

T.J. scanned the next page. "She floated."

"Wow," said LouAnne disgustedly. "And where did this travesty take place?"

Sherwood raised a pale hand and pointed to the picture window. "Why, it was just out there, dear," he said. "The picturesque Edwards Pond on our idyllic Village Green was the town's public place of judgment. I'm sure the event attracted a curious throng of onlookers."

"What came next?" asked Bortnicker. "Was she burned at the stake or something?"

"Contrary to popular belief, Bortnicker," said Sherwood in a patient tone, "witches weren't burned to death in the colonies. Hanging was the execution of choice."

"Did they lynch her, Big Mon?" he asked, as they all turned to T.J., who was bent over the ledger.

"It says here she would be tried the second week of August, 1662. In addition to the Town Council, some bigwigs from Hartford would be coming down to assist in the proceedings."

"Wait a minute," said LouAnne. "That means the trial happened three hundred fifty years ago *this week*. Pretty curious, don't you think?"

"Yeah," said T.J. "And here's something even more curious. The month of August, 1662, is ripped out of the ledger."

* * * *

The day's research had been fruitful, but before they left, the trio sought the historian's opinion. "Should we get started tonight?" asked T.J. "We've got everything set up, Mr. Sherwood."

"It would appear there's no time to waste," he replied. "I will leave the outside door to the auxiliary room unlocked and have the Museum's security alarm system disarmed. When would you figure to be back here?"

"After nine o'clock, when it's good and dark," replied T.J. "No sense in getting here any earlier."

"And you'll lock up after yourselves?"

"Don't worry," the boy assured. "In April we had to lock up the Baseball Hall of Fame every night. We're pretty responsible."

"Unless we get hexed, of course," said Bortnicker, making a feeble attempt at a joke.

"The other thing, Mr. Sherwood, we apologize, but we have a commitment tomorrow and might even not be back by tomorrow night," said T.J.

"Yeah," said Bortnicker, "we've been asked to throw out the first pitch at the Red Sox game in Boston tomorrow afternoon."

"One of the perks of stardom, I presume?" asked the historian with a trace of sarcasm.

"Something like that," answered T.J., his face coloring. "But we'll be here tonight, and after tomorrow, every night until this gets resolved."

"I believe you. Enjoy yourselves at Fenway Park. Isn't it curious, though, that the team who was supposedly the recipient of a famous curse wants to have *you* as a guest?"

Chapter Fifteen

"Dad, I really feel bad about you having to come pick us up so late," apologized T.J. as Tom transported the *Junior Gonzo Ghost Chasers*, attired in their stenciled black T-shirts, down to the Historical District for their first investigation. "But there's no sense just having you sit around the Museum for hours waiting for us to get done."

"No worries," replied his father, who after the Bermuda expedition was well aware of the methods employed in paranormal investigation. "There's a ballgame on tonight, and I have some work to finish as well so I can clear my desk and not be thinking about it tomorrow up in Boston. By the way, Bortnicker, thanks for saving me some work by cooking dinner."

"My pleasure, Mr. J.," responded the group's resident chef. "There was no need for a heavy meal anyway, since we ate so much at Archie Moore's. I just poked around in the fridge until I found some stuff to work with."

"Those shrimp and veggie kebabs were perfect for a light dinner," complimented LouAnne.

"Glad you liked it."

"Sorry your mom couldn't join us," said Tom.

"No big deal. She and a few of her girlfriends went out for a bite. She only would've liked the veggie part, anyway."

"So, gang, what are you hoping to accomplish tonight while I'm watching the Yankees?"

"I'm not expecting too much," confessed T.J. "The first time out on any investigation is for making sure the equipment functions and getting a feel for the area."

"This is our first real outdoor investigation with all the gadgets," explained Bortnicker. "Gettysburg doesn't count because we only had one measly camcorder that LouAnne brought from home."

"Ghost hunting has really gone high-tech, hasn't it?" observed Tom.

"Yeah," said Bortnicker, "and they're coming up with more doodads all the time."

"Are you sure you guys are dressed properly for this?"

"I think so," said T.J. "We have to wear the T-shirts for filming purposes, but even though it's pretty warm we all wore jeans and hiking boots, in case we have to go in the marsh."

"And we loaded up on bug repellent," added LouAnne.

"Good. Hopefully there aren't any really boggy areas—"

"Or quicksand," cut in Bortnicker.

"Which is why we have walkie-talkies," said T.J. calmly. "So let's not get all bent out of shape before we even start, okay? Jeez!"

"Don't worry, Big Mon," assured Bortnicker, breaking into his crooked smile, "it's all good in the neighborhood."

But as Tom pulled out of the parking lot, leaving the trio standing alone in the dark with the only sounds being those of crickets and barely rustling reeds from the marsh, even Bortnicker eased up on the bravado. "Mucho creepy," he muttered as they turned toward the unlocked Museum door.

Once inside, it was time to make a game plan and gear up. "Okay, guys," said Bortnicker as he stood before the array of devices he'd laid out on a table. "Here's all the stuff, with brand-new batteries. Each of you should take an EVP recorder, a camcorder, and a walkie-talkie. And I have a surprise for you," he said, handing them a headband with a small light attached.

"Bortnicker, really?" asked LouAnne. "This looks so dorky."

"You'll appreciate it when you're outside in the darkness. And I'll need you guys to set down two remote DVRs apiece. T.J., I think you want to position one near Jonathan Melrose's crypt, and maybe another on the back wall so it looks out on the marsh. LouAnne, why don't you put yours down on the Village Green near Edwards Pond and in the very center of the Green?"

"You got it."

"Okay," said T.J., "let's film a little intro." Bortnicker hefted a camcorder, pointed it at T.J., and nodded. "We're here at the Fairfield Museum and History Center, getting ready to go outside for our first investigation. We'll be concentrating on two areas: the Old Cemetery, which was established in the 1630s, and the Village Green, which was the center of activity in the town. We think we are searching for the ghost of Charity Blessing, a girl who was accused of being a witch in the summer of 1662, exactly three hundred fifty years ago. Some people in the area have reported seeing an apparition of a young woman in the areas we're going to cover. Hopefully, we'll pick up some EVPs or video on our ghost."

"Excellent, Big Mon," said Bortnicker, clicking off. "You're getting good at this—one take." He gave his buddy a high-five. "Remember to keep talking while you're walking around and filming," he advised. "Ask questions out loud and leave a good space for possible EVP response."

"This isn't our first rodeo, Bortnicker," chided LouAnne. "I think we know the drill."

"Sorry, you're right," he apologized. "Just be careful out there. I'll help you position the DVRs by walkie-talkie."

"Okay," said T.J. seriously, "let's bring it in." As had become their custom, they put their hands together in the center of their huddle. "One, two, three—"

Gonzos Rule! they cried in unison.

T.J. and LouAnne stepped outside. "Okay, Cuz," he said, "let's go set up our DVRs. Give a holler if there's trouble, and we'll come running." They both clicked on their headband lamps.

"Okay, take care," she answered before giving him a peck on the cheek and striding purposefully toward the Village Green.

"I'm heading towards the graveyard," he dictated. "The land was set aside in 1632, and eventually a low wall was built around it." Rather than go around to the front entrance, he sat on the side wall and swung his legs over. A few seconds later he reached Jonathan Melrose's tomb, next to which lay the newly dug plot of his recently deceased descendent. He set up a DVR, and called Bortnicker on the walkie-talkie. "How's this view?" he asked.

"Perfect, Big Mon," was the reply. "Now put one on the wall facing the marsh and you're good to go." This he did, and then, taking in his surroundings, began calling out to Charity Blessing.

* * * *

Meanwhile, LouAnne had set up both her DVRs and, with a little repositioning assistance from Bortnicker, began her own dialogue. "I'm trying to make contact with Charity Blessing. My name is LouAnne, and I'd like to speak with you. Are you here with me, Charity?" She paused for any EVP response. "Is this the pond where they ducked you?" She saw shadows darting here and there, but decided it was actually the partial moonlight playing off the trees and bushes. But she persisted, taking her path in ever widening arcs, swiveling her head from side to side and considering every sound, no matter how minute.

After a while, Bortnicker's voice crackled over the walkie-talkie. "Anything shaking out there, my dear?"

"Nada."

"Well, do another half hour or so and then I'll switch with you."

"Copy that."

* * * *

Two hundred yards away, T.J. wandered among the headstones, most leaning one way or the other and weathered, and kept up a one-way dialogue with Charity. But deep down, he knew that eventually he'd have to hop the fence and venture into the marsh. In fact, he'd felt it since they'd stepped outside the Museum. After much procrastinating, he took a deep breath, told Bortnicker he was going into Wolves Swamp, and climbed over the wall.

"Tread lightly, Big Mon," was the reply.

Immediately upon touching down with an uncomfortable squish, T.J. was assailed by mosquitoes and other species of insects; the repellent was somewhat effective, but not enough to keep him from swatting his exposed parts every few seconds. And then there were the six-foot cattails, which continuously brushed against his arms and face, disorienting him. Moving deeper into the marshland, he found himself breathing harder and harder as the labor of his shuffling in the muck mixed with his rising fear. He kept calling out to Charity Blessing, but his voice lacked the strength and conviction it had in the graveyard.

Then he heard it—a low, derisive laugh that seemed to be coming from all around him. He looked right, then left, trying to determine the source of the sound, to no avail. "S-show yourself!" he cried out, flailing at the reeds to create a corridor of vision. But it was useless. Suddenly it seemed that the surrounding cattails were swirling, closing in, clutching at him. T.J. turned to run but instead broke through the surface of mud, plunging down to his knee. He tried to yank his leg out but the mire sucked at him. In his panic, he fumbled for the walkie-talkie, dropped it, felt around for it on the ground, scooped it up again, covered with mud, and depressed the TALK button. "BORTNICKER! LOUANNE!" he cried, as the laughter began again, mocking him.

"On my way, Cuz! Hang on!" came LouAnne's frantic voice as she pounded toward the marsh. At the same time his buddy, clipping on a headlight, burst from the Museum door and sprinted across the parking lot. They crashed into the reeds together, screaming T.J.'s name.

"Over here!" he cried back, futilely trying to extricate his leg from the muck. But his comrades, like him, were totally disoriented by the high, thick reeds. LouAnne eventually reached him first, by this time on her hands and knees, smeared with mud. She saw his predicament, grabbed him by his upper arm and tugged, without success. Then Bortnicker was sliding in beside her, clamping on to the other arm. "One, two, three, pull!" he yelled, and T.J.'s leg came free with a popping *whush*. But there was no time to celebrate his extrication, for within seconds the temperature around the teens dropped precipitously, despite the humid heat of early August.

"What in God's name is going on here?" cried LouAnne as her breath came out in frosty vapor. But this was only the beginning of the onslaught. The wind picked up to where it was positively howling, and there was something else contained within it—a human shriek so piercing that it burned their eardrums and made it seem like the end of the world was at hand.

"Cover up!" yelled T.J. above the din, and the teens lay atop one another, holding fast, an island in a sea of insanity. The sound and wind built to a crescendo as they tightened their hold; LouAnne's nails were drawing blood on Bortnicker's arm but he didn't even notice. And then, just as it seemed the universe was about to explode, everything abruptly stopped, leaving the trio shivering and panting. A high, crackling laugh resonated above them, and then that was gone, too.

"Don't move," cautioned T.J., who lay, spread-eagled, atop his friends. "Just breathe. Let's make sure it's really over." They waited another minute until they could again hear the sounds of the marsh—crickets, the occasional croak of a toad, and the hum of mosquitoes. Slowly T.J. sat up and looked around, then sat back. "All clear, guys."

The other two *Junior Gonzos* rose up on one elbow; Bortnicker's glasses were covered with muck, and LouAnne had dark streaks in her blonde tresses. "Would somebody please tell me what just happened?" she asked wearily.

"I think whatever we were looking for just found *us*," replied Bortnicker, attempting to clean his glasses with his equally muddy T-shirt, "and it's not happy."

"Let's get out of this place," advised T.J. "Make sure you've got all the equipment." They snatched up dropped EVPs and camcorders and backed out cautiously, heads on a swivel, their nerves raw. Minutes later, they were in the parking lot of the Museum. "Come with me," said T.J. "We'll retrieve the DVR cameras together. No splitting up."

Once back inside, they sat around the equipment table, dripping globs of mud onto the floor, and reviewed the tapes. "Did you see anything in the DVR feeds?" asked T.J. as Bortnicker rewound the EVP recorders.

"Nothing. We had four cameras going simultaneously, but not even a shadow. I mean, you guys weren't out there but an hour when I heard you screaming, T.J. It isn't even eleven o'clock yet."

"Then it's up to the EVP tapes. Let's give a listen."

Bortnicker hooked up LouAnne's recorder to the computer and plugged in two sets of headphones, one for himself and one for her. Despite her repeated requests for communication, there was only dead air in the response gaps.

But T.J.'s EVP was another story. From the beginning, there were weird crackles and hissing sounds that he at first attributed to the reeds of the marsh. But once he stepped over the wall from the graveyard the responses gained a chilling clarity. As he and Bortnicker listened on the 'phones, their eyes widened.

"Charity Blessing! Are you here with me?"

I've been waiting.

"Show yourself if you're here!"

I make the rules.

"How can we help you?"

Too late.

"Did you harm Reverend Melrose?"

How dare you—

The next sounds heard were the low, menacing laugh, followed by T.J. plunging into the mud and screaming for his friends. Then came the grunting, squishing noises of him struggling to free himself, the calls of his comrades as they rushed to his aid, and finally, the rising crescendo of the wind, ending with that chilling laugh they all had heard.

The boys removed their headsets and sat back, blinking, as LouAnne took a turn listening. When she was done, they seemed frozen in their seats, too stunned for discussion. Finally, T.J. broke the silence.

"Okay," he said calmly, "here's what I'm thinking. First, we can't tell my dad what really happened out there. If we do, he'll never let us come back. Agreed?"

"Agreed," said Bortnicker, and LouAnne nodded. "But how do we explain being covered with mud, Big Mon?"

"We dropped one of the camcorders in a mud hole and had to fish it out," T.J. replied with a shrug. "Perfectly plausible."

"That's all well and good," reasoned LouAnne, "but the question remains: What the heck are we up against this time? Assuming it is Charity Blessing, is what happened out there an indication of what she's capable of? And if so, is it something out of our league?"

"Let me think about it a little," said T.J., while he dialed his dad for a pickup. "We're still pretty wound up here, and we've all gotta calm down. Maybe it's just as well we're taking tomorrow off to go to Boston. I think we need a day away from all this."

"Yeah," said Bortnicker, turning off the computer. "Let's just spend a relaxing afternoon at Fenway—no ghosts or witches allowed."

Chapter Sixteen

The Fenway trip was totally the Red Sox' idea, although the publicity it generated thrilled the execs at The Adventure Channel. Apparently, one of the teenaged daughters of the team's Board of Trustees was a big *Junior Gonzo Ghost Chasers* enthusiast, so when she became aware that two of the three ghost hunting team members were from Fairfield, a region that was neatly divided between Yankees and Red Sox fans, she mentioned them to her father, who didn't care much about ghosts but saw it as a marketing ploy to expand Red Sox Nation ever southward. Besides, their manager, Bobby Valentine, one of the greatest athletes to ever come out of the state of Connecticut, was a resident of nearby Stamford, so it couldn't hurt.

T.J., a casual Yankees fan himself, wasn't thrilled with the idea of throwing out the first pitch before the Sox' matinee game against the Texas Rangers (he had politely requested that all three of them, not just he, get to throw a first pitch simultaneously, to which the ball club agreed); but Bortnicker, a diehard Red Sox supporter who wore his battered and faded blue Sox ball cap with pride—when he could fit it over his unruly curls—begged him into submission. Besides, although T.J. was not the type of boy to idolize modern ballplayers, he did have an affinity for historic sites, and the lure of an insider's tour of Fenway Park, as well as the opportunity to step onto its hallowed playing field, had been too much to pass up. When LouAnne had thrown her support behind Bortnicker for the kids to do it, he'd caved easily.

The Red Sox had laid out a first-class itinerary for the trio, arranging for a limo to pick them up (along with Pippa, who had never even been to a Major League ballpark, and Tom) and transport them the 2½ hour trip up I-91 and the Mass Pike to Boston.

Spirits were high as the five travelers slid into the large red SUV at 8:00 AM that morning. The conversation was light, and the details of their encounters with Roberto Clemente up in Cooperstown were avoided in deference to the limo driver. Likewise, no mention was made of the previous night's harrowing experience, Tom having bought their camcorder story. Instead, they joked about whether they should throw their ceremonial pitches from the pitcher's mound or closer; all agreed that they could easily reach from regulation distance, and if any of them bounced it they would be mercilessly ragged on.

"The Sox have quite a day planned for you guys," said Tom, reading the itinerary printout with official Red Sox letterhead. "You'll have some time to walk the area around Fenway and soak up the game-day ambience. Then, we're to meet a team official in the business office who will give us a tour of the park; the three of you will end up in the Red Sox dugout where Bobby Valentine—he's the team's manager, Pippa—will personally greet you. And then, after the first pitch, we'll all watch the game from one of the team's luxury suites, with all the food and beverages you want."

"Way cool!" cried Bortnicker.

"All this because of a TV show," marveled Pippa.

"It's a little more than that," said Tom proudly. "According to the ratings, the kids' Cooperstown Special did exceptionally well for a cable TV show, and that was up against the MLB All-Star Game, which I thought was a gutsy move by The Adventure Channel."

"Which means we could basically write our ticket for one or more future specials," sniffed Bortnicker in his best John Lennon voice.

"I'm happy with the two we did," said T.J., looking out the window as the scenery flew by and inwardly revisiting the weirdness of the previous night. "We don't need another one."

"What do *you* think, LouAnne?" asked Pippa.

"Well," she said tactfully, "I could very well live without the drama at school that this all has caused. This past year was kind of rough." She stopped short of relating the horrible experience she'd suffered the previous winter and the sniping that came afterward from many students—even some of her former friends—who'd accused her of becoming stuck up over her fame. "But then again," she reasoned, "I've got college to think about in another year, and as of this moment I'm by no means a lock for a track scholarship. The trust fund money from these shows will be a big help to my parents."

"Guess you're outnumbered, Son," said Tom to T.J. playfully.

"It would appear," he replied resignedly.

They rolled up to Yawkey Way, one of the avenues bordering the venerable ballpark, at 10:30 AM. All the surrounding streets had been blocked off so that fans could mill around, visit the various souvenir stands and shops in the area, or maybe catch a bite to eat from the many pushcart vendors or local restaurant/taverns such as the famous Cask and Flagon.

It was a sundrenched morning with only moderate humidity, and the group easily made their way around, purchasing a couple souvenirs and taking photos next to the Ted Williams statue. Of course, despite the promise of unlimited eats later on, Bortnicker found himself succumbing to the temptations of the sausage & peppers carts from nearby Little Italy, and happily munched on a dripping sandwich as they strolled. "Just think," gushed Tom Jackson, ever the architect, "this building was opened the week the Titanic sank. And it's still going strong. Incredible!"

Then it was on to the official entrance, set in the park's outer red brick façade, where they were greeted by a fresh-faced intern named Carla Leber, who treated them like, well, TV stars. "I'm a big fan!" she proclaimed, shaking hands vigorously with all three of them. "I especially liked the diving sequence in your Bermuda show. I'm certified in SCUBA myself." She issued the group VIP passes encased in plastic, which they hung around their necks on Red Sox logo lanyards. "Follow me!" she sang enthusiastically.

They began their tour traversing the concourses under the stands, which were a hive of pregame activity, the food and souvenir vendors stocking their shelves and making preparations for the incoming crowd. Then it was upstairs to the glassed-in press box and skybox areas, followed by a trip down to the playing field where they actually got to go inside the fabled left-field wall of Fenway, more famously known as the Green Monster. As the manual scoreboard was accessible only through a

148

doorway at the left-field warning track, their venture inside was both mysterious and exhilarating.

"Wow!" cried Bortnicker, madly snapping photos on his phone. "It's all creaky and dusty in here."

"And it feels like an oven," added LouAnne. "I pity the people who work in here during the games."

Emerging into the fresh air and sunlight, Carla said, "All right, guys, one more stop. Let's go meet Mr. Valentine." They skirted the field, where batting practice was now in full swing, with infielders taking ground balls, outfielders shagging flies, and batters cranking arcing moon shots into the stands, where eager fans snagged them with gloves brought from home, bare hands, or scoop-style fishing nets. As they were passing one of the young Texas Ranger outfielders, he gave a quick whistle to get their attention, shot LouAnne a wink, and flipped her a ball, which she caught one-handed.

"Show off," joked T.J.

The embattled skipper of the Sox, Bobby Valentine, was just ending an apparently contentious session with a few Boston sportswriters in the home dugout. His team was hovering below the .500 level, and the notoriously critical Boston press, as well as the fans, were becoming more merciless with each loss. And yet, when Valentine encountered the kids he was quick with his trademark wry smile and a warm handshake, and motioned to them to sit on the dugout steps. "It's good to see some friendly faces from Fairfield County for a change," he cracked. "I take it you guys are Sox fans?"

"Well, I am for sure," said Bortnicker. "T.J. here, he's kind of a closet Yankee fan, and LouAnne's from Gettysburg, so she's big into the Phillies."

"Nothing wrong with that," said Bobby V. "My people here tell me you're a ballplayer, T.J. What school?"

"Bridgefield High," he answered with modest pride. "I was on the JV this year."

"Outfielder, right?"

"How can you tell?"

"You've got the build," said the manager. "Plus, I saw you walking along the outfield. You kind of glide."

149

"He batted .321 this season," offered Bortnicker. "I keep the team's stats."

"Not bad," said Valentine, who looked weary. "Maybe we should suit you up."

"I have a little trouble with curveballs," confessed T.J.

"Who doesn't? Well, we're glad to have you up here. Have fun throwing out the first pitch, and enjoy the game."

"Thanks, Mr. Valentine," said T.J. "Good luck the rest of the season."

"Yeah," he said, somewhat sardonically. "Now if only I could get those sportswriters to stop haunting *me*."

Carla led them to the end of the dugout, where they were handed team-issued Red Sox home white jerseys to wear over their *JGGC* golf shirts. Bortnicker was in heaven. "I'm never taking this off!" he crowed.

"Ewww," said LouAnne, wrinkling her nose.

As Tom and Pippa looked on proudly from the luxury suite above home plate, batting practice ended, the field was cleared, and the trio of ghost hunters marched out to the mound for their big moment. At home plate stood catchers Jarrod Saltalamacchia and Kelly Shoppach; they were joined at the last minute by David "Big Papi" Ortiz, the Sox' formidable designated hitter. The public address system crackled to life:

"Ladies and gentlemen, please turn your attention to the pitcher's mound where the Boston Red Sox welcome the stars of The Adventure Channel series *Junior Gonzo Ghost Chasers*, which recently was broadcast from the National Baseball Hall of Fame in Cooperstown. Let's give a warm Fenway welcome to T.J. Jackson, Bortnicker and LouAnne!"

The near capacity crowd provided a polite round of applause as the three teens gripped the brand-new MLB baseballs Carla had handed them. T.J. had thought he'd be a nervous wreck, standing on the mound of perhaps the famous ballpark on earth, but a quiet calm came over him—as usually happened in a tight spot—and he smiled. This *was* 'way cool'. "Okay, guys," he said, "on my count—one, two, three!"

The *Junior Gonzos* simultaneously effected a windup and threw. LouAnne, as could be expected, burned one in that Shoppach caught at the chest. T.J.'s loopy strike to Saltalamacchia came in waist high. But

Bortnicker, after an elaborate windup, saw his fastball fly over the head of the leaping—and laughing—Ortiz, all the way to the screen. The crowd went into hysterics, and the boy gave a dramatic bow.

"You hot dog," snickered T.J. as the kids jogged toward the ballplayers to retrieve their souvenirs.

"Nice toss," said Saltalamacchia.

"That's some arm you got," said Shoppach to LouAnne.

"Hey man, you trying to kill someone?" joked Ortiz as he handed a new ball to the still-beaming Bortnicker.

They were almost to the Sox dugout when T.J. felt a tug on his jersey. "Yo, my man," hissed Ortiz, "I gotta talk to you."

"Sure, Mr. Ortiz," said T.J. "Right now?"

"No, game's gonna start. Where they have you sitting?"

"One of the luxury suites behind home plate," he replied.

"Okay, I'll send one of the clubhouse guys up to get you. Thanks."

"No problem."

Carla escorted the threesome upstairs to the suite and bid them goodbye, but not before having them autograph a baseball for her. "I hope you guys do some more shows," she said in her Boston accent as they parted. "I'll be keeping an eye out for ya!"

"Good job, kids," said Tom before they stood for the national anthem down on the field. "You looked great out there."

"My, you really let that ball go, didn't you?" said Pippa to her son, her lips curling into a smile.

As soon as the anthem ended, Bortnicker lay siege to the buffet table, which included tubs of peanuts, Cracker Jack, popcorn and chips, as well as covered chafing dishes of burgers, hot dogs, sliced turkey, and veggie wraps for Pippa. Tom allowed himself a beer and Pippa sampled a glass of Chardonnay as the kids cracked open bottles of iced tea. An attendant checked in periodically to see if they needed anything more.

Unfortunately, the presence of the *Junior Gonzos* did not improve the Bosox' fortunes; they fell behind quickly in what became a wild game with plenty of scoring. The teens, whom had never experienced the panoramic views from a luxury suite before, were delighted to be there in any case. Even Pippa, though not a sports fan in the least, continually remarked on the beauty of the old baseball cathedral. "It's got good Feng

Shui," she concluded.

Finally, in the fourth inning, there was a quiet knock on the door and one of the "clubbies" appeared. "I'm here for T.J.?" he asked.

"Be right back, Dad," said the boy. "I have to talk to somebody. Guys, you want to come with me?"

"You got it, Big Mon," said Bortnicker, stuffing some peanuts into his pockets for the trip downstairs.

The clubbie took them down to the field level concourse and then through a door that led to a tunnel of whitewashed concrete. At its end was a staircase of unpainted concrete steps. "Sorry, miss," he said apologetically. "Up those steps is the locker room and, uh—"

"I understand," she said sweetly. "I'll just wait here for the guys."

"Lead on," said T.J. They ascended up and through a doorway that opened on the Red Sox' locker room, which had, of course, been off-limits during their earlier tour. Directly in front of them were two large brown leather couches arranged at ninety-degree angles so as to provide a good view of a large wall-mounted flat screen TV. To the right were a modern picnic-style table and benches fashioned from light wood with a couple boxes of baseballs waiting to be autographed. The walls of this surprisingly small room were an off gray, as was the neutral carpet. However, the large, open lockers were bright green, with the players' names and numbers on placards above them. A padded blue folding chair emblazoned with the Red Sox logo was set before each locker. The players' street clothes, extra bats, spikes and gloves were arranged neatly within the stalls, some of which had piles of fan mail on their floor as well.

"Somebody pinch me," rhapsodized Bortnicker.

Just then, the scraping of baseball spikes could be heard outside the locker room, and David Ortiz made his entrance from the doorway leading to the dugout. He was hatless, and sweating. "Okay, boys, I gotta make this quick, because I'm due up this inning," he said. He turned to the clubhouse attendant. "They need some sunflower seeds in the dugout," he said, which was code that he should make himself scarce. As soon as the door closed behind him, the slugger, who looked nervous, said, "So, you guys are ghost hunters, eh?"

"Yes, sir," answered T.J.

"And you, ah, really believe in that stuff?"

"We've seen some interesting things," said T.J., the understatement of the year.

"Really crazy things, in fact," added the more direct Bortnicker.

"Okay, then. Listen. I've got a teammate...he needs to talk to someone about some stuff. Will you do me a favor and listen to him?"

"Sure thing," said T.J.

"Julio!" called Ortiz. A light-skinned black man in a Red Sox uniform shuffled in from the trainer's room. Though nowhere as large in stature as Ortiz, he was still put together pretty well.

Probably a middle infielder thought T.J.

Ortiz said something to the player in Spanish, then clapped him on the shoulder. "Gotta go," said Ortiz. "*Gracias.*" He fist-bumped with the boys and jogged out of the room, leaving them with the mystery player, who appeared quite uncomfortable.

"Let's sit down," said T.J., motioning the man to the second couch. He and Bortnicker sank into the other plush sofa with a soft whoosh. "What can we do for you?"

"I, uh, do not speak English well, so forgive me, okay?" said Julio. "Plus, I am very nervous."

"Don't be," said Bortnicker disarmingly. "It's only us." He removed his Coke bottle glasses for a polish and smiled reassuringly.

However, this did little to calm the ballplayer, who kept casting furtive looks toward the locker room entrance. "First," he said haltingly, "I have to ask you. Have you really seen ghosts? No joke?"

"Yes," said T.J. quietly.

"And talked to them?"

Both boys nodded in assent.

Julio took a deep breath and played with his red wristbands. "The Red Sox, they called me up from Triple-A Pawtucket last week 'cause another guy got put on the disabled list. But the day I got called up, I also got a message from back in the Dominican, where I grew up. It was my mother, saying my grandma died. She helped raise me. We were poor, and my mother had to work—" A tear ran down his cheek and he looked at the ceiling to compose himself. "I'm sorry for crying."

"It's okay, man," said Bortnicker.

153

"It's that, I felt such guilt that I didn't go back for the funeral. I asked my father's advice and he said, 'Julio, this is your chance to go to the Major Leagues. You must do it.' So, I reported. And here I am."

"And you're feeling guilty," said T.J.

"*Si*. I can't concentrate at bat or on the field. My mind is with her."

"Well," said T.J. at that, "here's what I can tell you. It's true that Bortnicker here and I have seen ghosts. But I'm not like, uh, a medium, as they call it, someone who can contact the dead whenever they want.

"But on our last investigation, this spirit we met—" his mind flashed back to their incredible parting with the ghost of Clemente, who spoke personally to each of the teens before walking into the depths of Cooperstown's Lake Otsego—"he told me my mom, who died when I was young, was watching over me, and she was proud of me. If you were close to your grandma like you say, then I think she just has to be with you, and I also think she understands you have to chase your dream. Did she want you to be a ballplayer?"

"With her whole heart."

"Well, there you go, then," said T.J. warmly. "She's probably in here with us right now."

"You think?" said Julio, glancing around.

"Why not?" said Bortnicker.

"So if I were you," finished T.J., "I'd just try to relax and play some good ball."

Julio nodded. "Thank you, boys." He shook hands with both of them as they stood. "I'll make her proud."

Bortnicker, lightening the moment, added, "Tell Big Papi to stop pulling off the ball and keep his front shoulder in there."

"I'll tell him," Julio promised as he made for the door, a weight seemingly lifted from his muscular shoulders.

"Good job, Big Mon," said Bortnicker to his friend in the quiet locker room, which vibrated with the cheering of the crowd overhead. The Sox were probably mounting a comeback. "Hey, you think those burgers are still warm?"

"I wouldn't doubt it," said T.J. "Let's get out of here—LouAnne must be bored out of her mind."

"Okay, okay, in a second. But I've just gotta do one thing first." T.J.

stood, hands on hips, and watched his friend disappear around the corner into the spacious bathroom. "Wow! Too cool!" he called with glee while he took care of business.

* * * *

The ride home was markedly upbeat; the kids had decided not to mention the boys' encounter with Julio, explaining their absence away by claiming that a group of young *Junior Gonzo* fans had wanted to meet them downstairs. All of them, especially T.J., were starting to feel uncomfortable withholding information from their elders, but they felt it was all for the better.

"So, how's the investigation going?" asked Pippa innocently as they stood at the curb that evening after being dropped off on Tide Mill Terrace.

"Really good," said Bortnicker cryptically. "Who knows? We may be onto something. Too early to tell."

"Well, it's been a long day," said Tom, "but a memorable one. The Red Sox really outdid themselves."

"Yeah," agreed Bortnicker, "and I'm still stuffed to the gills. What a spread they laid out!"

"But I'm really bushed," yawned LouAnne, who, like her cousin and Bortnicker, hadn't gotten much sleep the night before, the events from the marsh playing in their heads in a continuous loop. "We running tomorrow, Cuz? Can't take two days off in a row."

"You know it," he promised.

They bid adieu to the Bortnickers and went inside. LouAnne, true to her word, slipped into her bed and was asleep within minutes.

But not T.J. He was on the phone to Jill Rogere.

Chapter Seventeen

"Thanks for getting together on such short notice, Jill," said T.J. as the trio squeezed into her 1990s Toyota Corolla sedan. "My dad got called into the office in Stamford and we had no way to get to Milford."

"No problem, folks," she replied, her eyes on the road. "Luckily, I work from home, so I was available."

"Let me do the intros, then. This is my cousin LouAnne, and—"

"Bortnicker," she finished. "You're quite the character on TV, my friend."

"Thank you—I think," he said with a grin.

"T.J. filled me in, pretty much, on what happened to you all in that marsh. It must've been terrifying."

They all nodded.

"Well, T.J. figured, and rightfully so, that the only way you could weather another encounter with this—whatever she is—is to talk to another witch. That's why we're on our way to Milford. My friend Deirdre is indeed a practicing 'white' witch, which means, basically, she's one of the good guys. What happened was, so many people were approaching her with questions and requests for assistance that she decided to give up her day job as a dental hygienist and open her own shop. As you can imagine, her presence in town raised more than a few eyebrows, but her business has been recognized by the Milford Chamber of Commerce, and nobody really gives her a hard time."

"Who in their right mind *would*?" said Bortnicker, attempting a joke.

Jill shot the teen a stern look in the rearview mirror as LouAnne applied a jab to the ribs. "Since you've given me the perfect segue,

156

Bortnicker, let me prepare you for this meeting. You'll find Deirdre Robin to be, at the very least, eccentric. But I assure you, when it comes to these matters she's dead serious. She'll size you up the minute you walk in the door, and if she senses one bit, one iota, of disrespect in your demeanor, she'll send you packing. And since you seem to be in dire need of her counsel, that would be foolhardy indeed. So my advice"— she again fixed Bortnicker with a look—"is to show deference to her beliefs and take to heart what she has to say."

"Sure thing, Jill," assured T.J.

"Yeah, sorry. Really," chimed in Bortnicker.

"Okay then," said Jill, lightening. "Now tell me what's wrong with my Red Sox."

As Bortnicker and LouAnne chatted away with Rogere about their heady experience up at Fenway, T.J. sat back and reviewed the morning. He and his cousin had taken yet another running route, down through Southport and then back up along Boston Post Road. They discussed the events of Wednesday night, and T.J. revealed the details of his phone call to Jill upon their return from Fenway.

"So she's kinda your 'sensitive' counselor?" LouAnne asked seriously.

"Yeah, I guess you could call it that," he'd replied. "She's helping me keep it all in perspective. It's been a real comfort."

"I can imagine, Cuz. I mean, it's not like you can look up people like her in the Yellow Pages, not that anyone really uses them anymore. Thank goodness she knows someone who can advise us on witch stuff."

They'd revealed their mid-morning destination to Bortnicker over a breakfast of homemade granola cereal and fruit, courtesy of Pippa. Bortnicker, temporarily replaced as head chef, had quietly sipped his coffee as his mates—once Pippa had left the room—gave him the lowdown. "If that's what it takes," he'd said finally, but he seemed dubious.

After calling Robert Sherwood and making a 2 PM appointment for another fact-finding session, T.J. felt he'd done all he could do at present. And now they were motoring up I-95 to talk to an honest-to-goodness witch. Incredible.

"How did you first meet Deirdre?" asked LouAnne, redirecting the conversation.

"Her mother, who is also a practicing witch, had a shop in Salem where Deirdre worked after school and on weekends. So, I went up there to visit the town when I was still in high school with this guy I was dating. We both walked in, and I started flipping through some books. Well, Deirdre, who was maybe a year or two older than me, came out of the back room where she had been doing a tarot card reading, walked right past me, and told my boyfriend to get out. He was offended, of course, and stormed out in a huff, and I was left standing there, open-mouthed. She turned to me and said something like, 'Listen, I don't know who you are, but I'm going to tell you right now: that boy is no good for you. No good will come out of a relationship with him.' Then she took me in the back room, read my cards—a very long reading, as opposed to those she does for customers that are purposely shorter so they'll come back—and what she saw, she said, confirmed her fears.

"So I left, totally conflicted, wondering if maybe she'd misread the situation, and this guy. And, of course, I was a little skeptical. Who wouldn't be? So I stayed with him. And within a couple months I was sorry I did. Let's leave it at that. Really, that first encounter convinced me of her sincerity, and her power."

"So, what is it that separates her from you, puts her on a different level?" asked T.J.

"It's what she believes. For her, established religion, such as what you and I believe in, has no value. She worships the earth, if you can understand that, and the symbols and materials she works with are different. But she can probably explain that all better than I can. And here we are."

They pulled into a small parking lot on a quiet side street in the heart of town where a cute yellow shingled cottage-style structure with an Old English sign over its front door announced it as The Majick Shoppe.

Jill led the way to the door; a tinkling overhead bell signaled their entrance. The ocher-hued walls were lined with varnished shelves chock-full of wands, chalices, pentacles, pendulums and Ouija boards, as well as candles, oils and crystals. Jars of herbs both large and small gave off a variety of scents, and there was a library section of books from paperbacks to hardcovers on everything related to Deirdre's vocation.

"Jill!" she called out, rushing from behind the counter to embrace her friend and administer a two-cheek European style kiss.

To say that Deirdre Robin was eccentric—in her appearance anyway—was an understatement. She was a stout woman, swathed in a black and purple caftan, with coils of multicolored beads around her neck and huge silver bracelets on both wrists. Her nail polish was black with silver accents, and her purple eye shadow – which matched the violet streak in her otherwise chestnut hair that hung to her waist—made her seem like she'd come from central casting. Turning from Jill, she shook hands first with T.J., then LouAnne. But when she took Bortnicker's she did not let go, and froze him with a steely glare. "You," she said seriously, "will not open your mouth for the entire time you are under my roof unless I tell you to. Is that understood?" He nodded quickly, his eyes bulging in panic, until she released her grip.

"Excuse me for a moment," she requested, and posted an *out to lunch* sign on the front door. "Follow me," she said, swishing towards the back room whose doorway was a beaded curtain. The kids gave each other a look, then trailed after her.

"I'll just poke around in the library," Jill called out sweetly.

They took their seats around a small circular wooden table with a thick burning candle in its center. As it flickered, it gave off a sweet smell not unlike pine needles. "Deirdre," said LouAnne tentatively, "may we film you for the TV show?"

"If you're respectful; but I retain the right to the final say on what makes it into the program. If you can't assure that, then this session is over."

"We promise that you'll have the last word," assured T.J., and that seemed to appease the witch.

"Jill is a dear friend of mine from way back," she began, "and told me you need help. And I am happy to provide that help. But before we get started I must tell you that I've seen both of these shows you've done, and I'm astounded as to how fortunate you've been—not only to come in contact with the various entities you've sought—but in how, rank amateurs that you are, you've managed to avoid putting yourselves in disastrous situations. I just don't know if you appreciate the forces you're dealing with in your so-called investigations.

"However," she continued, "Jill has assured me, T.J., that you are sincere, and that despite your commercial success you haven't developed a 'know-it-all' attitude. So that's in your favor.

"It's true that I'm a practicing 'white' witch, as was my mother before me. The religion, if you will, that I adhere to is called Wicca. It follows the cycles of the earth—the phases of the moon and the changing of the seasons. You'd be surprised how many people in our little County of Fairfield practice Wicca and/or paganism. Most of them keep it quiet for fear of ridicule or discrimination. But have no doubts: I do not embrace devil worship, or sacrifice animals. I'm not some voodoo priestess. My philosophy is to honor every living thing, our landscape, and the world we live in. Any questions so far?"

LouAnne cleared her throat. "Are all witches, or Wiccans, women?"

"No. The term 'witch' today is used to identify both genders."

"Are you able to, uh, cast spells?" asked T.J.

"Although Wiccans have the knowledge to cast spells, it is our responsibility to use the power wisely. Wicca teaches that what you do to another, you do to yourself. Wicca also teaches that it is always preferable to find a positive solution to our problems. So, why don't you tell me about yours?"

"Well," said T.J., "we're pretty sure we're investigating a witch from the 1600s named Charity Blessing, who lived in Fairfield. According to town documents and local history, she was accused of witchcraft and had to undergo an examination for witch's marks and a witch ducking. It seems like both tests went against her."

"What then?"

"That's where it gets sketchy. As far as we can see, there's no record of her trial, or what happened to her afterwards." He told Deirdre about the pages that had been removed from the town meeting minutes.

Ms. Robin gave a sarcastic chuckle. "Oh, there's a record, T.J. Somewhere. Those Puritans were pretty diligent about writing everything down. You've just got to find it." She paused. "But there's more to this situation, isn't there?"

"Yes, there is," he confessed. "And I'll tell you, but I don't think you're going to like it." He looked to his friends, who nodded for him to continue. And so, keeping it as plain-spoken as possible, T.J. told the

Wiccan what had happened in the marsh two nights before.

The entire time Deirdre was impassive; if she thought they were being reckless idiots she gave no indication. Finally, after a minute of contemplative silence, she said, "And what is it you want me to do here? Go to war with another witch on your behalf, one who might not even possess any powers and was erroneously accused, as were so many in that time? Even if I were sure she *was* a witch, I wouldn't go after her. I'm a Wiccan, not Clint Eastwood." She paused, no doubt reading the look of deflation on the faces of the teens. "What I can do, however, is arm you with some things to more or less protect you from whatever might get thrown at you."

"We'd appreciate anything you could do," said LouAnne. "Because the other night we thought we were goners out there." An involuntary tear made its way down her cheek.

Deirdre Robin, obviously moved by the sincerity of the teens, sighed. "I'll see what I can do," she said softly, "but there are no money-back guarantees on all this. Again, even if this supposed witch has powers, I don't know their extent. Wait here." She disappeared through the beaded curtain and the kids' shoulders sagged as they relaxed.

"This is heavy-duty, Big Mon," whispered Bortnicker, the first words he'd uttered since they had arrived.

"No duh."

"I say she's totally legit," stated LouAnne.

"I'm with you," agreed T.J. "Bortnicker?"

"Ditto."

A few minutes later Robin reappeared and sat at the table. "First and foremost," she began, "approach this person with respect. I've seen the provocative tact your friend Mike Weinstein takes on his show, the challenging, macho attitude—forget it in this case. Don't overstep your bounds. If she does interact with you, the conversation ends when *she* says it does. And although I won't jump to conclusions about this one, it does seem like something strong got called down on the three of you out in that marsh. So again, show respect.

"Now, as far as a protective shield, if you will. I'm giving you each a bottle of protection oil, and a crystal to keep in your pocket. In addition, I've prepared a small bag containing sage and black salt,

161

among other ingredients, to wear around your necks. I've attached them to leather lanyards for you. But you're still not done. I've written a prayer for you all to recite together before you go to see her. Hopefully, with all of these precautions, you'll be safe." She slid the paper across to the teens.

"Deirdre, I don't know how to thank you," said T.J., flashing his winning smile. "How much do we owe you?"

"Nothing," she replied. "Just a promise: that you won't take any stupid, unnecessary risks out there. This isn't Hollywood fantasy, T.J., not to me. It's the real deal, and it's serious. If you need me you know where to find me. Good luck."

* * * *

They grabbed a couple energy bars at T.J.'s house after being dropped off, hopped on their bikes, and pedaled down to the Historical District. It had been decided that although they would clue Mr. Sherwood in about their experience in the marsh, the meeting with Deirdre would be put aside for now. He awaited them this afternoon as on Wednesday, seated at his desk, but he wore a mask of concern.

"What's the matter, Mr. Sherwood?" asked LouAnne as they sat with him. "You don't look well."

"To be honest," the scholar said, "I didn't sleep at all last night, because of something that happened here.

"Knowing that your Boston trip precluded any activities yesterday, I ended up staying much later than normal, trying to find any sign of the missing information on Charity Blessing. By the time I left, around ten o'clock or so, I was tired and frustrated. I keep my van in the parking lot—it's been modified with a hydraulic lift to allow me to enter and exit with my wheelchair, and drive. You see, though I am confined to this contraption, I do somewhat have use of my right leg. My disability was caused, by the way, from a fall from a horse some twenty years ago.

"Anyway, the parking lot was deserted, but as I neared my car, I saw a shadow out of the corner of my eye—a silhouette, really—of a woman, standing before the edge of Wolves Swamp. And although I could not make out any distinguishing features, I felt it was following my every movement. To tell the truth, I was thoroughly frightened. I got myself up and in to the van and, as teenagers used to say, I burned rubber out of the parking lot. So tell me, my young friends: am I just a foolish old man who is letting his imagination run wild?"

"I don't think so, Mr. Sherwood," said T.J., "and here's why."

* * * *

"My word," said the historian after listening to T.J.'s account of Wednesday's adventure in the marsh. "Then perhaps I wasn't hallucinating after all. But now I'm filled with even more concern—for the three of you. Are you sure you still want to pursue this investigation?"

"If we don't, Mr. Sherwood, then who will?" asked Bortnicker. "We sure don't want what happened to Reverend Melrose to happen again."

"What you say is certainly commendable, but how do you know that you're equipped to take on this supposed entity?"

"We've done our research, sir," answered T.J. coolly, sidestepping their visit with Deirdre Robin, "and we feel we'll be prepared for what she—or it—might have in store. But I still wish we had a better handle on what happened to Charity Blessing after the ducking."

"Then it's back to the archives," Sherwood said. "There's one place we haven't checked yet. Come with me." They left the research library through a side door, passed a wide metal cabinet housing many rows of narrow pullout shelves for old maps, and came to a door, which read *No Admittance—Authorized Personnel Only*. "I give you 'the inner sanctum'," he said with a hint of playfulness. The inside of the room they entered reminded T.J. and LouAnne of the storage vault beneath the Baseball Hall Of Fame which they'd toured with the head curator. It was climate controlled, with movable shelves that could be accessed by the turning of a wheel on the side. Though not as vast as the Hall's storage area, it was clear that this vault held the Museum's most treasured artifacts and papers.

"I have a theory," Sherwood said as he maneuvered one of the rolling shelves out for inspection. It moved with a *shush* and then snapped into place, revealing compartments of varying dimensions. He pulled out one of them and removed an archival storage box. "Let's take this to the research room and have a peek inside," he said. They returned

Paul Ferrante

to the room and Sherwood donned white cotton gloves. As the teens looked on curiously, he removed the top of the box and lifted out an old book whose leather cover was frail and tattered.

"This volume was one of the first attempts to record the history of Fairfield," Sherwood explained. "It was written in 1800 by my ancestor, Cyrus Sherwood, who had served in the colonial army as a colonel during the Revolutionary War." He carefully started leafing through the ancient tome. "Ah, here we are," he said with an air of triumph. "How silly of me to not have remembered old Cyrus. If anyone could shed light on our mystery, it would be him."

"Does he talk about Charity Blessing?" asked T.J., wondering how a book from the 1800s could be of any help.

"Not in so many words," replied Sherwood. "But here's the thing: Cyrus mentions that in 1779, when it became apparent that the British were going to invade lower Connecticut by sea and march on Fairfield, it was decided that all town records, as well as valuables of the wealthier citizens, would be hidden in an existing tunnel that ran from First Community Church to the Old Cemetery. This was a good thing because, after coming ashore at what is now Compo Beach in Westport, the British attacked Fairfield and burned many of its existing structures, including First Community. The tunnel, however, was never found by the invaders, so the foresight of the Fairfield village leaders was rewarded. But it's what Cyrus says next that I find intriguing. According to this text, when the Revolutionary era colonials began packing these items away underground, they were surprised to discover some manuscripts and records, both governmental and religious, from the previous century."

"Why wouldn't church-related stuff just be stored in the church itself?" asked Bortnicker.

"A good question," replied Sherwood. "Could it be that the contents were too inflammatory?"

"Or would those papers prove an embarrassment to the church—or maybe its pastor?" asked LouAnne.

"Or the community in general?" added T.J. "For example, the persecution of innocent people who were accused of witchcraft?"

"Interesting theories, indeed," said Sherwood, gently closing the

164

book. "There is no mention as to where exactly this tunnel was, nor the location of the secret papers within that tunnel."

"Looks like we need to pay a visit to Reverend Stirling ASAP," concluded T.J., taking out his cell phone. He punched in the number the minister had given him at their first meeting but was disappointed to hear a voice message reporting that the Reverend Stirling would be out of town on business until tomorrow, and to direct all communication to his secretary, Mrs. Moose, in the meantime.

"Mrs. Moose? For real?" asked Bortnicker with a grin.

"For real." T.J. frowned. "Well, Mr. Sherwood, I think we've kind of hit a dead end here. I guess our next move is to check out this tunnel thing."

"I agree. Why don't you run over to First Community and speak to Mrs. Moose? But before you do, a word of advice about our Mrs. Moose: I have been a parishioner at First Community since childhood, and both I and my late wife have been involved in church activities. Mrs. Moose has been the secretary there since the 1970s, when Daniel Melrose became the pastor. Nothing happens in and around that place without her say-so, or at least her knowledge. She can be a bit of a gossip, but she's protective of her boss and the good name of the church. It's her life."

"I understand," said T.J. "Thanks for the heads-up."

* * * *

They walked the couple blocks from the Museum to the church, passing Town Hall and crossing Old Post Road before entering the church offices. Mrs. Moose was diligently going through some papers at her desk, reading glasses pushed down to the edge of her nose and attached by a cord, her blue-gray bouffant glinting in the fluorescent overhead light.

"Time to turn on the charm, Big Mon," whispered Bortnicker from the side of his mouth, as LouAnne suppressed a giggle. Indeed, the role of suave spokesman was T.J. Jackson's forte. His boyish charisma and earnest politeness never failed to warm the hearts of crotchety ladies. Even the cantankerous head of the Bermuda National Heritage Trust, Constance Tilbury, had cut him some slack during the investigation there.

"Mrs. Moose?" he inquired, reaching across the desk. "Please don't get up. I'm T.J. Jackson, and these are my friends Bortnicker and LouAnne. Reverend Stirling asked us—"

"I'm well aware of your investigation, T.J.," she replied with a firm handshake. "How is your father, by the way?"

"He's doing great, ma'am, thank you."

"Wonderful. He was such a help during our renovations. Reverend Melrose—" she paused and sighed at the memory of her former superior—"thought very highly of him."

"The feeling was mutual, ma'am. Now, I know Reverend Stirling won't be back until tomorrow, but could we ask you a few questions?"

"Well," she said modestly, "I don't know how much assistance I could be, but please ask."

"Would you mind if I video you, ma'am?" asked LouAnne sweetly. "I'm sure the Reverend mentioned the TV show—"

"Oh yes, yes," she replied, removing her glasses and patting her hair into place. "What would you like to know?"

"To begin, do you know anything about a tunnel under the church?"

A cloud came over the woman's face, mixed with a look of disappointment. "I'm afraid you'll have to turn off the recorder, dear," she said with a dramatic sigh. "What I can tell you is not for public consumption. Too bad, I wore my favorite blouse today." LouAnne clicked off the camcorder. "There is indeed a tunnel, but not *under* the church, per se. It begins in the boiler room and goes all the way to the Old Cemetery, or so I'm told."

"When was it dug?" asked Bortnicker.

"Sometime between the establishment of the graveyard and the construction of the first formal church structure on this site. Of course, you must know by now that the original First Community Church was burned to the ground by the British during the Revolutionary War."

"Yes ma'am," said T.J. "Do you know the tunnel's original purpose?"

"The answer to that question has never been clear. What I do know is that it serves no purpose today and thus is off-limits to the general public. We do have it checked every spring to make sure the winter freeze and thaw has not compromised its integrity. And then, of course, after Irene we had it checked for flooding."

"Was there any damage from the hurricane?"

"No," she said, "but..." Her voice trailed off and an air of discomfort came over her. She looked around, then motioned them closer. "Actually," she whispered conspiratorially, "the late Reverend Melrose had two DPW men check out the tunnel a couple months after the hurricane—he was deathly afraid of going down there himself, apparently—and they ended up scared witless, running for their lives."

The kids looked at each other. "Did they see something down there?" asked Bortnicker.

"I'm not sure," she replied, "but something frightened the daylights out of them. And nobody's been in that tunnel since."

"You've been a great help, Mrs. Moose," said T.J. "Would you please schedule an appointment for us with Reverend Stirling for tomorrow at 2:00 PM?"

The secretary checked the minister's calendar. "I'll pencil you in," she said. "And what is the nature of your visit?"

"We're going down in that tunnel," said T.J.

* * * *

Once outside, T.J. checked his watch. "Well, we got a lot done today," he said, "but really, we can't do anything more till tonight. Any ideas? It's only five o'clock."

"We don't have to go back to the house, necessarily," said LouAnne. "We have our shirts and stuff for tonight thanks to Uncle Tom doing the wash this morning."

"Yeah," said Bortnicker, "our clothes were caked with all that marsh mud."

"I've got an idea," said T.J. "Why don't we ride over to Subway, pick up sandwiches, and have dinner at Penfield Beach? We can eat in the pavilion there, and it's only a couple blocks from the Museum."

"Sounds like a plan," said LouAnne.

They pedaled to the sandwich shop on the heavily commercial Boston Post Road and ordered subs, chips, and sodas, then cut back through the Historical District to Penfield Beach, which, along with Jennings Beach, were the principal seashore parks that served the town,

Sasco being smaller and out of the way. Penfield featured a kiddie playground with swings and a newly remodeled pavilion that had replaced an1800s Victorian structure which had existed on the very same spot when Fairfield's beaches were the playground for the vacationing wealthy from Connecticut and New York. The low-slung facility, which had airy, glassed-in sides, housed ballrooms that could be rented for private or civic functions, bathroom facilities for beachgoers, and a concession stand and open deck that overlooked the beach and Long Island Sound. It had suffered some damage during Irene but was now functional again. As it was a fairly pleasant day, many beachgoers, primarily children with their mothers, were still frolicking on the sand or eating an early dinner on the deck.

"If they only knew," said T.J., his sunglasses hiding the concern in his eyes as he worked on his Italian sub.

"Yeah," said Bortnicker, in between bites of his chicken chipotle sandwich. "What do you think these fine citizens would say if we told them a witch was on the loose a quarter-mile from here?"

"That we were all nuts," answered LouAnne, nibbling on a barbecued potato chip.

"I called my dad and told him we'd be staying down here," said T.J. "He said to phone him when we need a pickup. We can throw the bikes in the back of the SUV."

"I need dessert," declared Bortnicker. "We could bike over to Tasteefreez and eat for free, but we'd better keep our distance for a while longer."

"They've got ice cream bars here," suggested T.J. "Of course, Bortnicker, there aren't any custom flavors, just vanilla and chocolate."

The team's culinary expert gave a theatrical frown. "It'll just have to do," he said sadly. "Anybody else want one?"

"No thanks," the cousins said.

"Your loss."

As he got up, T.J. asked, "Is it okay if the two of us take a walk?"

"How romantic," said Bortnicker sarcastically. "I'll be waiting for you back here, eating my Klondike Bar and pondering the meaning of life."

The cousins strolled along the water's edge, sidestepping little kids constructing sand castles, hiking boots slung over their shoulders and pant legs rolled up. Seagulls glided overhead, scanning the water and sand for food. "It's starting to cloud over," observed T.J. "They predicted thunderstorms later. Hope it holds off until we're done tonight."

"Don't take this the wrong way, Cuz," LouAnne countered, "but could we just get away from talking about tonight's investigation for a few minutes? We really haven't had a break all day."

"You're right, sorry," he said, taking her hand as they continued on.

"Can you believe it was just a year ago that we were walking on the beach in Bermuda?" she mused.

"Seems like longer," he admitted. "So much stuff has happened since then."

"Yeah," she said. "Let's see…you lived through a hurricane, the first TV special came out, I got jumped by that guy at school during the winter, we did the investigation in Cooperstown, you made the news down in Florida, the second TV show came out, we trashed the Tasteefreez and went to Fenway—"

"And maybe tonight we'll meet up with a witch from the 1600s."

She stopped walking and looked into his eyes. "It's been quite a ride," she said quietly.

"I know."

She drew him close and put her head on his shoulder. "I'm worried about you, T.J. Lots of people are pulling at you, and I know you're not thrilled with the whole celebrity thing—"

"It's okay, LouAnne, really," he said, inhaling the fresh scent of her herbal shampoo. "It's, like, I've been given this ability, and when people ask me for help, I can't say no."

"I get that," she said, "but I've got a bad feeling on this one, like maybe we're in over our heads. I'm scared."

"Me too," he admitted. "But, see, all these people here enjoying themselves on the beach, having a great time—they could all be affected by how we handle this case. I mean, if there is some kind of curse involved, who's to say it won't mess up the whole town?"

She pulled back and regarded him at arm's length. "And you really think the three of us can save them?"

"We'd have to try, at least. But no matter what powers you think I have, I can't do this alone."

"Don't worry," she assured him, her eyes brimming, "you know Bortnicker will never let you down, and if some witch comes after you, I'm seriously kicking her butt."

They kissed, the waves gently lapping at their feet, until a kid voice behind them screeched, "Ewww! No smooching in public!" Their spell broken, the couple turned and walked back toward the pavilion.

Chapter Eighteen

They left the idyllic seashore and rode back to the Museum in the early evening to set up the remote DVRs for later. LouAnne observed how quiet the surrounding neighborhood was and Bortnicker agreed, explaining that the large homes in the Historical District were fairly well spaced out, and that some of the owners were probably away on summer vacations, anyway. And, of course, the elementary school that bordered the Old Cemetery and marsh on the far side was empty for the summer. "So what you're saying," she surmised, "is that if something happens to us, nobody's going to come a-running."

"That's about the size of it," said T.J. "Think about it: did anyone notice the mini tornado we got hit with in the marsh on Wednesday?"

"Good point, Cuz."

Once the cameras were in place, they retreated to the command post and stretched out on the carpeted floor for a nap. Within minutes, they were sound asleep.

* * * *

At precisely 9:00 PM T.J.'s cell phone alarm sounded, and the *Junior Gonzo Ghost Chasers* groggily sat up and stretched.

"Man, that chipotle chicken sub is sitting heavy on my stomach," moaned Bortnicker.

"It might also be the five pounds of toppings you had them lay on it," cracked T.J. "I mean, *really*. Onions and jalapenos?"

"And let's not forget the ice cream bar at the beach," added LouAnne. "Or was it *bars*?"

"I only had two," he groused.

171

"Well, we're all set up," said T.J. "Who wants to take the first shift at the computer?"

"LouAnne, why don't you lead off," suggested Bortnicker. "I need to get outside and stretch my legs."

"No problem." She turned on the terminal and the 4-square screen came right up, clear as a bell.

"I think tonight we shouldn't split up," said T.J. "Cuz, Bortnicker and I are going to the graveyard first. If you see anything there or on the Village Green, get on the walkie-talkie."

"Sure thing."

The boys grabbed infrared camcorders, EVP recorders, and the headband lights. "Well, we've got the tech stuff squared away," said T.J. "Now, everybody make sure you have the stuff Deirdre gave us." He smeared a little protection oil on his forehead and his mates did the same. "Hope this doesn't attract mosquitoes," he mumbled as he re-capped the vial. "Everybody got their necklace on and the crystal in your pocket?"

"Check," said Bortnicker.

"Got it," said LouAnne, fingering the leather lanyard.

"Okay, then. Let's get together and say this prayer she gave us." They huddled, arms around each other's shoulders. T.J. read the prayer, one line at a time, and the others repeated it:

I dwell in the bright divine light
All goodness is attracted to me for my highest good
I am attuned with divine love and divine goodness
I give thanks for the divine light.

At the end he called, "One, two, three—*Gonzos Rule!*"

The air was somewhat cool outside with a rumble of thunder inland, as pop-up storms had been predicted for Fairfield County. The boys crossed the parking lot, their gazes darting, and hopped the low wall into the graveyard. No sooner had they arrived than LouAnne's voice came squawking over the walkie-talkie: "Guys, we have activity near Edwards Pond! Get over there!" Back the other way they went, scrambling over the wall and sprinting across the Museum parking lot to the Village Green, where they slowed to a cautious walk.

"I see something near the pond, under that big pine tree," whispered T.J. As they approached, the silhouette of a woman emerged. It seemed as if she was gazing out over the water. T.J. cleared his throat. "Hello?" he called. "Can we help you?"

For a few seconds the figure didn't budge. Then it wheeled, momentarily faced them, and started walking—gliding, really—across the mowed grass toward the marsh. The boys cautiously followed at a safe distance, Bortnicker filming as he moved along.

"Charity Blessing," called T.J., remembering what Deirdre had said about proper tone, "is that you? Please stop and talk to us." But the figure kept moving. Finally, it melted into the edge of the marsh reeds. "Don't," he said, grabbing Bortnicker's shirt. "She's not luring us into Wolves Swamp again. No way."

"I was hoping you'd say that," Bortnicker replied.

"We lost her," T.J. said over the walkie-talkie.

"What now, Cuz?"

"Back to the Old Cemetery, I guess."

Once again, the boys negotiated the wall. "I've got an idea," said T.J. "Come with me to Melrose's tomb." They picked their way over tree roots and fallen grave markers and stood before the marble slab. From this vantage point, they could look down into the marsh. "Film this," T.J. whispered to Bortnicker. "I've got my EVP recorder on. Ready?"

"Do it."

"Charity Blessing! Please come forward and talk to us! We will *not* come into that marsh. We're willing to wait here as long as it takes! I ask you to show yourself!"

"Big Mon," whispered Bortnicker, "look! Above the wall!"

It began as a dark shadow, then turned into a swirling, milky gray before going white. There followed a popping sound as the boys' electronic devices blew out. "Here we go! She's trying to manifest!" said Bortnicker.

Back at the Museum, half of LouAnne's computer screen went dark. "The cameras are out at the graveyard," she said to herself as she picked up her walkie-talkie. "T.J.? Bortnicker? Can you read me?" she called excitedly. Receiving no answer, she clipped on a headlight and rushed for the door. Fleet of foot as she was, the girl reached her friends just as Charity Blessing came into focus. As was their custom, the threesome took each other's hands to form a united front.

The apparition stood atop the low wall, or rather, hovered just above it. Even at 90% or so density, the teens could make out her features. The girl was striking, with flowing dark red hair and green eyes. And although her 1600s dress and cape billowed around her, they barely concealed the contours of a shapely figure.

If she went to Bridgefield High, the guys would be all over her, thought T.J.

The spectral girl regarded the trio with a mixture of curiosity and disdain. "And you are?" she asked.

"I'm T.J. Jackson," said their leader, "and these are my friends, Bortnicker and LouAnne."

The ghost cocked her head inquisitively. "T.J. *Jackson,* is it? Interesting. Allow me to introduce myself, then. My name, as you seem to have figured out, is Charity Blessing, of the town of Fairfield, in the Connecticut colony. And this," she added with a sarcastically dramatic sweep of her hand towards the marsh, "is my domain."

"Are you confined to that area?" asked LouAnne.

"This swamp, and the town square," she replied. "As you can see, I am not able to cross into the burial ground. I can thank the kind people of Fairfield for that."

"Could you tell us what happened to you?" asked T.J.

"Surely," she replied. "Ah, but where to begin?"

"Would you like me to tell you what we already know about you?"

Charity Blessing seemed amused. "Are you to say that I have been written about? Oh, that is rich. And what do the books claim, pray tell?"

"Well," he replied cautiously, "that in 1662 you were accused of witchcraft—"

"Lies!" she screamed, and the teens drew back. The girl quickly composed herself. "Pardon me, Mr. *Jackson,*" she purred. "Please continue."

"Okay," he said with trepidation, "from what we read, you were examined for what they called witch's marks, and it said they found some."

The girl shut her eyes and seemed to take a deep breath. "Proceed."

"And then," continued Bortnicker, "they had you take the water test, and—"

"I floated."

"Uh, yeah."

"But that's as much as we know," said T.J.

"Really?" she asked. "No mention of the sham of a trial I was forced to endure?"

"We haven't been able to find anything," said LouAnne.

The witch seemed pleased at this news. "Well, then allow me to enlighten you. I was hauled before our esteemed Town Council—including my sanctimonious, coldhearted stepfather—and a few exalted selectmen from Hartford, and forced to listen to the ravings of delusional hags and their cowardly husbands, whose approbation thinly veiled their wanton longing for me!" Her voice had continued to rise as she progressed, so that by the end it was shrill and piercing.

The teens, mightily trying not to betray their inner turmoil, swallowed hard, fearing another tornadal outburst raining down on them. Dreading her response, T.J. managed, "What was the verdict?"

"Guilty on all counts," she spat, "though I expected nothing less. And so, on a day much like this, they dragged me out to Gallows Hill in the middle of this godforsaken swamp and hanged me by the neck until I was stone dead. My last vision of this vale of tears was that of my poor mother, sobbing uncontrollably, as my stepfather and his cronies strung me up to the hoots and howls of our citizenry, who cheered as I twisted in the wind."

"That's horrible," gasped LouAnne.

"Indeed it was," said the girl matter-of-factly. "And then they carried me to a nearby ditch they had dug, dumped me in, and covered me up with not so much as a pine box to separate me from the elements." She turned and looked back over the marsh. "The hill, as well as the oak from which I swung, have long since disappeared...but I remained, decomposing in this wretched quagmire, until a great flood awakened me."

"Irene," said Bortnicker.

"Who is this you speak of?"

"She was—it was a hurricane," said the boy. "A terrible storm last summer. This whole area was under water."

"I see," she said with a mocking tone. "So a natural calamity

175

brought back this community's own manufactured disaster. How appropriate." Her eyes burned with hate and seemed to glow.

Clearly, they had reached an impasse. "Miss Blessing," said T.J., "what would you want us to do for you?"

"Do? For me? Are you presumptuous enough to believe you can actually help me, Mr. *Jackson*?"

"I don't know," he confessed. "But we've helped others...cross over."

"Indeed? Very well, then, Mr. *Jackson*. This is your charge, and it is simple: clear my name."

"But...how can we do that? It's 2012!" said Bortnicker.

She pointed to the boy, instantaneously causing him to crumple to the ground in pain.

"Stop it!" cried LouAnne, covering him with her own body. "He's trying to help you!"

The witch pulled back whatever she'd laid on Bortnicker, then crossed her arms over her chest and addressed T.J., who'd stood his ground. "My dear Mr. *Jackson*," she said flirtatiously, "I'm sure you'll find a way to assist this poor damsel in distress...unlike the forebears of your clan, whose bravery could be housed in a thimble." She licked her lips and looked to the heavens as if for guidance before putting him in her sights again. "I will give you three days," she warned. "Three days to reverse the injustice of three hundred fifty years."

"And what if I—if we—can't?" he asked.

She rested her hands on her hips and thrust out her chin, her mad eyes dancing with fire. "Then I shall bring down a plague on this town, the likes of which has never been seen. Do I make myself clear, Mr. *Jackson*?"

"Yes, very."

"Then I shall leave you." She vanished in a blinding flash, leaving behind only wreaths of smoke that evaporated into the gloom.

Immediately, T.J. was crouching beside his friends. "It's okay, Cuz, she's gone," he whispered in LouAnne's ear. She sat up, uncovering Bortnicker, who lay in place, his glasses askew. "You okay?" he asked his friend.

"Even my hair hurts," he replied, adjusting his glasses. "It was like she shot a lightning bolt through me—my legs just turned to jelly."

"Deirdre's stuff might have saved you from worse," T.J. said grimly. "Can you stand up?"

"Give me a minute, Big Mon."

"You got it." T.J. looked out towards the marsh. "I think I know what happened to Reverend Melrose," he reasoned. "Irene awoke Charity Blessing, and she came back looking for revenge. Who better to take it out on than the descendent of her stepfather, who she obviously hated? At his age, Melrose just couldn't survive the trauma."

"Makes sense," Bortnicker said from down below. "She wants us to clear her name, but I've got two questions: First, how do you go about clearing someone's name who's been dead three and a half centuries? And second, and I'm basing this on her little display just now, how do we know she wasn't really guilty, anyway? If she isn't a witch, I don't know who is."

"Those are great questions, man, which is why I believe stronger than ever that we *have* to search that tunnel tomorrow. I can just feel it."

"Uh-oh," said Bortnicker shakily as his comrades helped him to his feet, "we're in for it now. T.J.'s having a *feeling*."

Chapter Nineteen

The next morning T.J. and LouAnne came downstairs for their daily run to find Tom drinking a cup of coffee at the breakfast nook table. "Hold on a second, guys," he said, waving them over. "Let's talk for a few minutes."

The cousins nervously sat down and Tom closed his newspaper. "Okay," he began, "you didn't have much to say on the ride home last night, but I could tell something happened. And Bortnicker looked like he got hit by a truck. Is there anything going on that I should know about?"

"Gee, Dad," said T.J. carefully, "the investigation has been progressing pretty well—"

"Meaning what, Son? That you've found who or what you're looking for?"

"It's a 'who', Uncle Tom," confessed LouAnne. "A girl who was accused of witchcraft back in the 1600s."

"Here? In Fairfield?"

"Yeah," said T.J., "and the thing is, her stepfather was Reverend Melrose's ancestor. It's pretty complicated."

"And I take it you've spoken to her."

"We've had one real encounter so far."

"So, how close are you to some kind of resolution?"

LouAnne gave T.J. a look before answering, "I'd give it three more days, max."

"We're not investigating tonight," said T.J., "but there's a lot we have to accomplish during the day. It'll be sweet to have the night off."

"I agree. By the way, T.J., Rocco called last night. He said you and

178

Bortnicker could resume work next week, and to call him."

"Will do."

"And also, you lucked out—tonight's baseball game against Ridgefield has been canceled. Coach Pisseri texted and said Ridgefield didn't have enough players—too many kids away on vacation, I guess."

"Great. Now I don't feel bad about having to miss the game." The cousins started to get up.

"One more thing. How about a barbecue tonight? I bought some steaks and fresh picked corn."

"Sounds yummy, Uncle Tom," piped LouAnne.

"Is seven o'clock okay? I'll call Pippa and invite them over."

"You might as well," said T.J., "because you know Bortnicker's gonna want to cook. But what about his mom? She's vegan."

"I picked up a tofu burger for her," Tom said with a playful frown. "Now, I'll be working at the home office in Stamford today till about six. So we'll all meet here at seven."

* * * *

"Where to today, Cuz?" she asked as they stretched on the still-cool front lawn.

"Would you mind if we went down Pine Creek Road?"

"You mean near that golf course? The area where your family lived?"

"Uh-huh. Is it a problem?"

"Nope," she replied nonchalantly, though his request seemed somewhat curious.

They took off, as always, with an easy jog; by the time they'd crested Sasco Hill and turned down Oldfield they were practically sprinting because of the steep incline. Pine Creek Road was the first right-hand turn after they'd reached the bottom. It featured mostly large, modern houses with leafy yards; some had swimming pools out back, though the shore was only a couple blocks away. After making a left at the par-3 golf course, the teens continued parallel to the shoreline past an athletic complex that featured a baseball diamond and football field with goalposts. It was here that T.J. slowed to a walk, then stopped.

"You pull something?" asked LouAnne, hands on hips.

179

Paul Ferrante

"It was here," he said.

"What was here?"

"Jedediah Jackson's farm," he replied almost dreamily. "This used to be all meadow...and there were some cows and hogs."

"Is this another feeling, Cuz? Cuz?"

"Guess so," he said, snapping out of it.

"Well, okay then."

"But there's something else. I think Charity was here, back then."

"Well, maybe they had a daughter she was friends with, or she did sewing or laundry for them. That happened all the time in the old days."

"Yeah, maybe." He turned to his cousin. "Listen, uh, I don't know why," he said haltingly, "but a little part of me feels...sorry for her."

"Sorry?" she cried incredulously. "Are you serious? She zapped your best friend and probably had a hand in Daniel Melrose's death. Get real, Cuz!"

He started to say something, perhaps to argue, but thought better of it. "Yeah, you're probably right," he relented. "Let's get going." They resumed their run, LouAnne casting suspicious sideways glances at him the rest of the way.

* * * *

"Listen," said Bortnicker in hushed tones as he spooned cheddar-infused scrambled eggs onto his friends' plates, "I didn't say anything to my mom about last night, but I'm still a little sore. Charity got me good."

T.J. cut into a thick-cut ham steak. "Can you manage the ride down to the Historical District?"

"Yeah, Big Mon. But coming back up might be a challenge."

"Well, at least you can look forward to a steak dinner when you get here."

"I'm already on it. I stopped by your house and dropped off some homemade marinade for your dad to soak the meat in during the day." Bortnicker took a big gulp of coffee. "So, what's on tap for today?"

"We're meeting with Mr. Sherwood this morning; he left a text message last night that he'd found some 'interesting information' for us. Then we'll grab lunch and head over to the church. Reverend Stirling will be expecting us."

180

"And don't forget Mrs. Moose," added LouAnne.

* * * *

"Ah, there you are," said Sherwood eagerly. "Come in, come in." He rolled his wheelchair over to the conference table. "So, how did it go last night?" he asked. "Did our friend make an appearance?"

"She showed up, but she wasn't too friendly," said Bortnicker.

"Oh dear. What happened?"

"She's pretty upset," began T.J. "She feels she got shafted during the whole process—the witch's mark examination, the ducking test, her trial, everything. She said they hanged her on Gallows Hill in Wolves Swamp. Did there used to be a hill there, with a hanging tree?"

"Let's see." He spun from the table toward the map repository in the next room, the teens trailing behind him. "If you would be so kind as to pull the 1600s drawer, T.J.?" The boy slowly eased open the wide, deep drawer that allowed the old maps to rest unfolded between protective sheaths of vellum. "There's one that is, I believe, dated 1650," said the historian. "That should do."

"Here it is," said T.J., removing the parchment map of Fairfield carefully and laying it atop the squat metal cabinet.

"As you can see," said Sherwood, "at this time the town's environs only stretch a mile or so in every direction except east, where we have Long Island Sound. Now, T.J., find the Old Cemetery—"

"Got it," he said, tracing his finger lightly over the paper.

"Is Wolves Swamp labeled?"

"Yes. And here's the hill, about fifty yards in; it looks like a little knoll, really—probably wasn't much higher than its surroundings. But there's the notation 'Gallows Hill'. There must've been a tree of some size on it. Probably died and fell over long ago."

"That would be my guess."

"Charity told us they dumped her in a hole not far away from the tree, without even a crude coffin," said Bortnicker. "What a way to go."

"So, we've determined there was a hanging site in the marsh," said LouAnne as T.J. gently replaced the map. "But wasn't there something else you wanted to see us about, Mr. Sherwood?"

"Yes, my dear. Let's go back inside the research library." Once there, Sherwood produced a ledger that was close to disintegrating. "What we have here is the town register from January of 1662. You will notice that Charity Blessing is listed as the stepdaughter of Reverend Jonathan Melrose, and that there are no other siblings or step-siblings in that household.

"But what made me search out his book, T.J., was my curiosity about the listing for your family. As you know, Jedediah Jackson farmed down on what's now Pine Creek Road."

"Near the athletic complex?" asked LouAnne, an eyebrow raised.

"Why, yes," said Sherwood warily. "How could you possibly know that?"

"Lucky guess," she replied, shooting her cousin a look.

"Well, the focus of my research here is that although Jedediah had a fairly large family—not including children who had died at birth or infancy, from diseases and such—he ended up with four daughters and only one son, who's listed as Trevor. Ever hear of him?"

"No, sir," said T.J. uncomfortably. "Uh, how old would this Trevor have been in 1662?"

"It says here he was aged 18. That's not far off from you, is it?"

"Couple years," T.J. murmured.

"What I'm getting at is that according to this census, there was an oddly small number of Fairfield inhabitants in the sixteen to twenty age group at this time. Therefore, I would think, through social and church events and the like, Trevor Jackson would have to have been an acquaintance of Charity Blessing, who is of the same age group. Curious, eh?"

* * * *

"So this is the famous Pizza Palace," said LouAnne, genuflecting beneath its marquee in the strip mall on Black Rock Turnpike, a major thoroughfare which now divided modern Fairfield neatly in half. The teens had crossed Boston Post Road and traversed the three or so miles of the flat, winding North Benson Road, passing Fairfield University along the way, to reach their destination. Although there were more upscale Italian eateries in town, such as Quattro Pazzi, Centro's, and Tom's favorite, Avellino's, Pizza Palace remained the go-to restaurant for a pie and generous portions of pasta whenever the Jacksons and Bortnicker wanted to dine simply and heartily. It had also become the boys' pre-investigation good luck dinner site. The way things were going, figured T.J., they could use a little luck for what lay ahead. Even Bortnicker, who would normally be grumbling over the physical exertion expended in the lengthy ride, was uplifted by the vapors that emanated from inside as he helped open the door for his female friend.

The trio slid into a leatherette booth and ordered a large Seafood Supreme pizza with red sauce—well done—and a pitcher of Coke. "So this is where you guys come before every case, huh?" asked LouAnne, scanning the decor. "Not bad. And the food must be first rate since you keep coming back."

After what seemed like an eternity, the waiter arrived with their bubbling pie on a pedestaled chrome platter, along with plates, forks, and a stack of napkins. T.J. poured each of them out a glass of frosty soda. "Careful," warned Bortnicker, "the pie looks super hot."

"Omigod this is great," said LouAnne, carefully chewing her first bite. "They don't make pizza like this in Gettysburg."

"Speaking of food, I guess Rocco's missing us, Bortnicker," T.J. said to his friend, who was already removing his second slice from the pie. "He left a message that we can come back next week."

"Good. I'm down to, like, zero dinero," he replied. "Could you pass the garlic powder, please?"

"Easy on that," joked LouAnne as the boy vigorously shook a coat of powder over his slice, "we're going to be cooped up in a tunnel together in a little while." She turned to T.J. "So, Cuz," she said, dabbing her lips with a napkin, "you think Charity and Trevor knew each other?"

"Seems a good bet," he replied. "What with them being around the same age and all."

"Not to mention that he'd have to have noticed her," observed Bortnicker. "I mean, even for a nasty 1600s ghost, you've gotta admit she's pretty hot."

LouAnne administered a swift kick to his shin under the table.

"Oww! C'mon, I'm still sore, LouAnne!"

"Oops. Sorry," she said with a playful pout. But then, she met his eyes and gave a quick nod toward her cousin, who seemed to be drifting off in thought.

"Yo, earth to T.J.," said Bortnicker. "Whatcha thinking about, my brother?"

"What? Oh, nothing," he replied. "Who's gonna eat this last slice of pizza?"

"Well," answered Bortnicker, "we wouldn't want good food to go to waste," and he lifted the piece from the platter, all the time eyeing his best friend.

* * * *

After stopping by the Museum to gather their portable devices, the Junior Gonzos walked over to First Community and presented themselves to Mrs. Moose. "I'll buzz Reverend Stirling. And don't you all look so spiffy today!" she trilled.

"So good to see you again, T.J.," said Stirling, shaking his hand warmly. "And these must be Bortnicker and LouAnne. Welcome to First Community Church. Let's go talk in the sanctuary." They sat in the pews and the kids laid out their camcorders and EVP hand-helds. "My, that's quite an assortment of gadgetry," he remarked. He pointed to one of the EVP recorders. "What exactly does that do?"

"It can pick out sounds—maybe voices—that are at too high a frequency for the human ear," explained Bortnicker. "We've gotten feedback from different spirits on them during our investigations."

"Including this one?" asked the clergyman with a raised eyebrow.

"Well," said T.J., "we've gotten some interesting audio so far. But we also took some neat video on the Village Green with our infrared camcorder."

"What have you found so far?"

"Between working with Mr. Sherwood, who's been a great help, and our investigations, we're pretty sure we're on to something."

LouAnne broke in. "May I film our conversation for the TV show, Reverend?" she asked politely. "We'll edit it later on, of course."

Stirling paused for a second, then nodded. "Surely. I do appreciate everything you're doing for myself and First Community."

"As I was saying," continued T.J. in a narrative tone, "from the assistance of Robert Sherwood, chief historian at the Fairfield Museum and History Center, we've determined that the ghost of Charity Blessing, a teenaged girl who was accused of—and then hanged—for witchcraft in 1662, is haunting the section of the town's Historical District, including the Old Cemetery, the Village Green, and the nearby marsh, where she was executed and then buried."

As Stirling listened, his eyes widened. Then he remembered he was on camera and displayed a more composed façade. "What a tragedy," he remarked.

"Reverend, you're a clergyman," stated Bortnicker. "How did people—and the church—back then allow this kind of stuff to happen?"

Put on the spot, Stirling spoke carefully and thoughtfully. "Bortnicker, the religion practiced back in Puritan times was, frankly, harsh and rigid. This came about because of the threats the settlers perceived were all around them: Indian attack, disease, natural disasters. If things went wrong, there was the general feeling that God was displeased and that they were being punished for their sins—which simply elevated the paranoia, leading ultimately to the witch hysteria that overran the colonies in the second half of the seventeenth century, and culminating in the now-infamous Salem trials. It is not an era that I, as a man of God, am proud of. And I know that even our town, and First Community Church, played a role in this story. What I hope this all has taught us is that ours is a loving God, and that we, too, should never shun those around us, and try to be accepting of those whom we perceive as different." His sermon ended, Stirling motioned to LouAnne to turn off the camcorder. Then he asked T.J. if there was any relation here to what had happened to Daniel Melrose.

"We think so, Reverend. As it turns out, one of the chief players in the Blessing trial was Jonathan Melrose, the pastor of First Community. The thing is, he was also her stepfather."

"Good God. And he allowed her to go to the gallows?"

"It seems like it."

"And are you suggesting that she exacted revenge on Daniel?"

"Take it from me, Reverend," said Bortnicker, "she has the juice."

"But why now?"

"It looks like she was awakened when Hurricane Irene flooded her burial pit," explained T.J., "but there's more. This summer marks the three hundred fiftieth anniversary of her trial and execution almost to the day."

"And what do you make of the word 'curse' that she spoke to Daniel?"

T.J. grimaced. "Reverend, it's like this: she gave us a mission to clear her name, and we've got three days to do it, or else."

Stirling seemed alarmed. "Or else what?"

"Or else she's gonna lay something on this town the likes of which it's never seen," said Bortnicker. "Or so she claims."

"Do you think she has the power? What I'm getting at, I suppose, is whether she was, indeed, unjustly accused of witchcraft, as she claims. She seems pretty capable in that area, from what I've heard."

"That's why we have to go down in the tunnel today, Reverend," said T.J. "According to a town history written by Mr. Sherwood's ancestor, there might be records hidden away somewhere in that tunnel from the time of the British invasion."

"And we don't mean the Beatles," said Bortnicker/Lennon, prompting an eye roll from his teammates. Luckily, it also broke the tension in the room, and Stirling managed a tight smile.

"All right, kids," he relented. "I'll take you down there. But I should mention that there was, I believe, an incident a while back—"

"Mrs. Moose told us," said LouAnne, immediately covering her mouth at the gaffe.

Stirling waved her off. "No worries, LouAnne. Our Mrs. Moose knows all and says much. But that's why we love her. What I was getting to is that if I'm to allow you in there, we must take proper precautions."

"How about this," said T.J. "We'll stay in contact with you the whole time by walkie-talkie. If we see, hear, or feel anything that's not right, we'll end it there and come back."

"All right," said the clergyman. "The workers who did the last inspection—the ones who ended up running away—did declare the structure sound. So, the only thing that might be a problem for you is—"

"Charity Blessing," answered LouAnne.

"We'll deal with her," assured Bortnicker confidently. "It'll be like a Navy SEAL operation: in and out."

"Right. Follow me, then." He led them through a side door and downstairs to the cool basement, pointing out to them—as Daniel Melrose had to Paul Jarboe and Ken Trishitta months earlier—the charred ceiling beam that remained from the Revolutionary Era burning.

"Look at it this way," said Bortnicker. "Outside it's around ninety degrees with like one hundred percent humidity. We'll be cool and dry underground."

"How comforting," said LouAnne as Stirling removed the covering from the tunnel entrance. She got on tiptoe and peered into the hole. "We should just fit, if we crouch a little."

"Yes," said Stirling. "I'm around six-two, and I'm afraid that I wouldn't be much of an assistance all doubled over. I'll remain here on the walkie-talkie."

"Okay," said Bortnicker, "headlamps on." The teens attached their headlights and flipped them on. "I'll man the EVP recorder. LouAnne, can you handle the camcorder? T.J. will carry the walkie-talkie."

"No problem," she said.

Then, T.J. turned to Stirling. "Uh, Reverend, could you give us a minute alone?"

"Surely," he said, backing away and turning around.

The threesome huddled, arms draped over each other's shoulders. "Everyone got their witchy stuff on them?" Bortnicker and LouAnne nodded. "Okay, let's do the prayer." He murmured the lines and they repeated them earnestly, eyes closed, drawing strength from their shared touch. They finished and opened their eyes. "One, two, three—"

Gonzos Rule!

At this, Stirling gave a start. "Sorry, Reverend, it's kinda our thing," apologized Bortnicker.

"No need to explain," said the clergyman. "I admire your sense of teamwork and commitment to each other. Good luck."

"I'll go first," said T.J. "Give me a boost." In a flash, he was up and into the hole, dropping down on the other side and wiping off his jeans.

"What's it like in there, Big Mon?" called Bortnicker.

"Dark. Who's next?"

"I am." LouAnne took her boost from Bortnicker and nimbly maneuvered through the opening, T.J. easing her down on the other side.

"Here I come!" said Bortnicker and, with the aid of Stirling, he flopped through the hole and onto the dirt floor inside. "Thanks for catching me," he said sarcastically, dusting himself off.

Their devices switched on, the trio began their trek slowly, becoming acclimated to the small arc of light their headlights provided. The walls, comprised of packed, claylike earth, were a reddish-brown and studded with rocks. Every few feet crude wooden beams appeared overhead, some thicker than others. Thankfully, there was no water on the tunnel floor.

"And where does this tunnel go?" asked Bortnicker, narrowly avoiding whacking his head on the wooden beams.

"Supposedly all the way to the graveyard," said T.J. over his shoulder as he crept along.

"Listen!" said LouAnne a minute later. "I can hear something vibrating!"

T.J. looked up. "I bet we're right under Old Post Road," he said.

"Man, I hope these beams are legit," said Bortnicker. Indeed, wisps of dirt dropped down here and there between the planking, probably when larger vehicles were rolling above. Eventually the tremors stopped and they kept moving forward.

"We must be under Town Hall now," said T.J. "Jeez Louise, all I see ahead of us is dirt walls. Doesn't seem to be any place they could hide stuff."

"I think we're wasting our time, Big Mon," said Bortnicker disgustedly. "Old Cyrus Sherwood must've got it wrong."

"You guys can turn back if you want," said T.J. doggedly, "but I'm going as far as this tunnel takes me."

"Cuz, keep on going," said LouAnne. "We're right behind you." She gave the hesitant Bortnicker a little shove.

"I think we're getting near the other end," said T.J. "Notice how the floor is starting to slope upwards?"

"Yeah," said the reluctant Bortnicker, "but one thing—is it just me, or is it getting colder in here by the second?"

They had made it another twenty yards when T.J., fighting off a shiver, spied a different color ahead. Upon closer examination, an anomaly in the wall structure emerged. "Hey, check this out, guys," he said, waving them forward. "Something's built into the wall here!"

Indeed, an alcove about two feet deep that reached nearly to the tunnel ceiling had been dug out on one side and lined with rocks, fitted snugly together without the use of mortar. And right in the center was an aperture about two feet square. "It's a shelf, I think," he said.

"Let me see," said Bortnicker, nudging him aside. "LouAnne, give me a little light over my shoulder." He peered into the opening. "Pretty dark," he said. "Guess I'll just feel around."

Bortnicker was just beginning to extend his hand into the hollow when T.J. stopped him. "You hear that?" he said, squinting his eyes with the effort.

"Hear what, Cuz?" asked LouAnne, shining her light over Bortnicker's shoulder into the gloomy void.

"I thought I heard laughter from up ahead," he said.

"Well, go check it out, Big Mon, I'm trying to reach into this hole here."

T.J., turning away from his friends, took a step forward, then another. His breath was now a frosty vapor. The laughter, a low, menacing sound, became louder. He wondered if Bortnicker's EVP recorder was getting it. "Hey, I feel something!" cried Bortnicker behind him. "It's like a box! I can just touch it!"

Then everything happened very quickly. Something yanked T.J. forward so forcefully that he toppled headlong to the floor; the ceiling timbers behind him simultaneously gave way with a creak and a deafening crash, leaving a wall of dirt and rock between him and his friends. "Bortnicker! LouAnne!" he yelled, clawing at the formidable barrier. "Are you okay?" With his headlamp smashed and emitting only a trace of light, T.J. felt around on the ground for his walkie-talkie, located it, then realized Reverend Stirling had the only other one. The laughter he'd heard became louder, bouncing off the walls of the tunnel so intensely that he sank to his knees and covered his ears. Finally, he had the presence of mind to try to raise Stirling on the walkie-talkie. "Reverend, can you hear me!" he yelled.

"Hello, T.J.?" came a static-filled, barely discernible response.

"There's been a cave-in! I think they're buried!"

"What?"

"Bortnicker! LouAnne! Cave-in!"

"What? Say again?"

"Call 911!"

"What?"

Feeling the seconds tick away, T.J. Jackson rose to his feet, Charity Blessing's mocking laughter surrounding him like a fog. He broke into a crawling, scrabbling run, reciting, "they're not dead they're not dead they're not dead" like a mantra. The bottom continued to slope upward for another twenty yards until he smashed into a barrier, knocking him back on his butt. Laughter pealed around him. He shook out the cobwebs and refocused.

It was a thick door. Or rather, it had been. The planking was worn and in some places rotted. However, there was no handle or any other device that would suggest a way to get it open. T.J.'s shoulders sagged and he cried out in frustration. And then he heard it again—the voice from Florida, cutting through the maddening laughter to tell him, *You can do it.*

T.J. straightened himself up as much as possible and sized up his opponent. "I'm gonna pretend that door is a catcher blocking the plate," he said out loud. "He's waiting there with the ball in his hand, but I'm scoring!" With that, he backed up a couple steps, then lowered his shoulder and charged, crashing into the center of the door. The resulting crunch could have been the wood, or his shoulder, or both, but T.J. was undeterred. He backed up and charged again. And again. "I'm scoring!" he cried, on the edge of hysteria. "You're not stopping me!" Finally, on the fourth try, he crashed through the rotted planking to find himself at the bottom of a series of rough-hewn stone steps. Wiping the splinters from his face and hair, he crawled hand over foot to encounter what appeared to be a heavy stone slab. "Great," he muttered in exasperation. But this was quickly shaken off, and bracing himself on a step, he positioned his aching shoulder under the slab and lifted, his back and leg muscles straining with the effort. To his surprise, the impediment started to budge. He kept pushing, trying to slide the slab upwards and sideways at the same time. Then, finally, he saw it—a blessed sliver of sunlight. At this, he doubled his efforts, cursing every wasted moment.

Chapter Twenty

One thing about the Old Cemetery, thought Gertie Bartholomew, *it sure is restful.* Yes, Fairfield had its beaches and parks; but even the Village Green was too noisy for her. She didn't appreciate the judgmental looks and snidely whispered comments of its patrons, either. That's why she took her daily afternoon respite in the graveyard. It was peaceful and serene, with only the birds in the trees as her co-inhabitants.

Gertie's favorite spot was near the wall closest to the Museum parking lot's entrance. There were a few old crypt-like tombs under a shady maple that provided the perfect venue for her to spread out a modest snack of tinned sardines and crackers, or maybe Vienna sausages, along with one of those tasty Capri Sun drinks, and enjoy the solitude.

So when one of the weather beaten gray slabs across from Gertie began to slightly rise and then slide, it got her attention in a hurry, and she dropped her sardine and saltine sandwich in the dirt. But what tore it was the frenzied grunting that came from underneath, sounding like some demon was trying to free itself from the depths of the ancient tomb. When a dirty, bloodied hand reached out from under the slab, she lost it. "Jumping Jehosaphat!" she screamed, grabbing her cart and dashing for the gate. "Run for your lives! It's a zombie attack!"

* * * *

Once the slab had been moved sufficiently for him to squeeze through, T.J. climbed over and out of the empty crypt and lay on the ground, gasping for breath. In the distance, he heard the blare of oncoming fire trucks—and maybe an ambulance. As the figure of Reverend Stirling came sprinting up Beach Road toward the Old Cemetery, blowing by a screaming old woman with a handcart who was running the other way, T.J. remembered the cell phone in his back pocket and speed dialed Susan Morosko's number.

* * * *

"Okay, you're sure on this?" asked the fire lieutenant, whose name tag read Halloran.

"Yes!" said T.J. feverishly, the clergyman's calming hand on his shoulder. "They're buried in an alcove in the tunnel wall, but they're not dead!"

Lieut. Halloran, a stocky, mustachioed veteran firefighter in full gear, looked over his shoulder at his men, who awaited orders as they geared up. "How do you know they're alive?"

"I just know!" the boy cried.

"Okay kid, okay," he said. "How far back was the cave-in?"

T.J. did some quick mental calculating. "About twenty yards—not far from that wall, on a line with First Community."

A firefighter hopped the wall and started looking for any telltale indentation in the ground. "Can't see any dips here, Loot!" he called.

"Right," said Halloran. "Hassey, Zadravec, get this slab offa here!"

Within seconds the two burly firefighters had removed the top of the entrance crypt completely. "Grab a pickaxe and some shovels and follow me!" He made his way down the worn stone steps to the remnants of the door. "Hassey, hand me that pickaxe." With a few violent chops, the lieutenant made short work of the planking. Then he turned to his men. "Even if those kids found refuge in that alcove, they've got ten minutes of air, max. I don't know how much dirt came down around them, but we don't have time to go all the way to First Community and take the long way. What we need to do is shore up the area next to the cave-in on this side and go in aggressively. You guys remember your Confined Space Entry training?"

"Yessir!" they barked in unison.

"I need two-by-fours, pronto!" Halloran said into his shoulder radio. Then he pushed on toward the cave-in, his men right behind.

* * * *

Topside, T.J. waited with Stirling and Detective Morosko, who had come roaring up in an unmarked cruiser with a black-and-white right behind her.

"Don't worry, T.J.," she said, gripping his arm. "These guys are the best at what they do. But how do you know they're still alive?"

Because the voice told me. "I just do," he said miserably. "This is all my fault. They wanted to turn back, but I had to keep going." Distraught, he buried his head in Morosko's shoulder.

* * * *

"See anything, Loot?" said Zadravec as he shined a flashlight over Halloran's shoulder. They had reached the wall of crumbled dirt and rocks; behind them, Hassey was pounding the two-by-fours into the ceiling as fast as he could.

At first, it seemed to Halloran that the fallen dirt and rock barrier reached solidly to the tunnel ceiling. But as he pried the top layer away, a small space appeared. "Zadravec, from the top, start shoveling this out with me!" They began scooping the earth, furiously throwing it back and pelting Hassey, who hardly noticed. And then, Halloran put his gloved hand on Zadravec's chest to stop him. "Listen!" he whispered. What they heard made their jaws drop.

* * * *

"Anything?" asked T.J. of a young firefighter who stood nearby, listening to his shoulder radio for instructions from his superior.

"Not yet—wait!" he said. "Lieutenant, come again?"

The radio crackled loud enough for T.J., Morosko and Stirling to hear. Halloran, between grunts of exertion and the crunching of shovel thrusts, said, "I hear singing!"

"Singing, sir?"

"Yes, singing!"

"Singing *what*?"

"This might be before your time, son, but there's this song called 'Fixing a Hole' on the Beatles' *Sgt. Pepper* album—"

T.J. fell to his knees in delirious relief.

* * * *

Underground, Halloran and Zadravec picked up the pace, removing dirt as quickly and efficiently as they could in their restrictive surroundings. Finally, a huge drift of sediment fell away to reveal a bedraggled teenaged boy and attractive blonde girl hugging each other tightly, buried to their waists in a stone-lined alcove. They were dirty and haggard looking, but alive. "What kept you?" said the boy in a strange British accent.

* * * *

After sharing a long, emotional group hug, the trio sat together with Stirling, Morosko and Sherwood, who had wheeled himself from the Museum at the sound of the sirens, and tried to make some sense of it all. The firefighters, after receiving heartfelt thanks from the teens, had replaced the tunnel entrance slab and departed, as had the EMS team, who found Bortnicker and LouAnne incredibly filthy, but in perfect health.

"You kids are so lucky," said the detective admonishingly. "Personally, I think you were out of your minds to go down there."

"It would seem to have been an ill-advised move," agreed Sherwood.

"Then please blame me," said Stirling, "not the kids. I gave them the authorization, and accept full responsibility."

"Listen," said T.J., "what happened, happened. But now it's over, and nobody got hurt—"

"Just dirty," said Bortnicker, smiling crookedly and shaking soil out of his scraggly mop.

"Well," said Morosko, "it's been quite a day. I'll have a police van take your bikes home for you, and a cruiser will drop you off there."

"Thanks, Detective," said LouAnne. "Now, all I want is a shower." Morosko shook hands with all of them, giving orders to a patrolman on her way out of the Old Cemetery.

Stirling looked around, his eyes finally resting on the tomb of Jonathan Melrose. "I would love for you young people to tell me this is over," he said, "but that would be wishful thinking, I suppose."

"Oh, I don't know," said Bortnicker cryptically, "we might be closer than you think."

"Very well, then," said Sherwood. "I'll be here at the Museum tomorrow if you need me."

The *Junior Gonzo Ghost Chasers* climbed into the police cruiser, basking in the air conditioning on this oppressively hot day, and enjoyed the short ride home from the graveyard in silence. Once the police car dropped them off, T.J. asked Bortnicker, "Okay, so what makes you think this is almost over?"

Bortnicker turned to LouAnne and gave her a wink. "Because, Big Mon," he said, "just before we got buried back there I felt the edge of a box. I had to go in up to my shoulder to get a grip on it; I was pulling it out when the ceiling collapsed. It was heavy, made of lead, probably, but there was something inside."

"What?"

Bortnicker reached under his shirt into the front waistband of his jeans and pulled out a weathered, leather-covered folio. "This." He handed it to T.J.

"You think this is it? The trial document?" asked the amazed boy as he fingered the cracked leather of its sheathing.

"It has to be," reasoned LouAnne. "Charity Blessing didn't want us to get at it, so she buried us—almost." She gave a look of steely defiance that T.J. had seen when she ran competitively.

"I'd say we have a little reading to do after dinner tonight," remarked Bortnicker.

"But first, can I *please* take a shower?" begged LouAnne. "And Bortnicker, hit the mouthwash, okay? Being smooshed up against you in that tunnel wasn't pleasant. I *knew* that garlic powder was gonna come back to haunt us!"

* * * *

"I feel guilty being so far away while this was all happening," said Tom as he nursed a beer on the Jacksons' patio. It was still hot in the early evening, but a cold front was supposed to pass through within the next few days to alleviate this stretch of sweltering weather.

"No big deal, Dad," said T.J., sipping his iced tea as Bortnicker grilled away in the background, whistling a Beatles tune. "All things considered, it was over pretty quickly, thanks to the fire department."

"What also helped," said Bortnicker, "was that because the area is so quiet, the news people never found out about it. Then it would have been a real circus."

At that moment LouAnne, radiant in a pink sundress, made her entrance. It was the most dressed up that she'd been the whole week, and as always, her beauty made T.J. pause in awe. "I couldn't believe how much dirt came off me in that shower," she announced. "I've never been so happy to get clean."

"I'd say you did a commendable job, my dear," remarked Bortnicker through the grill smoke.

"Me, too," agreed Tom, who couldn't help but notice his son's mesmerized stare. "You look great, kiddo."

"Thanks, Uncle Tom," she chirped, giving him a peck on the cheek. "How are those steaks coming, Bortnicker?"

"Patience, fair maiden," he cautioned, "you can't rush perfection."

LouAnne looked around. "Hey, where's your mom?" she asked the cook.

"Believe it or not, she has a date tonight. She's meeting some guy for dinner down in Greenwich at this swanky vegan restaurant. I think they met during a Feng Shui consultation or something. But that's okay; she doesn't appreciate an exquisitely grilled T-bone anyway."

"Well, I think it's good your mom is getting out and dating," said Tom as he applied sour cream to his baked potato. "She's a nice lady and should be able to have some fun."

"Yeah," said Bortnicker, "I guess so."

"How's it going with you and that sweet Ms. Cosgrove from Bermuda, Uncle Tom?" asked LouAnne.

"It's going. I'm glad I was able to get over there on Memorial Day weekend."

"Speaking of Bermuda, Bortnicker," teased LouAnne, "we haven't heard from Ronnie while I've been here. Why don't we Skype her tomorrow?"

"A capital idea!" he said, buttering an ear of corn.

As the famished foursome attacked their steaks, Tom again expressed his concern over the current investigation. "This undertaking of yours has gone a whole lot further than I expected it would," he said. "Are you *sure* you've got it under control?"

"No question, Dad," said T.J. confidently. "That cave-in today was just an accident. Could've happened at any time." The teens, as usual, had decided among themselves to withhold certain information so as not to panic their elders.

"Okay, you know I trust you guys to do the smart thing, but that doesn't stop me from worrying. Great steak, Bortnicker."

"Did you expect anything less, Mr. J.?"

* * * *

After the table had been cleared, the *Junior Gonzos* anxiously retired to the rec room to go through the folio. They had just settled onto the couch when T.J.'s cell phone buzzed. "It's Mike Weinstein," he said with a smile, "calling to check up on us."

"Dudes!" boomed the celebrity ghost hunter. "What's the matter, you too big to talk to me anymore? I have to call you?"

"Sorry, Mike," said T.J. sheepishly, as he put them on speakerphone. "Where are you, anyway?"

"You're not gonna believe this. We're in Boston, where we just finished an investigation of the Old North Church—you know, Paul Revere and all that—and we're flying to Romania to check out this castle they say belonged to Dracula!"

"Cool," said T.J., shaking his head. Same old Mike. "Well, things have been kinda hectic around here—"

"To say the least," broke in Bortnicker.

"I'm listening."

Taking turns, they related the details of their adventures to date, leaving out nothing. When they were done, Weinstein let out a low whistle. "Dudes, this is some serious stuff. And you say you've got footage?"

"Mike," replied Bortnicker, "between the EVPs, video, and interviews with a bunch of people—and wait till you see Deirdre the witch, she's a show all by herself—we'll have more than enough."

"You even got stuff in that tunnel?"

"Yeah, before the cave-in. Haven't seen it yet, though, but it should be mucho creepy."

"Fantastic. Another hit special. No wonder the suits at The Adventure Channel can't get enough of you. So, do you anticipate a bang-up ending?"

"Mike," said T.J., "of course we want an exciting ending, but remember, we've got a responsibility to my town to think about. In fact, if *nothing* happened from here on, you'd still have a cool show."

"Solid, T.J. Well, take care and be safe. I don't have to tell you how jealous of you guys I am; your success rate on seeing ghosts is off the chain." He paused. "And by the way, my man, did your little sit-down with my friend Jill prove me right?"

T.J., coloring in front of his friends, replied, "Ah, that would be a 'yes', Mike."

"Weinstein does it again!" he crowed. "Well, gotta go. They're boarding our flight."

"Say hi to Dracula for us," said LouAnne.

"Yeah, don't get bit," added Bortnicker.

"Will do. Adios, dudes!"

"All right," said T.J., who was always exhausted after talking to his ghost hunting mentor, "are we finally ready to check out this stuff?"

"Read away, Big Mon."

Chapter Twenty-One

August, 1662

The meeting house in Fairfield was square, unadorned and functional. A raised platform for the judging panel had been constructed for the trial, and extra seats were added behind the pews, for the sensational nature of the event would surely attract both the concerned and the curious.

Charity Blessing, attired in plain, somber clothes, sat stone-faced beside her mother in the front pew. Her stepfather was seated with the Fairfield councilmen to one side of the room. Jurymen chosen from the immediate area had their own section on the other side. By the time the court was called to order, the meeting house was packed and stifling.

The magistrates began by administering the oath of office to the Crown's prosecutor, James Hill, who had come from Hartford. Then, the jurors were sworn in as well.

Hill, a powerfully built man with thick brown hair and a broad nose, began his monologue in a rich baritone that reverberated in the meeting house. "We are here today before God to determine the innocence or guilt of Charity Blessing, who is accused of practicing witchcraft in this community.

"The accused has met numerous criteria for the convening of this court. They are as follows: notorious defamation by the common report of the people, the cursing of another person that led to death, the practicing or implementation of spells or potions, the presence of a Devil's mark upon her body, and the failing of a trial by water. If it is proven here that the accused, Charity Blessing, is guilty of these numerous charges, it will be the duty of our jurymen and judges to

199

bestow upon her a fitting punishment."

The entire time Hill was speaking, Mary Blessing wept quietly, knowing full well that any emotional outburst on her part would prompt a removal from the room. Her accused daughter, however, remained stoic as the charges rained down on her. One by one, Hill then brought forward witnesses to attest to Charity's guilt, which they claimed stemmed from her tutelage in the satanic arts by the slave woman named Clarisse, who had lived in town for over a year until her unexplained disappearance.

Abigail Osborn testified that Charity was contrary and argumentative, especially in her criticism of Abigail's household remedies, which she claimed were useless. Hannah Penfield swore that Charity had tried to put her husband under a spell with the intention of stealing him away from her. Jeremiah Perry told of Charity looking crossly at his prized ox, which fell ill and died shortly thereafter. Probably the most dramatic testimonial came from Julia Robinson, who claimed that after a falling out with Charity, her daughter began experiencing agonizing convulsions or paralyzing trances, and blamed them all on Miss Blessing's witchery. Martha Robinson had died at age 16 earlier in the summer.

Various other citizens, some of them men, said that Charity had come to them in dreams, sometimes in the form of a demon, which had resulted in the withering of their crops or the premature spoiling of their food stores. Others had seen her in the fields, picking herbs for her potions, and noted that on numerous occasions she had suggested remedies for various persons' ailments that went far beyond the knowledge of local women.

Then, Harriet Nichols and Goody Ogden, the women who had examined her for the witch's marks, recounted their damning findings of a few weeks before, and the men who had bound and thrown her into the pond came forward to recount their experience with the floating girl.

The fact that Charity Blessing had a haughty and somewhat contrary personality surely worked against her. So did the fact that her beguiling beauty was the source of much jealousy among the plain, weatherworn women of the town. Still others bore a grudge against the girl because of the transgressions of her father, a brutish, quarrelsome drunk who had managed to alienate most of the townsfolk before he was killed in a hunting accident.

After what seemed like hours of testimony, the Crown's prosecutor asked Charity if she would like the opportunity to refute any or all of the charges before her fate was handed to the jury. Despite the fact that her life hung in the balance, the girl rose, faced the courtroom, and said simply, "Since it is obvious that I have been brought here through a conspiracy of hatred and lies, the fact that I am innocent of all these charges is inconsequential. But if you are waiting for me to throw myself upon the mercy of the court, you will be disappointed. I'll not give you the satisfaction of watching me beg for my life."

This brought forth a collective gasp from the courtroom, and a wail from her mother, who fainted dead away and had to be carried from the room by Jonathan Melrose, who cast condemning glances at his stepdaughter the whole way.

When Hill asked the jurymen if they needed time to deliberate upon the evidence presented, they solemnly looked at each other, shaking their heads. Then the eldest of them, Samuel Sturges, declared that the jury had found Charity Blessing guilty on all counts. At that, Hill bowed to the judges and took his seat across the aisle from where Charity Blessing, rock solid, still stood.

John Thorpe, the presiding judge, who like Hill had been sent from Hartford to conduct the proceedings, then rose from his seat on the platform and pointed down at the girl, who faced him defiantly. "Charity Blessing, as the king's representative, I hereby decree that by the law of God and the law of the colony, thou deservest to die. Tomorrow at sunset, you will be taken to a proper venue and hanged by the neck until dead. May God have mercy on your wretched soul."

Chapter Twenty-Two

It was the same vivid dream he'd had every night since the investigation began, starting with himself and LouAnne jogging down Pine Creek Road on a pleasant summer morning. But then, as they were pounding along, their surroundings would begin to change. Gone were the upscale houses with BMWs or SUVs parked in their driveways, to be replaced by knee-high meadow, which would force them to labor in a kind of dreamy slow-motion. Then he would realize he was no longer clad in his Bridgefield High Athletics T-shirt, shorts and New Balance 1240s, but a blousy, scratchy shirt, knee breeches and high stockings with clodhopper-type shoes that shifted with each stride. He would look at LouAnne to complain, but she would race ahead, swishing through the tall grass. Gathering all his strength, he would put on a burst of speed, but then she would look back and it wasn't LouAnne anymore, it was Charity Blessing, and she was leading him toward the marsh—

T.J. sat up in bed in a cold sweat and checked his alarm clock: 6:00 AM. He sank back down, allowing his heart rate to stabilize, glad that he and LouAnne had agreed the night before to cancel this morning's run in deference to the traumatic near-burial she and Bortnicker had experienced the day before. It was just as well. The *last* thing he wanted to do this morning was go for a run.

* * * *

Bortnicker, aware that his friends would be coming by earlier for breakfast because of their canceled workout, rolled out of bed and shuffled to the bathroom, took a quick shower—he was *still* finding dirt from yesterday—dried off and shook out his curly mop, and threw on

202

some shorts, sandals, and a T-shirt. He was bounding down the stairs, planning out this morning's menu, when the smell of brewing coffee reached him. Which was strange, because Pippa disapproved of her son's affinity for the dark Colombian blend he counted on to get his morning rolling. "Hey, Mom," he said, turning the corner into his kitchen, "you didn't have

to—"

What he saw stopped him cold. A man was sitting at the kitchen table, sipping from a coffee mug. And though the glasses he wore were more of a modern style, and his hair was a little shorter and flecked with gray, the stunned boy was looking at a future incarnation of himself.

"Hello, Son," said Nathaneal Bortnicker. "What's happening?"

* * * *

LouAnne was lounging in bed, reveling in the comfort of the air-conditioning and the prospect of a day off from running, when there was a light knock at the guest bedroom door. "I'm awake," she said with a yawn.

T.J. poked his head inside. "Looks like we're on our own for breakfast, Cuz," he said. "Bortnicker just texted me that he has some stuff he has to do. He'll be over a little later."

LouAnne pouted; she looked forward to her friend's culinary delights each morning.

"Don't worry," laughed T.J., "there's bagels and stuff downstairs. We'll throw something together. Why don't you lay around for a little longer?"

"I was hoping you'd say that," she smiled.

* * * *

It wasn't until around 9 AM that Bortnicker finally showed up. T.J. and LouAnne had toasted the bagels, along with some cold cereal, to go with their tall glasses of orange juice. Tom had grabbed a bagel and filled a travel cup before taking off.

"Morning," grumbled their friend as he smeared cream cheese on his bagel.

"So, why no breakfast this morning?" chided T.J. "LouAnne's all disappointed. What's up?"

Paul Ferrante

"Oh, nothing," he replied nonchalantly, "except that my long-lost father has decided to make an appearance."

"What!" his friends cried in unison, milk and cereal dripping from their mouths.

"Yup, in the flesh. Came down to start breakfast and there he was having coffee, like it was the most natural thing in the world."

"Wow," said T.J., who'd never laid eyes on the man—Bortnicker had never even seen fit to show him a picture. "So, why, uh, what's he doing here?"

"Beats me," he replied casually. "You didn't make coffee, did you?"

LouAnne blinked, then shot her cousin a concerned look. "So," she said carefully, "then it was your dad your mom was out with last night?"

"Appears so." He crunched into his bagel.

"No, no coffee, Bortnicker, sorry," said T.J. "Do you, uh, want to talk about it?"

"Not particularly," he replied absently. "I should know better than to eat sesame bagels. The seeds always get stuck in your teeth."

"For sure," said LouAnne, trying to fill the dead air.

Taking the hint that the details of his friend's encounter with his father were off-limits, T.J. changed the subject. "I've got a call in to Mr. Sherwood for a ten o'clock meeting this morning so we can go over the trial account," he said. "I'm sure you all had the chance to think about what we read. I want to get your opinions."

"About what?" asked LouAnne.

"Well, do you think she was really guilty of those charges?"

"Of course she was," snapped Bortnicker. "If you haven't figured out the mayhem she's capable of, you haven't been paying attention."

"That still doesn't prove she was casting spells and wreaking havoc on people back then," returned T.J.

"Wait, are you *defending* her?" moaned LouAnne. "C'mon, Cuz, she was guilty as sin."

"We don't know that."

At this, the girl threw up her hands in exasperation. "Bortnicker, would you talk some sense into this hammerhead?"

The boy, who seemed to be in no mood for any type of confrontation, simply shrugged his shoulders.

204

"I guess this discussion isn't going anywhere," concluded T.J. "But there is someone I wanted to talk to before we see Sherwood. Bortnicker, you think you could dial up Ronnie Goodwin on Skype?"

For the first time all morning, his friend brightened; the image of Bortnicker's first romantic friend, a vivacious island girl from Bermuda, would improve anyone's day.

* * * *

"Well, if it isn't my esteemed ghost hunting friends," Ronnie purred in her Bermudian lilt. "I'm here at the dive shop, getting things in order for the day's first excursion. How's the weather there, mates?"

"Hot and sticky," said T.J. "Good beach weather, though. How about there?"

"A bit overcast, but passable," she replied. "Most importantly, we've been lucky so far to get through hurricane season unscathed. So, what are you guys up to?" she said with a toss of the corkscrew curls that framed her mocha skin.

"We're investigating a girl from the 1600s, Ronnie," said Bortnicker. "A real tough customer. She got hanged for witchcraft—that is, she was accused of being a witch."

"Yes," said the girl, "I remember reading about the Salem witchcraft trials in my history class over here. A nasty business. Of course, they'd had similar trials in England beforehand. People just brought their crazy ideas across the pond with them when they settled in the States."

"Ronnie," said T.J., "what happened in this case was, the girl was supposed to have learned about spells and stuff from a slave woman who had passed through the town. Now, I remember that your ancestors on your mom's side were brought over to Bermuda as slaves from Africa to work on the plantations, right?"

"Oh, yes," she said with a touch of bitterness. Indeed, their investigation in Bermuda of a famous buccaneer-turned-gentleman planter had led to the discovery that he had fathered a child with Ronnie's ancestor, a slave, which prompted an uprising by his workers, who had murdered him. It was still a sore spot with her, obviously. The teens could read it on her face.

"Listen, Ronnie, maybe we should just drop it," suggested

Bortnicker.

"No, no," she replied with a sigh and a dismissive wave. "It's all right. But what would you want to know from me?"

"Ronnie," said T.J., "did your mom ever tell you about the...customs of your ancestors? Like, did they ever practice—"

"Voodoo, T.J.? Is that what you're getting at?"

"I guess so."

"Well," she said, "like slavery itself, it's kind of complicated. Let me try to explain as simply as I can. My mother's people, including the woman named Maruba who bore Sir William Tarver's child, were from coastal West Africa, a region that today is called Senegal. What they practiced, actually, is called Vodun, pronounced vo-doo. It was their traditional religion."

"What were their basic beliefs?" asked Bortnicker.

"To begin, let's get something out of the way. Vodun, or voodoo, is *not* evil. Its literal translation is 'spirit'. Someone who is a practitioner is simply trying to communicate with spirits. It all centers around the elements of divine essence that govern the earth. There are deities that control the forces of nature and human society, as well as the spirits of bodies of water, trees, rocks, and what have you. They also believed in things like saints and angels as well, which is why voodoo, as it's come to be called, blended so nicely with Christianity, especially Catholicism."

"Sounds a little like the beliefs of a modern 'white' witch we met over here," said LouAnne. "The girl in this case was believed to have learned about potions and stuff to cast spells from a slave woman. Does that sound right?"

"Oh, yes. You see, in Vodun, all creation is considered divine and therefore contains the power of the divine. That's where medicines such as herbal remedies come in, and objects called fetishes, which can be anything from statues to dried animal parts. People who practice vodun use the medicines and fetishes for healing or spiritual rejuvenation."

"You really know your stuff," remarked T.J.

"Why, thank you. After our little investigation last summer, I decided to learn all about my ancestors—the good, the bad, and the strange. Vodun is a combination of the three."

"And you think a white girl in the 1600s could be taught by a slave to make the potions and maybe lay a curse or whatever on someone?"

"If she really bought into it, why not? You see, T.J., for my people these beliefs offered some measure of protection and peace of mind in an otherwise hostile world. The girl you speak of might have turned to these measures if she felt put upon, or ostracized."

"Bingo," muttered Bortnicker.

"The question is," said Ronnie, "were her accusers able to actually prove she did harm to others? Unless she was caught in the act, this would be a bit dicey, don't you think?"

* * * *

The trio rode down to the Historical District no more unified in their appraisal of Charity Blessing's conviction than they'd been before their talk with Ronnie. It was another scorcher, even though some thunder boomers had rumbled through in the early morning hours; but the Museum provided some respite.

"So this is the folio that Jonathan Melrose squirreled away in the tunnel wall," Sherwood marveled, leafing through its pages with gloved hands. "And no wonder; it reflects badly upon himself and his cohorts. It seems that there was no shortage of citizens to come forward and testify against Charity Blessing."

"Seriously," agreed Bortnicker. "The only thing they didn't get her for was littering."

"Then, my friends, I have to pose this question: If, as she warns, something very regrettable could befall our town due to our inaction, are we still compelled to try to clear her name?"

The teens looked to their leader for direction. "I say we do it," T.J. stated flatly. "We don't have a choice."

"That's what I figured you'd say all along," said Sherwood, "even before you found the book. So I did a little asking around. There is a way that we can give Charity Blessing what she desires."

"How?" asked T.J.

"A governmental pardon."

"You're kidding," said Bortnicker.

"Oh, quite the contrary," said Sherwood. "And, believe it or not, we wouldn't be the first. I did some research last night, and there are currently eleven individual petitions that have been filed to clear the names of accused witches executed in the state of Connecticut between 1647 and 1663. In 2008, a resolution was introduced to our state's General Assembly to acknowledge the existence of witch trials for the purpose of granting posthumous pardons. However, the state Board of Pardons and Paroles said it doesn't have the power to grant these, and the resolution died.

"Then, various descendants of these accused people, who were mostly women, began contacting their state representatives, and applying pressure via the petition route. At this particular moment, the movement has stalled somewhat. However, seeing as how the welfare of our community might be affected by the outcome of a request on our part, as opposed to simply removing a negative stigma from a family ancestor, I think we might have grounds for action; we must then hope our plea will find a sympathetic ear."

"Like whose?" asked LouAnne.

"Well, dear, here in Fairfield we have what's called a first selectman, as opposed to a mayor. He or she pretty much serves the same function. And our first selectman, Patrick Weese, by all accounts has an 'in' with our current governor, whom he campaigned heavily for, hosting a 'town meeting' event right here at the Museum a couple years back as a way for the then-candidate to meet the people. I think that if Mr. Weese contacts the governor, he won't be 'blown off' as you young people say."

"But how do we get an appointment with Mr. Weese?" asked T.J.

"We already have one. And if we don't get cracking, we're going to be late."

* * * *

Fortunately for the group, the travel distance to the office of First Selectman Weese was less than the length of a football field, as Town Hall lay just across the Village Green, where tents were being set up for an afternoon arts and crafts fair. Flanked by his friends, T.J. pushed Sherwood's wheelchair out of the paved parking lot entrance and up the sidewalk along Beach Road to the wheelchair-accessible entrance of Town Hall.

They went inside the white Colonial building past the portraits of long-dead town officials and dignitaries, to the office of the first selectman, where none other than Detective Susan Morosko and Reverend Stirling were waiting outside. "I figured I'd summon all the heavy hitters," said Sherwood. "Shall we?" Stirling opened the door and they walked past the empty secretary's desk and into the spacious office, where the first selectman awaited them.

"Well, well, Robert," boomed Patrick Weese, coming around from behind his cherry wood desk, "I didn't expect such an entourage. I don't know if I can seat you all." He shared a warm handshake with the historian.

"I thought of that, Pat, so I brought my own chair," joked Sherwood as the kids pulled up seats next to him. "Thanks for coming in on a Sunday."

"Not a problem, Robert. I was going to drop in on the arts and crafts fair, anyway."

Morosko and Stirling, who had rushed over after First Community's morning service, sat together on a side couch.

Weese, who seemed to be alternating terms with his counterpart from the opposing political party, was in his 40s and trim, though not as rangy in size as the clergyman. He had an engaging smile and an easy manner that served him well as a politician. The first selectman settled back into his padded rolling chair and said, "Now what can I do for the *Junior Gonzo Ghost Chasers?*"

"You know who we are?" asked LouAnne.

"But of course. T.J. and Bortnicker here have established themselves as local celebrities, and have been a source of pride to our community. And, T.J., what you did saving that poor woman down in Florida was simply outstanding. I think there might be an official commendation in your future."

"There's no need, Mr. Weese," said the boy with his trademark modesty. "And while we're all here together filming a show that's going to feature our town"—he paused for effect—"we really need your help. It could be a matter of life and death."

Weese leaned forward on his elbows. "Tell me about it."

"Well," said T.J., "way back in 1662..."

209

By the time he was done, with contributed bits from Bortnicker, LouAnne and Sherwood, Weese had loosened his tie and downed an entire glass of water. He looked over at Stirling. "Stephen, you think this Charity person had a hand in Reverend Melrose's death?"

"I'm keeping an open mind, Patrick," he replied.

"Detective?"

"If I didn't think there was a threat I wouldn't be here, sir," she said. "And I can vouch for the sincerity of these kids."

"As can I," added Sherwood. "They've been dogged in their search for the truth."

"And have put themselves in harm's way for it as well," said Stirling, remembering the events of the previous day.

"Wow," said Weese, drumming a pencil on his desk and thinking hard. "Let me look up something." He turned to his computer terminal and started typing, making some mistakes in his haste, until his desired site was found. "Okay, folks. According to the Connecticut Law Library's judicial website, pardons in this state can only be granted by the Board of Pardons and Paroles, who can also grant commutations from a death penalty imposed under Connecticut law. There is an attached application, also classified as a petition, that has to be filled out and submitted to the Board of Pardons and Paroles. The application form includes information on what kind of documents or character references have to be included to make your case.

"It also says here the Governor himself has no authority to grant pardons or commutations, only reprieves. And such a reprieve is only temporary, lasting until the ending of the next session of the General Assembly."

"I understand that, sir," said T.J., masking his loss of patience, "but we don't have time to go through that kind of government red tape. We've got thirty-six hours, give or take, to get this girl officially pardoned."

"But what can I do?" pleaded the distraught politician.

"You can get on the phone, Patrick, and call your good friend the governor and make him see the urgency in all this!" thundered Sherwood, whose veracity took everyone in the room aback.

"Okay, okay, folks," said Weese, who had clearly been blindsided by the magnitude of this meeting and its implications. "I'll speak to the governor today, if at all possible. It is a Sunday, you know. I'll get back to you if and when I have news. More than that I can't promise."

"Sir, your best effort is all we can ask for," said T.J., who was quite the politician himself.

"Which is what your constituents expected when they voted you in," added Bortnicker, who was not.

* * * *

Back in the Town Hall foyer, Morosko looked at her watch. "Well, I'm back to the office. Thanks for calling me, Robert. You helped spice up an otherwise ho-hum day. Kids, give me a heads-up when you know what your next move is."

"We sure will. Thanks for coming, Detective Morosko," said LouAnne, her admiration for the female law enforcement officer evident.

"And I must be getting back to the church," said Stirling, "but not before sampling some homemade treats at the fair outside."

"Thanks for helping out, Reverend," said T.J.

"No need for thanks," he replied. "It was me, after all, who got you into this mess. You know where to reach me."

"And I'm going to tidy up my research materials before spending a pleasant afternoon on my back deck with a cold drink and a good book," said Sherwood.

The remainder of the group exited onto the busy Village Green; the arts and crafts fair was now in full swing, and traffic was snarled on the Old Post and Beach roads. It certainly was a festive day in Fairfield, but Bortnicker wasn't feeling it. "I'll take Mr. Sherwood back to the Museum, and then I'm going to the command post to go through the audio and video and mark the good bits for the production people."

"Don't you want some help?" asked LouAnne.

"Nah, it's kinda dull work, and I need some alone time, anyway. Why don't you two enjoy the fair? It's after noon, and all the beaches are probably mobbed."

"Good point," said T.J. "What about dinner?"

"Think about someplace to go and then text me," he said, the implication clear that he had no plans of returning home anytime soon.

"You got it," said T.J. "Well, Cuz, it's on to the fair."

It was a large operation; the entire Village Green was occupied by a tent city that featured local artists, photographers, sculptors, and the like. LouAnne purchased a Victorian style handcrafted birdhouse for her parents back in Gettysburg; T.J. picked up some homemade kettle corn for them to munch on as they promenaded hand-in-hand. "It's kinda weird," he said, finally, licking his fingers of caramel coating. "Here we are, right near this pond where so much bad stuff happened, and people are laughing and enjoying themselves, just oblivious."

"Well, Cuz," she countered, "would you have ever known—or cared—about witches in Fairfield if we hadn't been put on this case? Can you blame people for living in the present?"

"Guess not. Because as nostalgic as people get about it, a lot of things in the past sucked."

At that moment, they were walking just past the pond when they saw a youngish man—a real one—in full Revolutionary War Colonial dress, talking to a small group of people next to a sign index of the historic buildings sprinkled here and there. "Welcome!" he said with a nod of recognition. "I'm Wally Meltzer, the head of educational programs at the Museum. We're just starting a tour of the Colonial buildings here on the Village Green. Care to join us?"

T.J. and LouAnne looked at each other. "Sure," he said. They tagged along behind the group, hand in hand. There were three structures in all, each different in its design and purpose.

"These buildings date back to the Revolutionary War era and slightly afterwards," said Wally as they approached their first stop, the Sun Tavern. "George Washington actually stopped in here once." From there it was on to the Old Town Hall and an early schoolhouse. As would be the case with all the buildings, they were mostly shells; there were few furnishings or decorations in any of them. At one point in the schoolhouse, Meltzer pulled them aside and whispered, "Mr. Sherwood speaks very highly of you guys. He says you're conducting a most interesting case."

"No doubt about it," smiled T.J.

"You must be dying in that uniform," observed LouAnne.

"You have no idea," he replied, mopping his forehead. "All in the name of history." He lowered his voice a few octaves. "Don't worry," he promised, "I won't blow your cover. It's surprising nobody's pointed you out already."

"That's the way we like it," said T.J., who hated the limelight.

They were leaving the last building, the Old Town Hall, when LouAnne asked T.J. if he'd "felt" anything in the structures. "Nope, nothing," he replied. "I guess 'cause they were all built after Charity was long dead. Edwards Pond, on the other hand…"

"Speaking of feelings, what're we going to do about Bortnicker? I've never seen him so down. What do you think happened between him and his dad this morning?"

"I have no clue. Maybe he'll loosen up over dinner; food usually puts him in a good mood. You know, the cooking thing's become a bigger hobby for him than his model trains, not that he doesn't still work on his layout, which takes up most of his basement. In fact, he's even mentioned maybe majoring in what they call 'Hospitality Industry Management' in college, or going to a culinary school."

"Wow," she said. "And what about you, my darling cousin? Any ideas about your college major?"

"Well," he said, "don't laugh, but…I'm kinda leaning towards journalism."

"Really."

"Yeah. I actually like to write, and I've become much more of a reader, probably because of all the cases we've been on."

"What kind of books are you into?"

He chuckled. "Historical fiction, actually."

She laughed and hugged him. "You're a riot, Cuz," she said.

"And what about you?"

"What do you think of me majoring in physical therapy?"

"You mean like sports medicine?"

"Yeah. I want to be able to figure out what's wrong with me every time I get hurt."

"Like in Bermuda?" he said mischievously.

"You had to bring it up," she said, punching him in the shoulder, much like Doris Barrett would slug Morty. "Dropping out of that 5K race when I was in the lead just killed me."

"Don't I know it," he smiled.

* * * *

"You must've been reading my mind, Big Mon," said Bortnicker as he slid into the booth with T.J. and LouAnne at the modern-chic Flipside restaurant on Post Road, the boys' favorite burger place. "I haven't really eaten since breakfast, so this is exactly what I need. LouAnne, this joint has any kind of burger you can imagine, in a medium or large size. And the fries are good, too."

"Wow, you aren't kidding," she agreed, pouring over the extensive menu. "I have no idea what to choose."

"I like the Alpine burger," said T.J. "That comes with Swiss cheese, caramelized onions and sautéed mushrooms."

"The Santa Fe also looks good," she said. "Jalapeno jack cheese, salsa and avocado. Yum. What about you, Bortnicker?"

"He gets the large size burger with *everything* on it," said T.J. "Every single time."

The trio placed their order. As the waitress set tall sweet teas in front of them, LouAnne got things rolling. "So, how did the editing go, Bortnicker?"

"Not bad. With the interviews, they'll have a ton of footage. The tunnel stuff was especially creepy. It gave me goose bumps just looking at it."

"Was Charity's shadow pretty clear that time we followed her from the pond?" asked T.J.

"Oh, yeah. With computer enhancement, it'll come out just fine. Proving once again that we're the best."

"Of course, we can't mention the possibility she caused the death of Reverend Melrose," offered LouAnne.

"Or the fact that she's put a curse down on Fairfield," added Bortnicker. "We wouldn't want our neighbors to get hysterical."

The burgers arrived and the teens dove in, which cut down considerably on the rate of conversation. It wasn't until they were mopping up ketchup with their few remaining fries that LouAnne could bear it no longer. Throwing down her napkin onto her plate, she looked Bortnicker in the eye and said, "So, are you gonna talk to us about your dad or what?"

"Not much to tell," he mumbled as T.J. motioned to the waitress for their check.

"Try me," she challenged.

"Okay," he said. "So, anyway, you know my dad hasn't been around most of my life. He left my mom when I was like two years old. Incredibly, I think she still loves him." He shook his head at the thought. "Apparently, since then he's been moving all around the country. He never stays in one place for more than a couple years, though."

"What does he *do*?" asked T.J.

"Well, according to what he told me this morning, it's kinda government related."

"You mean, like the CIA or something?"

Bortnicker gave a snort of derision. "I wouldn't bet on it being anything as important as that," he said. "What matters is that he sends the money every month from whatever he does."

"Did he at least say he missed you?" asked LouAnne, her eyes starting to tear.

"Of course he did. What else was he gonna say? And he told me he's really proud of the TV stuff and how I've become the man of the house, yada-yada-yada."

"I bet he really is proud of you," she said.

"I hope so; it's just hard to believe anything that has to do with him."

"So, is he staying a while?" asked T.J.

"Nope. He's probably gone already. Mom just let him sleep on the couch last night because she felt bad sending him to a hotel. Apparently, they had a pleasant dinner together and did a lot of catching up, whatever that means."

"But what made him show up so suddenly?" asked LouAnne.

"He told me he really missed me and Mom—yeah, right—but I bet it was my grandfather getting on his case. I think he was kinda guilted into it."

"Yeah," said T.J., "having met your grandparents, I can see they'd be good at that. But still, he didn't have to do it."

"I know," relented Bortnicker quietly.

"What's he like?" asked LouAnne.

"What's he like? Well, he's got a sense of humor, I guess, and in a way he's kinda charming. My mom's always said that about him."

"What's he look like?" asked T.J.

"Picture me in thirty years."

"No way."

"Yes way. It's kinda weird, actually."

"So, uh, how did you leave off with him?"

"In a roundabout way, he told me that he was on the way to figuring things out, 'getting his life in order' was how he put it, and that he'd be in touch with us, and not just because somebody'd got on his case about it."

"Do you trust him at all?" asked LouAnne.

"I really want to," he admitted, "but with a guy like my dad, you can't get your hopes up."

"But you left the door open?"

"Just a crack," he said with a crooked smile.

"Hey," said T.J., thinking back to their Cooperstown trip, "did you tell him you gave his old baseball glove to Roberto Clemente's ghost?"

"I'm saving that story for next time. Hopefully." He looked at his Mickey Mouse watch. "Hey, Big Mon, it's still early and the DQ is just down the road. Who's up for a Blizzard? I'm buying."

* * * *

After a very long wait at the window, the teens carried their desserts to a side bench and watched the Post Road traffic go by. "You sure you guys won't get in trouble for this?" asked LouAnne as she spooned her Reese's Pieces medium-sized Blizzard into her mouth.

"Nah," replied Bortnicker as he dipped a long red plastic spoon into T.J.'s large cookies n' cream shake. "Rocco doesn't care, as long as we show up for work at his place."

"Hey, you've got your own!" said T.J., pulling his cup out of reach as his cell phone buzzed. Everything stopped. He handed the Blizzard to Bortnicker, whispered, "Don't eat it all," and wandered off to find a quiet place to field Patrick Weese's call.

He returned a few minutes later, ashen, his lips bloodless from being

216

pressed together. "It's a no-go," he said simply as Bortnicker handed back his shake, which he promptly tossed in a nearby garbage can. "Weese apologized up and down, said the governor heard him out, but in the end he told Weese the story was just too far-fetched to base a piece of legislation on. The fine people of Connecticut would think he'd gone off the deep end. And then the governor added that if he did this for Charity Blessing, it'd open up a whole new round of litigation from those other petitioners, blah blah blah. We're dead in the water."

"So what do we do now, Big Mon?"

"As I see it there's only one thing to do here. We have a date with Charity tomorrow night, and we're not standing her up."

Chapter Twenty-Three

August, 1662

"It is time, child," announced a somber Jonathan Melrose, the members of the Town Council behind him, as he unlocked the tiny room in the meeting house that had served as a jail cell for Charity Blessing. The girl sat on the plank floor in the corner of the room. Next to her was a tin plate with a piece of moldy bread that lay untouched, and a bucket provided for her bodily functions. When the minister extended his hand to help her up she looked at him with dark-rimmed eyes, grabbed onto a chink in the rough wall beside her, and pulled herself up without assistance.

The last rays of sunlight hurt her eyes as she stepped outside the rear entrance, where an oxen-pulled cart awaited. The cart was three-sided with large wooden wheels, the back end open for when it would pull away from the tree. The fact that this final public humiliation of her would come not before sunrise, when few would be in attendance, but later in the day when chores were done, came as no surprise to Charity. She was to be made an example of.

A stool was provided for Charity to step up to the flatbed of the wagon. Her hands were bound behind her, and stoically she mounted the vehicle that reeked from the manure it usually carted. A procession, led by her stepfather, followed behind as the driver cracked his whip and the oxen began to plod across the Village Green towards Wolves Swamp. A path had been beaten down leading from the grassy area through the reeds; nevertheless, the surface was muddy and uneven, and Charity had to balance so as not to topple over into the vegetation when they hit a rut.

218

Because her wrists were bound, she could not swat at the mosquitoes that tormented her in the sopping humidity. Her previous experience at the ducking, she knew, should have prepared her for the expectant, anxious faces of the spectators. Even so, their sense of anticipation turned her stomach.

After what seemed an eternity, they finally reached Gallows Hill, with its hanging tree, in the marsh's center. A noose had been prepared from 1¼-inch rope that had been boiled and stretched to eliminate spring or coiling. The knot had been lubricated with soap to ensure a smooth sliding action.

With some difficulty, the driver maneuvered the cart up the side of the small hill underneath the solid branch from which the noose hung motionless in the still of the sunset. There was barely enough room around the cart for the Town Council members and her stepfather. Her mother, who trailed behind, looked to be in a state of shock, for which Charity was sorry. She noticed that Trevor Jackson was present at the side of his father, stone-faced, to witness the final act of this farcical play. She also noticed that a shallow pit had been dug some distance from the hill for her burial; because of the nature of her crime, she could not be interred in consecrated ground.

Once the crowd, restless in anticipation and the August heat, was more or less in place, one of the men leaped up into the cart and fitted the noose around her neck. John Thorpe, who had stayed in Fairfield following the trial, faced the gathering and opened a scrolled proclamation, which he began to read after a dramatic clearing of the throat:

"Whereas Charity Blessing has been found guilty of the crime of witchcraft by a jury of her peers, her punishment will be conducted in the name of His Majesty, Charles II of England, and John Winthrop, governor of the Connecticut colony, on this third day of August in the year of our Lord 1662."

A lusty cheer went up from the crowd, which was quickly subdued by Reverend Melrose, who asked the gathering to bow their heads and join him in the reciting of the Lord's Prayer. As they chanted piously, she stared at Trevor Jackson, who couldn't help but steal a peek at her; when he caught her glaring at him he quickly lowered his eyes again.

219

The prayer finished, Thorpe asked Charity if she had any last words, or wanted to recant for her crimes. She paused, looked to the sky, and then faced her fellow Fairfielders one last time. "My only crime," she said, "was in having the hope that you—" she looked directly at Trevor, who remained expressionless—"would have the sense to see the folly in all of this. But I tell you this here and now, so mark me: the Village of Fairfield will rue the day of my dispatch from this world, and I will return to dance on your graves."

With that, Thorpe nodded to the driver, who again cracked his whip. For seconds afterward, the only sound that could be heard was the creaking of the rope against the bark of the tree branch. Later on it would be well discussed amongst the townsfolk how quickly Charity went, how she neither kicked nor struggled—and how, despite all the injustices visited upon her, she left this world *smiling*.

Chapter Twenty-Four

"I wish we had a beach in Gettysburg," said LouAnne as they crunched along the shoreline of Sasco Beach. "I'd run on it every day."

"You'd get bored with it," countered T.J. "At least on the battlefield you can take a bunch of different routes."

"Yeah, maybe. I guess any training program gets old after a while. Still, the resistance of the sand gives you an extra level to the workout. I like that."

"And the sea breeze doesn't hurt, either."

"Hey, Cuz," she said as they made the turn at the Southport Canal, "notice how the wind has picked up a little today?"

"Uh-huh. They're saying there's gonna be some nasty thunderstorms later that'll finally break this heatwave."

"But it won't change our plans, will it?"

"We were given a three-day deadline. Tonight's the night, no matter what." His jaw was set; LouAnne knew there was no changing his mind. Not now.

* * * *

Things were back to normal—if one could call it that—at the Bortnicker residence. Nathaneal had left again for parts unknown, and Pippa was out on their back deck, meditating and practicing yoga, a veggie shake at her side. Her son, conversely, was pulling out all the stops: eggs Benedict with crispy bacon and hash brown potatoes.

"Cleaning out the fridge, huh?" joked LouAnne.

"Eat up. I think we'll need all the strength we can get later on," he replied, pouring himself an extra-large coffee.

"Are we trying to film tonight?" asked T.J., sprinkling salt on his hash browns.

"We can bring a hand-held or two out there," answered Bortnicker, "but I wouldn't get my hopes up. Last time she blew out everything we had."

"And another thing," said LouAnne, mopping up some Hollandaise sauce with her wheat toast, "I think that when we have it out with her, we do it from the graveyard."

"I agree," said T.J. "The last thing we're gonna do is let her lure us into the marsh; that's *her* turf. And have you noticed, she won't come inside the wall of the graveyard? The most she can do is hover over it—"

"And zap us from there," said Bortnicker.

"Just make sure you all have your handy-dandy witch protection stuff," said LouAnne. "She might not be too pleased with what we have to tell her."

* * * *

With an entire day to kill, it was decided that the threesome would finally spend some time lounging at the beach. Sasco was chosen for its close proximity. They packed some soft coolers with sandwiches and snacks, grabbed some towels and sunscreen, and were off on their bikes.

"Sorry we don't have waves like Bermuda, Cuz," apologized T.J., pointing to the foot-high swells. "If we were at the ocean beaches on the other side of Long Island, they'd be a lot bigger."

"So that's Long Island across the way?"

"Yup. It looks a little hazy 'cause of the humidity."

"And this water is Long Island Sound, right?"

"Uh-huh."

They unrolled their towels. "Sorry we don't have an umbrella," said Bortnicker. "Too much to carry."

"No problem, guys," she said. "I'll just spray on a lot of sunscreen." She stood in the sunlight and peeled off her Beatles T-shirt, revealing a stunning one-piece that accentuated her athletic curves. As she swept back her blonde tresses, Bortnicker stole a look at his buddy, wiggling his eyebrows; T.J. frowned back at him, though he was equally impressed.

"Another thing," said Bortnicker, as she settled back onto her towel between them, "we don't have any pink sand—but at least they rake the beach every night—"

"Will you two stop apologizing!" she cried. "Okay, so it's not Bermuda. I get that. But you guys are so lucky to have all these beaches just for your town. I'd *love* to live on the water here."

"Not if there was a hurricane, you wouldn't," replied T.J. "You should've seen it, Cuz—Irene really trashed this beach, and all the others. Not as horrible as the ocean side of Long Island, but pretty bad."

"Well, look at it this way," she said philosophically, "you had the big storm last August, so you've gotta figure you're okay for a while." She took out a paperback and started reading.

"Ready to jump in?" asked Bortnicker. "It's almost high tide, so we won't have to walk out three miles to go swimming."

"Sure. You coming, Cuz?"

She tilted her head and looked over her sunglasses at the dark blue water. "Uh, I think I'll pass, guys. If I can't see the bottom I'm not going in."

"Suit yourself." They took off like a couple of banshees and hurtled into the Sound.

LouAnne sighed and went back to her book. Since it was Monday the beach's population was sparse, with mostly all adults sitting quietly and soaking up some rays or reading. Sasco was less kid-friendly than the other beaches, so it was blessedly quiet, except for one of Bortnicker's occasional yelps as he wrestled with T.J. in the water. It seemed so incongruous to her that these typical teenaged boys—with her help, of course—were being called upon to bail this community out of what could turn out to be a colossal mess. She was especially concerned for her cousin who, because of the abilities that had been bestowed upon him, seemed to be carrying the weight of the world on his shoulders, though he tried to exude an air of confidence. And she vowed to herself that tonight, no matter what, she'd shield the boy she loved from harm.

* * * *

"Great fajitas, Bortnicker," said Tom as he and Pippa started collecting the dinner plates on the Jacksons' patio. "You sure know how to punch up leftovers."

"It was a snap, Mr. J.," he answered proudly. "The steak was already grilled from the other night, so all I had to do was cut it up and add some onions, peppers, salsa and spices. No big deal. Throw in a little beans and rice, and bingo—Mexican dinner a la Bortnicker."

"So, what are we looking forward to tonight, gang?" asked Pippa, who seemed a bit melancholy after the departure of her husband.

"Well," said T.J., downplaying the gravity of the situation as usual, "if Dad'll drop us off around nine, we'll try to get things wrapped up tonight. We'll give you a buzz for a pickup, if that's not too much trouble."

"None at all," replied Tom. He thought for a second. "Hey, Pippa, would you like to take in a movie, and maybe a late dessert at Avellino's?"

"That would be nice, actually," she replied, which caused T.J. and his buddy to exchange a quizzical look.

* * * *

Dressed in their *Junior Gonzo Ghost Chasers* T-shirts, the trio exited Tom's SUV and looked to the skies. The weather had deteriorated steadily since the afternoon, and a stiff breeze had kicked up. Grayish-purple clouds obscured the moon. "Storm front's coming in," observed Bortnicker.

"Hope it holds off till we're done," said T.J.

"Don't count on it," said his cousin.

They let themselves in to the command post to find Robert Sherwood sitting at their computer terminal. "Amazing, all the paranormal contraptions they've developed. This branch of science, if you will, seems to be exploding."

"Are you sure you want to be here, Mr. Sherwood?" asked Bortnicker.

"Wouldn't miss it for the world," he answered with a chuckle. "An old man like me could use a little excitement every so often. If you'll excuse me, I'll be up in my office with a pair of infrared binoculars I've borrowed for the occasion. Good luck, and please try to stay safe. If the situation becomes precarious, no one will fault you for bowing out."

"Thanks, Mr. Sherwood," said T.J. "Tell you what—if you see anything crazy starting to happen to us, call Detective Morosko, and tell her to bring reinforcements."

"Will do." He wheeled out of the room.

"Good guy," said Bortnicker.

"Yeah," agreed T.J., "if it weren't for the wheelchair, I think he'd be out there with us." He took a deep breath. "Well, guys, this is it. Let's bring it in." They huddled. "Everyone got their witchy stuff?"

"Yup."

"All right, then. Repeat after me..." They recited Deirdre's prayer, eyes shut tight, drawing strength from one another, trying not to tremble. "One, two, three—"

Gonzos Rule!

* * * *

When they exited the Museum, having decided to forgo the stationary DVRs, it was raining. Nothing too heavy—yet. But the wind was rising, and the smell of swampy decomposition wafted in off the marsh.

"Let's go in the front entrance this time," said LouAnne defiantly. "No more of this hopping-the-fence nonsense." The boys shrugged and followed her as she pulled open the creaking wrought iron gate and strode inside the graveyard. They passed the re-sealed crypt from which they'd exited the now unusable tunnel and made their way to the tomb of Jonathan Melrose, its white marble shining in the gloom. The rain's intensity picked up. Bortnicker hefted a camcorder and LouAnne clicked on her EVP recorder. They nodded at T.J., who closed his eyes for a moment, steeling himself.

"Charity Blessing!" he called in the pelting droplets. "We've come here to see you, as promised. Show yourself, please!"

Nothing.

"Once more, with feeling," said Bortnicker in a shaky John Lennon voice.

"Charity Blessing," barked T.J., "we're getting awfully wet out here. If this is your idea of a joke—"

A crack of thunder, followed by a blinding flash that split a maple tree in the far corner of the graveyard, brought the teens to their knees. "Get up!" yelled T.J. to his friends, refusing to kneel in fear. "We've had just about enough of this, Charity Blessing!" he cried into the steady rain. "Show yourself—*NOW!*"

"Getting colder, Big Mon," said Bortnicker. "Here she comes!"

LouAnne suddenly yelped, then dropped her steaming EVP recorder; Bortnicker let go of his camcorder just before it exploded into shards of metal and plastic.

There was first the telltale black silhouette, followed by the familiar milky white-to-solid materialization as Charity Blessing returned to her perch atop the outer wall. Though the rain was drumming at a roar, she spoke normally and with perfect clarity. "So here we are, then," she began.

"Hey, T.J., check it out," said Bortnicker sideways, "she's like, perfectly dry." Indeed, it seemed as though the witch of Fairfield had a force field around her. She hung suspended in air, arms crossed, staring down at the sopping teens.

"There is no need to take a disrespectful tone with me," she said in a lecturing manner. "The last thing you want at this moment is to raise my ire—"

CRACK! Another bolt of thunder flew down, striking a telephone pole across the street and throwing the surrounding area's houses into darkness.

"Good God!" cried Robert Sherwood as he started dialing Susan Morosko on his cell phone.

Across Old Post Road, the sanctuary in which Reverend Stirling was praying went dark. Sensing that his young friends were in trouble, he ran for the church's front door. It wouldn't budge. He tried the other entrances. It was no use. Someone—or something—had locked him in.

* * * *

The *Junior Gonzo Ghost Chasers* rose to their feet, their jeans beneath the knees now covered in mud, not that they noticed. The wind was howling by now; nearby mighty oaks and maples lush with foliage were swaying in the wind like the palm trees of Bermuda in a tropical storm. The report of cracking branches resounded throughout the Historical District.

"You were given a task to perform," said Charity, the wind giving her words an eerie, echoing effect. "Have you done it?"

T.J. stepped forward. "We took your case to our first selectman, who contacted the governor of Connecticut, asking for an official pardon."

"And?"

"The governor refused."

Charity's eyes glowed in anger; she threw back her head and let forth a withering scream that nearly blew their eardrums out. But T.J. wasn't backing down. "We tried our best!" he yelled back at her. "We've done everything we could, including risk our lives, to learn about you and clear your name!"

"How commendable," she said, her voice dripping with sarcasm. "And what did you learn, pray tell?"

"That you lived in a time of intolerance, where people could be persecuted for their beliefs."

"Bravo," she said with a mocking applause.

The rain continued in sheets.

* * * *

Upon receiving Robert Sherwood's frantic call, Detective Morosko ran outside onto Reef Road and signaled a patrolman who was just pulling his cruiser up to headquarters. Jumping into the front seat she barked, "Beach Road Cemetery—on the double!"

"Yes, ma'am!" answered the fresh-faced officer, and gunned the motor. They burned rubber down Reef Road, flashers and siren going, and hung a left onto Old Post Road. The tree at the corner of Old Post and Rowland seemed to come out of nowhere, crashing down in their path. The officer swerved and skidded in the ponded water, and the cruiser's passenger door broadsided the trunk with a sickening crash. Seconds later, Morosko came to. Shaking the cobwebs, she saw the officer slumped sideways, out cold behind his deployed airbag. Winking away droplets of blood, she squirmed from behind her airbag and out her shattered window, called for assistance, dropped to the flooded street, and started running.

* * * *

"So you have failed me again, *Trevor*," said Charity. "Powerless in my time of need."

"Trevor?" said Bortnicker. "What the—"

"He did his best!" screamed LouAnne, her blonde locks plastered to her head. "What more do you want?"

Charity ignored the girl and gave an eerily sensual grin as she extended her hand. "Come with me, *Trevor*," she invited enticingly.

T.J., stupefied, managed a "Wha—"

"Come with me, my love," she beckoned, her voice sweet as honey. "I'll take you to a place where we can be together, *forever*. I could make you so happy. And I can show you things…things you've always wanted to know…people you've always wanted to see. You understand, don't you?"

"Yes," he whispered, and started to step forward, at the same time feeling so out of touch with his body that his feet seemed to be leaving the ground. It was crazy, but he *longed* for her, had to have her—

"NO!" screamed LouAnne, who grabbed two fistfuls of his shirt front and yanked him to her. "No, T.J.! You can't do it!"

He mumbled, "But I have to go—"

That's when LouAnne slapped him—hard—across the face, the rain's wetness accentuating the *whack* of her skin on his. Pulling him nose-to nose, she pleaded desperately with him, half sobbing: "Don't you get it? Listen to me, Cuz. She didn't come back here to clear her name— she came back here for *you!*"

T.J. brought his hand to his stinging face and thought, *What's happening to me?* He felt powerless, drained of all resistance. However, his friends were neither, and they got between him and Charity.

"No way!" yelled Bortnicker, practically blind from the hair in his eyes and dripping glasses. "You want him, you've gotta go through *us!*"

"You'll have to kill me first!" cried LouAnne like a girl possessed. "You can't have him! He's not Trevor! He belongs to *me!*"

T.J., totally sapped by the ordeal, tried to speak up, but yielded to the defiant exhortations of his friends. And then, for the last time, he heard that same voice, its timbre calm and empowering: *Don't believe her. Your place is here.* Reaching deep within himself for strength, he squared his shoulders, staring down Charity Blessing through the swirling wind and rain. "You've gotta leave this place," he said firmly. "This is not your—"

The next thing he knew he was being yanked down forcefully by his friends. There was a series of pop-pop-pops as a bloodied Susan Morosko, her elbows propped on the top of a broken tombstone behind them, emptied the magazine of her Glock automatic pistol into the apparition's chest, the bullets passing clean through into the wind and rain. This precipitated yet another bloodcurdling yowl from the witch, whose pointed finger sent the detective tumbling backwards.

One more time, T.J. Jackson rose to his feet. "Go, Charity," he now said, in a voice that sounded oddly older and antique. "It is over."

Charity Blessing gazed at T.J.—or was it Trevor?—with a mixture of love, hate, and pity. "Very well, then," she hissed as LouAnne and Bortnicker, using T.J.'s sopping shirt for purchase, climbed back up to his side. "But mark me, the day of reckoning for this vale of tears is at hand. Remember me when it comes!"

With a final, earsplitting explosion Charity Blessing blew apart and was carried away on the gale winds, leaving the teens holding each other in the rain.

"It's gonna be okay," they repeated over and over. "It's gonna be okay."

Epilogue

The hurricane that would come to be known as Superstorm Sandy, among the largest and most devastating Atlantic storms in United States history, slammed into the coast of Connecticut on October 29, 2012, as a post-tropical cyclone with hurricane force winds.

In an onslaught that dwarfed Irene, Sandy pummeled Fairfield's shores with unprecedented storm surges, while trees fell like matchsticks for miles inland. The Historical District was blacked out and rubble-strewn for days after, populated only by police and uniformed National Guardsmen. At Sandy's height, seawater from Long Island Sound came within a stone's throw of Old Post Road and Town Hall. Most of the Old Cemetery on Beach Road, because of its slight elevation, was spared. However, the tunnel that almost claimed the lives of Bortnicker and LouAnne was flooded beyond repair, and subsequently was filled and sealed off by the Department of Public Works. Paul Jarboe and Ken Trishitta were all too happy to take part in the project.

For some ten days in late October and early November, the residents of Fairfield tried to deal with the reality of over 1,000 trees down, 1,000 homes flood damaged, 5,000 citizens evacuated, six homes washed out to sea with dozens more condemned, and the loss of electricity to thousands of families.

Tide Mill Terrace, again spared from the almost biblical flooding incurred by those at sea level, nevertheless was devastated as branches or whole trees indiscriminately crashed down upon houses, garages and cars. Curiously, this was not the case at #65, where some freak of nature caused the property to avoid the presence of so much as a fallen twig.

Even more curiously, the Jacksons, who had again taken in the Bortnickers to ride out the storm, could not explain later why their house was the only residence for miles around not to lose power. Even the utility workers, who would be toiling around the clock for weeks to restore some semblance of normalcy, could not fathom this anomaly.

But one person could. For when T.J. Jackson slipped outside at the storm's height, he could swear that within the apocalyptic winds of Sandy could be heard the keening wail of the witch of Fairfield, still in search of her lost love.

Author's Note

It was great fun writing about Fairfield, the place I've called home since 1998. Because of this, just about every locale named in the book is real, except for the Tasteefreez on Boston Post Road. If you ever get the chance, you might want to check out the various establishments and sites mentioned, including the three beaches. From an historical perspective, the Fairfield Museum and History Center, as well as the Village Green and the Old Cemetery—and the former Wolves Swamp beyond, which is now a fraction of its original acreage—are pretty much as I've described them (though Edwards Pond, which still remains, was drained long ago, leaving only its bowl-like imprint), as is First Church Congregational (not First Community) at the corner of Beach and Old Post. You will find the staff at the Fairfield Museum most helpful; Robert Sherwood is a fictional character, but he is based on the late Rod MacKenzie, who was by all accounts a remarkable historian and helpful to all.

As for the history of witchcraft in Fairfield County, both Goody Bassett and Goody Knapp really did exist. Charity Blessing, a fictional character, was based on a young woman named Mercy Disbrow (sometimes spelled Disborough), who was tried for witchcraft in 1692 in Fairfield and convicted, but later pardoned. She was, so the legend goes, quite attractive.

Finally, the one-two punch of Hurricane Irene and Superstorm Sandy, which provided a framework for the plot's timeline, dealt punishing blows to Fairfield. As I write this in 2014, there are still a few condemned houses along the beachfront awaiting demolition or replacement, as is the pavilion at Penfield Beach, which was just recently given the go-ahead for restoration.

But overall, Fairfield, Connecticut, is a great town with much to offer. I hope this book will encourage those who live here to explore its history, and those who don't to come for a visit and enjoy its attractions and welcoming atmosphere. Who knows? You just might see Tom's SHAGWA tooling around town—I know *I* have.

About the Author

Paul Ferrante is originally from the Bronx and grew up in the town of Pelham, NY. He received his undergraduate and Master's degrees in English from Iona College, where he was also a halfback on the Gaels' undefeated 1977 football team. Paul has been an award-winning secondary school English teacher and coach for over 35 years, as well as a columnist for *Sports Collector's Digest* since 1993 on the subject of baseball ballpark history. Many of his works can be found in the archives of the National Baseball Hall of Fame in Cooperstown, NY. His writings have led to numerous radio and television appearances related to baseball history.

The **T.J. Jackson Mysteries** series has led Paul to speak at the 150th Anniversary Battle Commemoration in Gettysburg, PA, and the National Baseball Hall of Fame during their 75th Anniversary celebration.

Paul lives in Connecticut with his wife Maria and daughter Caroline, a film director/screenwriter.

Please visit Paul's website: **www.paulferranteauthor.com** for information on the **T.J. Jackson Mysteries** and his other writings; also visit **www.facebook.com/tjjacksonmysteries**.

The T.J. Jackson Mysteries

Last Ghost at Gettysburg
Spirits of the Pirate House
Roberto's Return
Curse of the Fairfield Witch